LION OF STEEL

A Medieval Romance
Sons of Christopher de Lohr
Part of the de Lohr Dynasty

By Kathryn Le Veque

Trade Paperback Edition

Text by Kathryn Le Veque
Cover by Kim Killion

The characters and events portrayed in this book are fictitious. Any similarity to real persons, living or dead, is purely coincidental and not intended by the author.

WWW.KATHRYNLEVEQUE.COM

ARE YOU SIGNED UP FOR KATHRYN'S BLOG?

You'll get the latest news and information on exclusive giveaways, exclusive excerpts, coming releases, sales, free books, cover reveals and more.

Kathryn's blog followers get it all first. No spam, no junk.

Get the latest info from the reigning Queen of English Medieval Romance!

Sign Up Here

kathrynleveque.com

A powerful spinster, a lonely woman, and a hunky knight are front in center in this gripping tale of passion, meddling, betrayal, and the truest of loves.

It's ***Douglas de Lohr's*** *turn to shine!*

As the fifth son of the Earl of Hereford and Worcester, one of the most powerful men in the realm, Douglas has his share of power and prestige also. Rather than linger in his father's mighty shadow, or even the shadow of his important older brothers, Douglas is about to carve a path for himself that will either shatter his will to live… or make him the most impressive de Lohr son yet. It all begins when his father asks Douglas to go to the aid of the sister of an old friend, to an enormous castle in Devon where legends live and chaos reigns.

Lady Isabel de Kerrington is the sister in question, the heiress to the Earldom of Axminster and mistress of mighty Axminster Castle. A spinster all her life, she rules Axminster with an iron fist. But there are wolves at her door. She has requested that her brother's old friend, Hereford, send help and it comes in the form of Douglas.

He walks into a strange, new world.

Another member of this strange, new world has been living a bland, loveless existence. Lady Misery Isabella Ruth d'Avignon has been at Axminster since childhood. Mira, as she is known, has been part of Lady Isabel's world for many years and Lady Isabel looks upon Mira as her own daughter. It is Mira who helps Douglas gain his bearings in a castle that has only known instability as of late. Acquaintances become friends, and friends fall in love.

But there is a danger lurking at Axminster.

What starts out as a harmless annoyance quickly turns deadly when a former ally visits. A jealous young woman thinks to use this former ally against Mira, driving her away from Douglas, but what she unleashes threatens to destroy both Axminster and the House of de Lohr. She has launched a spark into a powder keg with unintended, and explosive, results. The implications are so far reaching that it seems all hope is lost. Can Douglas save the woman he loves? Or will she become the sacrifice?

It's an edge-of-your-seat ride in this epic de Lohr saga!

House of de Lohr motto

Deus et Honora

God and Honor

AUTHOR'S NOTE

Finally! It's our darling Douglas' story.

Let me start off explaining the Tale of Two Douglases. This happens in my universe, on occasion, when I have two characters that have the same name. Kieran Hage is one. Douglas de Lohr is another.

Where else does he pop up, you ask? "Douglas de Lohr" is a secondary character in *Tender Is the Knight*, a d'Vant series novel. It was the first one I ever wrote in that series. Originally, "that" Douglas was indeed supposed to be a son of Christopher and Dustin, but as the years passed and I started the Sons of de Lohr series, I realized it couldn't have been because of the time frame. So, I made it so "that" Douglas is just a distant relative. Fair enough. Because, honestly, I would have been so disappointed to miss out on "our" Douglas' story. I think Peter de Lohr summed it up best—I love what he said about his brothers in *Lion of Hearts*:

Curtis is the strong one, Roi is the smart one, Myles is the fearless one, Douglas is the wise one, and Westley is the lively one

And in that statement, you know what you're dealing with when it comes to the de Lohr brothers. In this book, we're dealing with the wise one—Douglas. I wouldn't want to miss that story.

Now, we've got some super-fun cameos in this novel. I've added two characters who have been mentioned before in other books from long ago, so I'm going to tell you who they are so you know immediately and aren't distracted from the story trying to figure it out. The first one is a character that has been mentioned but we've never met—Jonathan de Wolfe, older brother of William de Wolfe (*The Wolfe*). If you've read *The Wolfe*, then you know that William has two older brothers—Robert, the Earl of Wolverhampton, and Jonathan, who serves the Earl of Norfolk, Roger Bigod. That was established in *The Wolfe*. But what we find out is that Jonathan has a wee bit of a background with Bigod and there's some trouble there. I won't give it away, but I love his story.

The second cameo is none other than a man we've heard quite a bit about in at least three books, the father of the Lords of Thunder, Antoninus de Shera. In this book, he's been married to Honey (Olivia Charlotte de Lohr) for quite some time and his sons are young men. We also get to see Grayson de Winter (we did meet him in *The Thunder Lord*) and his young adult son, Davyss. Yes, THE Davyss de Winter (*Lespada*).

On a side note with the House of de Winter, it was never mentioned in *Lespada* (the de Winter novel), but Grayson de Winter is the Earl of Radnor. It was implied, but not named. That was a title passed on to Davyss, but as he mentioned in *Lespada*, he doesn't like politics and only wants to be a knight, so he never speaks of the fact that he's really an earl. The de Winters are the war machine of the monarchy, and knights to the bone, and things like earldoms don't mean a whole lot to them (but if you've read *Lespada*, you know they mean a lot to Davyss' ambitious mother, Lady Katherine!). Anyway—fun facts about the House of de Winter. They are the Earls of Radnor and their property, as mentioned in the book, is all of Radnorshire. The reason they have so much property in Norfolk is because Lady Katherine is the sister of the Earl of Surrey—and Surrey really did claim much of Norfolk.

Now, on to our heroine—she has a GREAT name. You're going to get a kick out of it. Her surname—d'Avignon—is a name you've seen frequently in the Executioner Knights series, as it belongs to Caius d'Avignon (*Winter of Solace*). In this book, the heroine is the daughter of Caius' older brother, Silas, so that's how they are related—though it isn't mentioned in the book. But for those of you who like to keep track of family trees, now you know.

As I usually do in the de Lohr books, here's a quick family tree on who all of the children of Christopher and Dustin de Lohr are and whom they're married to. It gets updated with each successive book in the series. A very helpful family list!

- Peter (*The Splendid Hour*) Lord Pembridge, eventually Earl of Farringdon. Garrison commander Ludlow Castle
- Christin (*A Time of End*) Married to Alexander de Sherrington, Garrison commander of Wigmore Castle
- Brielle (*The Dark Conqueror*)
- Curtis (*Lion of War*) Earl of Leominster (heir apparent to the larger Earldom of Hereford and Worcester), Baron Ivington
- Richard "Roi" (*Lion of Twilight*) Earl of Cheltenham
- Myles (*Lion of Hearts*) Lord Monnington of Monnington Castle, a Marcher lordship—Lordship of Doré
- Rebecca
- Douglas (*Lion of Steel*)
- Westley (whose middle name is Henry and he was sometimes referred to as "Henry" when he was young) (*Lion of Thunder*)
- Olivia Charlotte (the future Honey de Shera from the Lords of Thunder series) Countess of Coventry

A quick mention that there is a scene in this book that involves chess. Chess was indeed played by Medieval folk, but I've used language that is more modern so the reader can better envision what moves have been made with what pieces. Chess evolved from an Arabic game in the ninth and tenth centuries and the pieces were slightly different, so I've used modern pieces for ease in understanding.

Oh, and one last thing before you jump into this story. As loyal readers know, the Executioner Knights and the House of de Lohr are quite involved with one another. Peter de Lohr ends up running the spy ring at one point, but the involvement of the rest of the brothers was explained in *Lion of Twilight*. Just as a reminder—

Christopher had mostly been a warlord, though he'd worked closely with William Marshal as the man manipulated the politics and players of England. Peter, Christopher's son, had been a great Executioner Knight, now mostly retired due to his age, while Christin's husband, Sherry, and even Christin herself had been spies during their younger years. Truth be told, Roi had been involved with them in his younger years as well, as had Curtis. Douglas and Westley had avoided the service because Christopher had other duties for them, but Myles de Lohr—the great middle brother—was a fully fledged Executioner.

Wherever there was need in England, the Executioner Knights—and the de Lohrs—answered the call.

As you can see, Douglas and Westley weren't involved with them like the others were, and I didn't want you, as the reader, to think it was a mistake or an omission. Douglas and Westley have a different path than their elder brothers, which is revealed (for Douglas) in this tale.

Lastly, I want to point something out—several of my big series, de Lohr and de Wolfe included, take place in the thirteenth century during the reign of Henry III. Henry reigned for fifty-six years, which is a crazy-long amount of time. He assumed the throne at nine years of age and reigned until he died at seventy-two. Therefore, all of my great families have something to do with him at some point during his reign. Fun fact: at fifty-six years, Henry's reign was still only the fifth longest! No kidding! The list of longest-serving monarchs (top five) is Elizabeth II, Queen Victoria, George III, James IV, and then Henry. Talk about longevity!

Now, the usual pronunciation guide:

Mira: MEER-uh

D'Avignon: phonetically, it's davin-yawn (like filet mignon, the "g" is silent, giving way to a "n-y" sound)

Axminster: Just the way it looks—ax-minster

And with that, get ready for what is one of the more interesting and detailed stories in the Sons of de Lohr series—and it's got some wild twists and turns, courtesy of characters who were determined to do what they wanted to do and not necessarily what I wanted them to do. Such is the life of a writer—listen to the characters!

Happy Reading!

Kathryn

CHAPTER ONE

Year of Our Lord 1247
Axminster Castle
Seat of the Earls of Axminster

THE RAIN WAS pouring.

The thunder was pounding.

Lightning streaked across the sky as the battle for control of Axminster Castle entered its third day. Three days of severe weather, chaos, blood, death, and frustration.

But the battle, in truth, had started long before the armies took the field.

It all began when a certain Lord Rickard Tatworth of Tatworth Castle, about ten miles to the north of Axminster, offered for Lady Isabel de Kerrington's hand. As the sister to the Earl of Axminster and heiress to the earldom because her brother was childless, she was considered a prestigious marital prospect, if not a little old, and Tatworth had ambitions that he should be the next Earl of Axminster when Eduard de Kerrington keeled over. The man was of bad health, anyway, and that wasn't a secret. He was married, once, but his wife had produced no children.

That left Lady Isabel as a very great prize.

But Isabel was also quite intelligent—and past childbearing age herself—so when Tatworth began to send missives of his admiration and even love for her, she burned them. Eduard thought it was quite hilarious that his spinster sister should have a suitor, which only made Isabel furious. Even at their ages—with Isabel at forty years and Eduard at fifty years and four—they fought like siblings often fought at much younger ages. Eduard teased and Isabel was stoic until they were alone.

Then she used any weapon she could get her hands on against him.

Axminster, however, continued on as a great seat of training and learning in spite of the antics of the brother and sister who were at her helm. Eduard was a great earl, benevolent and generous to his vassals, and Axminster had become a training ground for royal troops because of his relationship with King Henry III. Eduard was a personal friend, a man who had supplied the king with both support and money when he needed it, and Henry had a high regard for Axminster.

He had an even higher regard for Lady Isabel, who had created a school of manners and learning for the daughters of the nobles of England, a school of such reputation that everyone wanted to send their daughters there. Under Lady Isabel's tutelage, young women learned skills and grace to become some of the finest ladies in all of England and highly sought-after wives. *Axminster Angels*, they were known as. Young ladies with the most excellent grace in all the land.

Even if their patroness, Lady Isabel, chased her brother around the castle with a hot fire poker from time to time.

Not surprisingly, the de Kerrington spinster was a formidable woman, and when Tatworth started his campaign of love and devotion, Isabel was not only annoyed, she was also embarrassed. It was made worse by Eduard's taunting, but that taunting caught up with him. Through karma or fate or divine humor, Eduard was teasing her one night and laughed so hard that he choked on a chicken bone. It pierced his throat and he died of an infection almost a month later. Though Isabel was saddened, it seemed that she had the last laugh in the courtship of Lord Tatworth.

So she thought.

As the heiress, and calling herself the Countess of Axminster after her brother's death, Isabel ruled Axminster with an iron fist, far stronger than her brother ever had, but Lord Tatworth, only seeing a vulnerable woman—because the man was clearly blind—and enraged by her constant rejections, decided to take matters into his own hands.

And that's why the battle was raging.

Tatworth fielded a large army. Reinforced with an ally in Richard St. Martin of Wardour Castle, he threatened to march on Axminster and force Lady Isabel to marry him. She refused, in no uncertain terms, but she also secretly sent word to an Axminster ally who had the biggest army she could think of—

Christopher de Lohr, Earl of Hereford and Worcester.

Hereford could field thousands of men. She knew this because she'd heard her brother speaking of the man he fondly called "Chris." But she didn't only send word to Hereford—she also sent word to the Earl of Coventry of Isenhall Castle, Antoninus de Shera, as well as to Roger Bigod, the Earl of Norfolk at Arundel Castle. Those men alone brought thousands with them, and when Norfolk brought his own reinforcements in the House of de Winter, it turned out to be ten thousand men against Tatworth's four thousand. A four thousand he had been very proud of until de Lohr rolled down from the north like a ball of fire.

It had been three very long, very difficult days.

Axminster, as a royal training ground, had about a thousand men inside the castle, which was kept bottled up while Tatworth and St. Martin tried to scale the walls and gain access. Once de Lohr and Bigod arrived, however, it turned into a massacre because Tatworth's men refused to leave. They didn't merely try to defend themselves—they fought like banshees, and when they'd managed to capture a few of Norfolk's men, they cut them into pieces and launched them back at the surrounding army.

There were pieces of chopped soldiers all over the place.

Even now, Hereford's men were walking around a pile of limbs and other meaty parts, which had been collected from the mud and placed in an area near the surgeon's tent. But there were still things sticking up out of the mud, and as the thunder continued to roll overhead, there was a meeting taking place in the tent of the Earl of Hereford and Worcester. His blue tent with yellow lions was recognized all over England. The meeting hadn't started yet because they were waiting for one man, who quickly came from the direction of the castle and dashed into the tent. Shaking himself off, he pulled his helm off to reveal a flushed, wet face and soaking hair.

"How nice of you to join us, West." The man standing near a cluttered table, surrounded by a half-dozen soaking, smelly men, glanced up at the latecomer. "Any late news to bring us?"

Westley de Lohr, the youngest son of the Earl of Hereford and Worcester, nodded his head at his eldest brother. "Aye," he said. "My apologies for being late, but this was just hurled over the wall. One of our men picked it up."

He was holding up a rock with something strapped to it, and handed it over to Curtis, who was not only his father's heir but also the Earl of Leominster in his own right. It was evidently a rock wrapped in oilcloth that was held on with a pair of belts. Curtis set the rock on the table as he and another man fussed with the ties on the belts.

"Careful, Curt," the man said. "It's dripping water on whatever is inside."

Curtis acknowledged the advice from another de Lohr brother. Douglas de Lohr was three years older than Westley, the fifth of six de Lohr brothers, but the brother with perhaps the most maturity and wisdom out of all of them. He was also highly intelligent. But the brains and good character he had were encased within a form that sent many a maiden swooning. With his long blond hair, sky-blue eyes, and muscular body, he looked like a Viking god.

Tales of Douglas de Lohr's beauty were legendary.

"Right," Curtis said, peering at what seemed to be underneath the oilcloth. "It looks like vellum."

Douglas took the rock from the table and finished stripping off the leather belts. The oilcloth fell away and a piece of folded vellum did indeed slip out, falling to the ground. Curtis quickly retrieved it, opening it up and reading it as the men in the tent crowded around the table.

"What does it say, Curt?"

A tall, powerfully built man had asked the question. He was older, with dark hair that was turning to gray and the worn lines of a face that had seen much in his lifetime. He also happened to be Curtis' brother-in-law. Antoninus de Shera, Earl of Coventry, was married to Curtis and Douglas and Westley's youngest sister, Olivia Charlotte, otherwise known as

Honey. He had a great sense of humor but was impatient at times.

"Well?" Antoninus demanded again. "What does it say?"

Curtis finished reading it and handed it over to Antoninus. As the man took it, reading it greedily, Curtis turned to the group.

"It seems that Lady Isabel wants to open the gatehouse and let her army into the fight," he said, raking his fingers through his dark blond hair. "I cannot say that I blame her. If we open the gates, it is a two-front battle."

"But we also risk Tatworth men rushing into the fortress and attacking the keep," another man said. Attention turned to Grayson de Winter, Earl of Radnor, a man who was a close friend of de Shera and de Lohr. He was also the one in command of not only his men, but of Norfolk's army as well. "We have to be prepared to send men in to protect the keep. There are about fifteen women in that structure that I'm sure Tatworth would love to get his hands on, not to mention the greatest prize of all in Lady Isabel."

Curtis nodded. "I realize that," he said. "Grayson, can you organize the defense of the gatehouse? Let no Tatworth man into the bailey. I will maintain my post out here on the walls. We have Tatworth where we want him and I would like to see this battle over by nightfall."

Grayson nodded, glancing at his son and heir next to him. Davyss de Winter, something of a knightly prodigy at his young age, nodded firmly. With Grayson and Davyss in charge of the gatehouse, surely no man could make it through their line.

"Good," Curtis said, looking at the other men crowded around the table, all of them taking a turn reading the missive. "Then it is settled. If Lady Isabel wants to open the gates, let her.

We will end this skirmish once and for all."

"As if you could stop her from opening that gate," Antoninus said with a twinkle in his eye. "Honestly, I'm surprised she's not out here with us, swinging a sword. The woman is formidable."

The men chuckled to varying degrees because he was correct. Isabel de Kerrington was a strong, determined woman if there ever was one.

"There is great truth in that statement," Curtis said. "I think it will be a task simply to prevent her from leaving the keep and taking a stick to Tatworth. The man's very life is in danger if she gets half a chance."

"Must we send men to protect him, then?" Douglas quipped.

Everyone laughed at the expense of Tatworth, and Lady Isabel to a certain extent. Curtis shrugged his big shoulders.

"Quite possibly," he said. "She will be furious enough to beat him soundly about the head and shoulders. But what we must do is protect the keep in case Tatworth men get by me or Grayson. Douglas, that will be up to you. Choose the men you would take with you carefully and go to the keep. You will be the last line of defense if anyone slips through."

Douglas nodded. He already had his squad in mind, men he'd worked with for years. Men he trusted.

It was going to be a long afternoon.

CHAPTER TWO

THE STORM HAD worsened.

But the time Lady Isabel was ready to raise the portcullis and purge her army from Axminster, the storm was so bad that it was buffeting men about with wind and rain. The Tatworth army had taken a stand when they saw that they would now be fighting on two fronts and had dug in, which had made it difficult to move them away from the gatehouse. It was like tides of men, each pushing against another until there was very little movement at all.

But it was a enough movement for Douglas and his men to get into the bailey.

It wasn't only Grayson and the de Winter war machine that protected the gatehouse—there was also a line of Axminster men to reinforce them. They were on the interior of the gatehouse while the de Winter men were on the exterior. Douglas had to push through them in order to get to the keep, and they weren't entirely welcoming about it. He had to explain to them that he'd been sent by Hereford to protect the keep, and only after too much discussion and a lot of frustration did the Axminster men finally let him through.

At that point, the sky was dark gray with clouds and the wind and the rain made it difficult to move. Everything was blowing them in different directions and, given they were on the top of the hill, no one wanted to roll down a slope.

Axminster Castle was referred to as a spur castle, meaning it sat atop a natural hill, or a spur of a hill, and used the steep sides as protection. There were a series of earthworks at the bottom of the hill for defensive measures that had been heavily used, and the gatehouse was at the top of a switchback road that was, at this point, slick with mud, and part of it had collapsed in a landslide.

Once inside the bailey, it was as if two castles were linked together—there was a large bailey just beyond the gatehouse followed by an even larger bailey flanked by curtain walls that that ran the length of the top of the flat hill, with outbuildings and an enormous great hall. The keep was anchored at the end of the long central bailey. Enclosed in its own small bailey, the tall, square building was five stories in height. It was enormous, covering the entire south side of the hill fortress.

It was that enormous keep that had Douglas' attention.

With the keep in sight as the storm howled around them, Douglas, Westley, and another knight, plus about seventy de Lohr men, rushed toward it. The third knight was none other than Jonathan de Wolfe, a vassal of the Earl of Norfolk. He also happened to be the brother of the Earl of Wolverhampton. Most importantly, he was also the brother of William de Wolfe, Baron Killham, who was largely considered the greatest knight in the north of England. The scourge of the Scots, they called William. Jonathan wasn't an earl, or even a prestigious warlord, but he had something else.

Raw, brute strength.

Jonathan had the dark de Wolfe good looks, and hazel eyes that were gold in some light, but he was taller and wider than either of his brothers. *Beastly* was how some people described him. Wolfie, as he was called, was a follower, not a leader, a man with more brawn than brains, which was particularly needed at this moment. Like a rare few of his knightly contemporaries, he was a Blackchurch trained, something even his younger brother couldn't claim. The Blackchurch Guild was the premier training facility for knights in England, if not the known world.

That made him an extraordinary tool in a situation like this. As the group of de Lohr soldiers approached the keep, Douglas put de Wolfe on the stone stairs that led to the entry.

"Wolfie!" he shouted above the storm, pointing to the keep entry. "You will not move from that spot, not for anyone. Do you understand me?"

Jonathan nodded firmly, leaping onto the slippery stone steps and miraculously not losing his footing. He was heading up the stairs when the shutters of a small lancet window that was positioned about eight feet above the mid-flight of stairs suddenly opened. Had Jonathan not seen it, and had he not been quite fast on his feet, he would have been covered by a pot of boiling water. The women inside were screaming at him, throwing boiling water from the window to try to get him off the steps, but he stood out of range and tried to explain who he was.

They didn't believe him.

Now, Jonathan was trapped on the landing in front of the entry door, which was bolted, with no way to go down the stairs unless he wanted to expose himself to more scalding water or worse. Since he was out of the line of fire from inside the keep, he simply stood guard in front of the door, watching the distant gatehouse, watching a surge of allied men coming in beneath the raised portcullis. Douglas, standing below the stairs, was watching the same thing from a different vantage point.

And that was when he heard it.

Thump!

Above the wind and rain, he'd heard it. He turned to see Jonathan with his hand on his helmed head and a large iron pot at his feet. Shielding his eyes from the rain, Douglas could see a window high above the entry landing, and there was movement. He could see an arm. Someone had evidently dropped the pot on Jonathan's head from a great distance. Poor Jonathan was trying to shake off the stars he was undoubtedly seeing.

That brought Douglas up the steps.

"Ladies!" he boomed above the bad weather. "I know you can hear me, so listen well. I am Douglas de Lohr. My father is Christopher de Lohr, the Earl of Hereford and Worcester. We were asked to come on Lady Isabel's summons to help defend Axminster against Tatworth and the man you are trying to kill, the one at your door, is Jonathan de Wolfe, who is the brother of the Earl of Wolverhampton. Stop trying to smash the man. He is here to defend you!"

No one could shout like a de Lohr. His voice echoed off the stone and he knew very well that they were hearing him inside. On the landing above him, Jonathan was trying to pull off his helm, but the iron pot had evidently dented it. It took him three tries and a long, hard pull to finally pop it off his head.

There was blood running down the side of his face.

That set Douglas off.

He took the steps to the landing where Jonathan was standing, unmolested by hot water or flying pots, and began to pound on the door.

"Open this door at once!" he shouted. "You have injured this knight. Open this door or I will bring a battering ram and smash it down!"

He pounded and kicked, demanding entrance, and finally heard a bolt move. He stopped pounding, but he was still furious. Grasping Jonathan by the arm, he pulled the man over to the door about the time it lurched open.

Several frightened faces were on the other side.

"Here," he said to them, shoving Jonathan in their direction. "Tend his head and allow him to lie down for a time. God knows what damage you have done."

There were several young women who stood aside as Jonathan stumbled over the threshold. One woman in particular, an older woman with carefully coiffed red hair, seemed to take charge of him.

"We did not know he was an ally, Sir Douglas," she said, grasping Jonathan by the arm and forcing him to bend over so she could see the damage. "A scalp wound. They bleed terribly. He will be well tended."

She turned him over to the women surrounding her and they led him off, hovering around him, while the red-haired woman and two or three other young ladies remained. The woman with the red hair faced Douglas.

"I am Lady Isabel de Kerrington," she said in a voice laced with confidence and authority. "It is on my request that your father sent men. I am deeply grateful. I hope you will tell him that."

Douglas stood on the doorstep as the rain pounded on him. "You might have shown your gratitude better than by trying to kill a knight sent to assist you," he said.

"We could not be sure it was not Tatworth."

"You know the Tatworth standard, do you not? Wolfie was not wearing it."

"It could have been his ally."

Douglas lifted an eyebrow. "He is wearing Norfolk of Arundel," he said, growing annoyed. "You are a woman well versed in the politics of England, enough to know the standards of every important warlord that matters. Moreover, Arundel is your ally and he was clearly wearing the standard. I will not argue this with you, Lady Isabel. And I will tell my father that you are grateful for his assistance. But please try to be more careful with the men who are helping you hold on to your castle."

Isabel knew he was right for the most part, but it was also true that because of the storm, she and the other ladies really couldn't see Norfolk's distinctive colors because they were darker and the tunics were wet. But she didn't argue. There was no point. With a slight nod in his direction, she excused herself to see to the care of the knight they'd tried to brain. Two of her charges went with her while the third one remained behind.

Douglas watched the woman disappear into the darkness of the keep, trying to decide if he was offended by her attitude or if he simply didn't care. He was weary from three days of fighting, and that was beginning to affect his temperament. He wasn't quick to temper by nature, but he might make an exception in the countess' case. With a weary sigh, he was preparing to turn away from the door when he heard a soft voice.

"Please do not be angry with us, my lord," she said. "Lady Isabel has not slept since the attack started and she is only doing what she feels is best. She would defend this keep single-handedly, I think."

Douglas turned to the source of the voice. A woman came out of the shadows, wearing something white. Until his eyes adjusted to the dim light, all he saw was a flowing, pale garment. Like a wraith would wear. Or an angel. It turned out to be a simple linen garment, but on her, it seemed like gossamer. The woman's movements were graceful, her stature short but her figure pleasing. But when he got to her face, the real pleasure took hold. She had a sweetly oval face, with a little nose and little chin and enormous green eyes.

He was taken aback by what he saw.

"I am not angry," he managed to say. "I do not think any of us have slept much since we arrived. If I was sharp or loud with Lady Isabel, then I apologize."

She smiled with rosebud lips that parted into a delightful expression. "I have heard Lady Isabel speak twice as sharply and thrice as loudly," she said. "You were not nearly as frightening as she can be, my lord."

He couldn't help it. He grinned because she was. A woman like that—tiny, sweet, pixie-ish—there was no way he couldn't smile in return. She was like a fragile little doll, porcelain and pristine, and Douglas had a hard time believing she was real.

He'd never seen such perfection.

"I see," he said. "Then mayhap I should come in here and sit amongst the women and let her take charge of the army outside."

"She would do a tremendous job of it."

He snorted. "I suspect she would," he said. His smile faded as his gaze lingered on her, like moth to flame. "What is your name, my lady?"

Those bright green eyes glimmered with mirth. "Lady Isabel would box my ears if I told you my name without our being properly introduced," she said. "But I suppose there is no harm, considering the fact that there is no one around to introduce us. I am Lady Misery Isabella Rosalie d'Avignon."

His eyebrows lifted. "Forgive me, but… Lady Misery?"

"Aye."

"*Misery* is your name?"

She chuckled. "I have a twin brother named Payne," she said. "Payne and Misery. My mother spent three days laboring to give birth to us and refused to name us anything other than what she was feeling at the time of our birth."

He stared at her in disbelief. "And your father allowed this?"

"He died about a month before we were born. We were named out of grief."

Douglas could see the overall picture, including a woman in mourning. It made some sense as to why her daughter bore such a horrific name. "A pity," he said. "I would have thought your name to be something glorious like Eleanor or Elizabeth or Katherine."

She was smiling as she shook her head. "I am afraid not," she said. "But if it makes you feel any better, I am known as Mira. The first letter of each of my names—M-I-R-A. My grandmother refused to call me Misery, too."

"Ah," he said with approval. "Mira. That is much more suitable."

"And your name, my lord?"

"Did you not hear me shout it before I tried to kick your door in?"

She laughed softly. "I confess, I did not," she said. "I was one of the ones boiling water to drop on unsuspecting knights."

He frowned, but he was jesting. "Then *you* are to blame."

"I confess, I am."

He quickly returned to a smirk. "To answer your question, I am Douglas de Lohr," he said. "My father is the Earl of Hereford and Worcester."

"Christopher de Lohr?"

"You know him?"

Mira shook her head. "Nay," she said. "But I wrote the missive requesting his assistance. Since the death of Lady Isabel's brother, the situation at Axminster has been… difficult. Tatworth has been persistent."

"So it would seem."

"Your presence is most welcome."

His smile turned into one of those devastating gestures that had caused many a maiden to swoon, but for Mira, he meant it. He wasn't trying to get something out of her or force her to his will, as he'd been known to do on occasion. Douglas liked women and they liked him in return. But for pretty little thing like Mira…

It was genuine.

"Thank you, my lady," he said. "Your gratitude is appreciated. Would you do something for me?"

"Of course, my lord. How may I be of service?"

He pointed to the ceiling. "Can you check on my knight?" he asked. "That was a nasty blow. I would like for you to keep a close eye on him and report to me when I return. Will you do that?"

She nodded eagerly. "I will, my lord."

"Thank you."

With that, he dipped his head, silently excusing himself, and then turned for the entry door, which was still open. He paused a minute before heading out into the rain, pulling his helm down a little to help keep the water out of his eyes, but he couldn't help himself from glancing over his shoulder to see if Mira was still standing there. Maybe he just wanted another glimpse of her before he headed out into the elements. To his pleasure, not only was she still in the entry, but she was right behind him as he headed out the door. When he looked at her curiously, wondering why she was following him, she indicated the soaked oaken panel.

"I must bolt the door after you leave," she explained. "But I will see to your knight immediately."

He simply nodded his head and continued on, out into the driving rain and down to the series of baileys where the Hereford and Norfolk armies had very quickly subdued Tatworth and St. Martin. With the added men from inside Axminster, it had only been a matter of time before Tatworth and his ally were finally forced to lay down their arms. By the time Douglas hit the gatehouse, he had reports from multiple men telling him multiple things.

Unfortunately for Douglas, his mind was still back in the keep.

Mira.

He would remember that.

CHAPTER THREE

"AND HE HAS been harassing me ever since," Lady Isabel told a roomful of men. "Tatworth wants to marry me, assume the earldom, and merge the lands. It would give him a very large property and make him quite wealthy, but I have no intention of marrying the man, and my rejection has driven him mad."

In the great solar of Axminster Castle, a two-storied chamber with a small staircase that led to a catwalk around the upper portion of the chamber where records were kept, the men gathered about could easily believe Lady Isabel's statement. They'd just spent three full days battling Tatworth, who had dug himself in and refused to move until Douglas and Grayson split the Tatworth-St. Martin army and conquered them. But given the prize of Axminster and the glory that was the castle itself, not one man could really blame Tatworth. Axminster was a fine prize.

But it was a prize that Lady Isabel retained.

"Tatworth and his men are prisoners," Douglas said. His helm was off, his long hair tied up into a messy bundle at the back of his neck. "He wants to negotiate his surrender but, frankly, there is nothing to negotiate. I can demand that he surrender his castle to you, and you would be a rich landowner, my lady. What is your pleasure?"

Isabel smiled weakly. "I do not want Tatworth Castle," she said. "It is enough for me to manage Axminster, but I appreciate your sentiment, Sir Douglas. Mayhap… mayhap if de Lohr were to station men at Tatworth to help me oversee the place, I would consider it."

"Then we must be clear on this, Lady Isabel," Curtis spoke up. "Now that Tatworth is subdued, if you do not wish to confiscate the castle as the spoils of war, what do you want to do with Rickard Tatworth?"

Isabel cocked her head. "What do you mean by that?" she said. "What is there to do but send him home?"

"So he can attack you again?" Curtis said, trying to convince her to think the worst in a situation like this and plan accordingly. "May I be frank, my lady?"

Isabel gave him a stone-faced expression, hiding her irritation at a man who was trying to give her orders. "Please."

Curtis knew she didn't mean it, but he was going to say it anyway. He'd spent the past several hours with Lady Isabel de Kerrington, and although he hadn't known her before his march on Axminster, even in the few hours he spent with her he could see what kind of a character she was. Determined and stubborn was where she started. Where she ended, he couldn't even guess, but he knew one thing—she was used to doing things her own way and didn't like to be told what to do.

That was going to make this conversation very interesting.

"My lady, I suspect you haven't been involved in many sieges or battles," he said. "Is that a correct assumption?"

Oh, but she had to be called out for anything that anyone

might consider a shortcoming. Isabel was standing in a chamber with more than a half-dozen seasoned warriors and now she was being forced to admit that she didn't know much about battle.

It wasn't going to be easy for a woman of her considerable pride.

But she had to be honest.

"Axminster is a peaceful demesne," she said evenly. "I am not a trained warrior, my lord. I have not had the need to participate in any sieges or battles. But that doesn't mean I do not understand the quality of mercy."

Curtis could see that she was defensive. They all could. "This has nothing to do with mercy and everything to do with protecting Axminster," he said. "If I may speak plainly about this situation, my lady, my sense is this—Rickard Tatworth was greatly offended when you refused his offer of marriage, so much so that he attacked Axminster. You were so concerned that he might succeed in breaking down her walls that you sent word to my father and to Coventry and Norfolk. We were able to subdue Tatworth, but if we simply send him back home, as you suggest, he will only consider that a weakness. It will not keep him from attacking you again. Are you prepared for that?"

She wasn't. With a heavy sigh, she reluctantly shook her head because she knew she was defeated by his logic. "Nay," she said. "What would you suggest?"

Curtis glanced at Grayson, at Antoninus, before speaking. They had already discussed this earlier and were about to present a united front against a very headstrong lady. Curtis was to be the one elected to speak with her about it because he happened to be married to a very headstrong lady himself. He knew how to handle them.

He hoped.

"My lady, I know this is difficult," he said. "But you must understand that we are your allies and we are trying to help you. I'm sure you believe that."

"I do."

"Then believe me when I tell you that this is for your own good," he continued. "We will send Tatworth home, but his army will be distributed among our armies and we will replace his with men who are loyal to us and a knight to command them. We will also station a knight here, at Axminster, and about five hundred de Lohr men. I know it does not sound like a lot, but these are highly trained men who will help reinforce your own ranks and keep your fortress safe until Rickard can be trusted again not to charge Axminster and, subsequently, force you to do something you do not wish to do."

Isabel was listening carefully. "Axminster only has about four hundred regular men," she said. "We've never needed a substantial army, but you are aware that royal trainees are sent here by the king and trained by my brother's knight, Eric le Kerque."

"I know, my lady."

"Then you are suggesting doubling that amount with de Lohr troops?"

"Aye, my lady."

"This is to become a de Lohr garrison, then?"

Curtis shook his head. "Nay, my lady," he said. "We will be here to protect you."

"But—"

"Tatworth is subdued, but St. Martin is not," Curtis pointed out, interrupting her because she was growing defensive again. "He has run back to his castle and left Tatworth to face punishment. The last thing you want to do at the conclusion of a battle is let your guard down, my lady. We believe stationing troops here will show Tatworth and his allies that your guard is up and will remain up until they settle down and behave."

He'd left no doubt about what their intentions were and what they thought she should do. Isabel's gaze lingered on Curtis before moving to Antoninus, Grayson, and finally Douglas and the big knight they called Wolfie. It was a ridiculous name for so big and rough a man, but it was his name all the same. They were all looking at her, waiting for her response, but the truth was that she could only respond one way. She had to agree with their terms and suggestions because if she didn't and Tatworth came back on Axminster, she seriously doubted they would come at her call again.

That meant she had to accept their help.

"Very well," she finally said. "How long?"

Curtis shook his head. "What do you mean?"

"How long will your men be here?

"Several months, at least."

Isabel had to think on that. Folding her hands, she put them against her mouth as if praying as she slowly and thoughtfully made her way to a large, carved table that was near the hearth. A table that had been carved from exotic wood, with legs carved into the shape of lions. It had belonged to her grandfather. When she finally sat, it was with great contemplation.

"If you feel that is best, then I will agree," she said, looking up at the men around the table but mostly at Curtis. "But I will make myself clear, Lord Leominster. Axminster is a prize property and we have a function that cannot be interfered with. We are a royal training ground for soldiers. I personally mentor ten young women from the finest families in England and there are more to come. I will not have a gang of soldiers not under my command interfering with either function. Is that clear?"

Curtis nodded. "It is, my lady."

"I will tolerate no interference from the de Lohr men," she continued. "I assume you are leaving a knight in command?"

Curtis nodded, pointing to Douglas. "My brother," he said. "I believe you have already met Douglas."

Isabel cocked an eyebrow as she looked at Douglas. "He raised his voice to me before we were even introduced," she said. "I remember him well. Sir Douglas, I hope we are going to get on with one another."

Douglas nodded. "I will do my very best, my lady."

"No more raising your voice to me?"

Douglas cleared his throat. "As long as you do not throw pots of boiling water on my knights, I do not see the need, my lady."

The men in the room fought off smiles because they'd heard the story. Lady Isabel seemed rather embarrassed by that comment. "No more boiling water," she assured him. "Is the knight we offended remaining here as well?"

Douglas nodded. "He is, my lady."

Her gaze moved to Jonathan, standing back in the shadows with Westley. The boiling water hadn't done any damage, luckily for her, but the man still had an egg-sized lump on the back of his head.

"I shall try not to offend him again," she said before returning her attention to Curtis. "I will accept your recommendations, Lord Leominster. I pray it discourages Rickard Tatworth enough to leave me alone and prey on someone else."

Curtis nodded. "That is the hope, my lady," he said. "But

please utilize Douglas if you need to. He is a seasoned knight, and quite intelligent, and his advice is sage. He is also deadly with a broadsword and fearless in his actions. And de Wolfe is a Blackchurch-trained knight. They do not come any better or any braver than him. Both men will be at your disposal."

Isabel passed another glance at Douglas as if appraising him, so much so that when she looked the other way, Douglas closed his eyes and shook his head faintly as if already leery of what he was about to face with her. It hadn't been his idea to remain with the de Lohr troops, but Curtis', so he'd essentially been forced into it. Curtis had his own properties to administer as well as their father's, because Christopher was quite old these days and although sharp mentally, physically, he was old and weary. Curtis had therefore stepped in to help and Douglas had been assisting him, but Curtis wanted Douglas to remain at Axminster because he felt it was more important at the moment.

Douglas wasn't so sure.

"I have le Kerque at my disposal as well," Lady Isabel said, jolting him from his thoughts. "He is a fine knight also."

Curtis nodded. "Indeed, he is," he said. "But he manages the royal troops. He trains them. That is where his focus should be. Douglas and de Wolfe will be here to manage everything else for you and he will work well with le Kerque. They have known one another from times past."

Isabel didn't seem too keen to continue the conversation at that point. Things were not moving the way she wanted them to, not really, so there was no real use in arguing about it. For a woman perpetually in control, that was a difficult thing to acknowledge. Therefore, she simply nodded her head and moved away from the table.

"Whatever you believe is best, my lord," she said. "I do not suppose I will be much help from this point forward, so I will beg my leave at this time. Make whatever arrangements you need to make and please inform le Kerque of your intentions. I should like him to know what is happening so that we may have order and organization once your armies pull out."

Curtis watched her head to the door. He could sense her disappointment in her loss of complete control, and the truth was that he understood. But it had to be this way.

"My lady, I realize you are not happy with de Lohr troops here," he said. "But believe me when I tell you that we are doing it for your safety and the safety of everyone at Axminster."

"Would you be happy?" she said, not looking at him. "Having strange troops at your home? It is simply an adjustment. We shall become accustomed to them."

"Would you rather have Tatworth troops, then?"

She paused in the doorway, turning to look at him. He was telling her, very nicely, that this was the best the situation could be and she would have to accept it. Whether or not she wanted to.

"I've told you that I am grateful for your assistance," she said steadily. "I am grateful for everyone's assistance. My brother would have been grateful, also. I am concerned, however, that I am creating a burden now that you feel the need to leave some of your army with me. It was not my intention to create a burden for you after the job of fighting off Tatworth was done."

Curtis shook his head. "It is no burden, my lady," he said. "My father would want us to ensure you were protected and that our efforts were not wasted."

Isabel simply nodded. Forcing a smile as if to reinforce her statement of gratitude, she quit the solar, shutting the door softly behind her. No one said anything for several long seconds, making sure she was well away before they did. In fact, Antoninus went to the door, carefully opened it, and peered outside before shutting it again.

"She's gone," he confirmed quietly.

Curtis took a long, deep breath and sat heavily in the nearest chair. It was the first time he'd shown his exhaustion since the battle began, and as he sat, so did Grayson and Antoninus. Everybody began hunting for chairs except for Westley, who began hunting for wine. He found some in a nearly empty pitcher and grabbed it by the neck, draining it, without offering some to anyone. When he put it down and smacked his lips, he found himself looking at a roomful of men who were glaring at him to varying degrees. Realizing why, he headed for the door.

"I'll find more," he muttered.

"And food," Douglas said, kicking him in the arse as he walked by. "You'd better bring all you can find. And hurry about it."

Westley didn't take kindly to the kick, but Jonathan got in behind him and pushed him toward the door before he could take a swing at Douglas.

"I'll help you," Jonathan said. "I do not trust you not to eat everything and tell us you could find nothing."

Grinning, Douglas looked at Curtis, who rolled his eyes as Westley and Jonathan quit the chamber. When they disappeared, Douglas laid his head against the back of the chair and emitted a weary sigh.

"She wants us to defend her castle, yet she does not wish for us to remain and ensure Tatworth does not return," he muttered. "The woman even wants him released with no punishment. If we do that, what is to deter him from coming back and trying again?"

"*You* are the deterrent," Curtis said. "Whether or not Lady Isabel likes it, you and de Wolfe are the deterrent. She is simply going to have to accept it."

With his head still against the back of the chair, Douglas rolled it in the direction of his brother so he could look at him. "And why can you not leave Westley here instead of me?" he asked.

Curtis scratched his head wearily. "Quite honestly?" he said. "Because Westley does not have the patience you have. He would fight with her and she would see that as a weakness. You will not fight with her because you have patience, and with a woman like that, it is the only way to assert control. Unless Grayson or Antoninus would care to remain behind."

Both Grayson and Antoninus shook their heads quickly. "Not me," Grayson said. "I've already given you de Wolfe, though I can spare Davyss as well if Douglas would like his sword. It might be good for him to do something on his own for a while and not be under his father's constant supervision."

"Absolutely," Douglas said. "I can use Davyss. I would feel better with him at my side."

"Good," Grayson said. "He shall remain, then. But be cautious, Douglas—he may be hell with a sword, but he is very much a young man when it comes to his wants and desires. I've seen the ten young women that are under Lady Isabel's tutelage. My son may consider that a hunting ground, so make sure he keeps his mind on his tasks. Do not let him be idle."

Douglas smiled wearily. "He has barely seen twenty years," he said. "I would *hope* he would be a little unrestrained with his wants and desires at that age."

Grayson cocked an eyebrow. "I do not want, or need, any de Winter bastards," he said. "Just keep him focused. That is all I ask."

Douglas continued to smile in response to a father who was perhaps a little stern with his eldest, and very virile, son. "I have a father who also went to great lengths to ensure his sons were restrained at that age," he said, looking at Curtis. "Remember? Papa was not terribly encouraging when it came to us and female companionship."

Curtis put a weary hand over his face. "Christ," he muttered. "That is an understatement. I recall a feast at Winchester Castle when a de Leybourne lass caught my eye. You know the family? From Cornwall. Her name was Catherine. As it happened, I caught her eye also, and we shared a few dances before I fetched two cups of watered wine so we could sit and talk. We found an alcove with these beautiful oriel windows and sat in the night breeze, perfectly respectably, and speaking about anything that came to mind."

Across the room, Antoninus spoke. "That does not sound terrible, Curt," he said. "I cannot believe Chris objected."

Curtis shook his head. "You have not let me finish," he said, wagging a finger at the man. "My mistake was in closing the heavy brocade curtains to give us some privacy, and the next I realize, a hand reaches in, grabs her by the arm, and yanks her out of the alcove. Then the curtains collapse on me and I'm being beaten through the curtains. As it turned out, the lady had two brothers and a father who took exception to my closing those curtains. My father agreed. He was the one who yanked her out and let those de Leybourne fools beat me with sticks through those heavy curtains."

Douglas burst into soft laughter. Even Grayson and Antoninus grinned. "I stand corrected," Antoninus said. "Your mistake was closing those curtains. You *are* a fool."

Curtis sighed. "I know."

"Were you injured?"

"Hardly bruised. The curtains were so heavy that the blows barely made contact."

"Then you were fortunate," Grayson said. "Alas, I only have two sons, so I cannot fully relate, but I do know that both Davyss and Hugh carry the hot de Winter blood. You *will* look out for Davyss, won't you, Douglas?"

Douglas nodded with confidence. "I shall throw curtains on him and beat him if he gets out of hand."

"I would be grateful."

The conversation quieted, at least for the moment, because it was the first time in days that these men had had the opportunity to sit still and quietly. Grayson found a chair and, once he tipped his head back, was instantly asleep. Antoninus found a bench underneath one of the lancet windows, and even though it was a small bench, it was enough for him to get his head and torso on it. He, too, closed his eyes and faded off almost immediately.

That left Douglas and Curtis as the last men standing.

Literally.

"What now?" Douglas said quietly, his eyelids begging for sleep. "Am I to be subservient to a countess who has no battle experience, or do I have some independence?"

Curtis was feeling his exhaustion like the others. Probably more because not only had he been commanding the allies, but he'd been fighting as well. He could hear the disdain for Lady Isabel in his brother's question.

"You are subservient to her unless you know that whatever

she wishes or commands will either put everyone in jeopardy or get everyone killed," he said. "In that case, you have my permission to do what is necessary to ensure the safety of everyone. I hope that is clear enough because I cannot make it any clearer. Use your judgment, Douglas. It has not failed you yet."

Douglas sighed heavily. "Something tells me that this assignment is not going to be a simple thing."

"Probably not."

"I do not want to be here longer than three months, Curt."

"Understood."

Curtis sat down behind Lady Isabel's big table and put his head down on the worn wooden tabletop as Douglas finally laid his head back on his chair again and closed his eyes. It took very little time for their snoring to join those of Grayson and Antoninus, and when Jonathan and Westley returned sometime later bearing food and drink, it was as if they'd walked headlong into a chamber full of thunder. The defense of Axminster Castle was finally over.

Now, the real battle was about to begin.

CHAPTER FOUR

Six Weeks later

"DO YOU SEE him?"

"Who?

"*Him!*"

There was a good deal of craning necks and gasping and even some shoving as several young women strained to catch a glimpse of something that had their attention.

Some*one* who had their attention.

He had since nearly the day he arrived.

It was a bright and sunny day in the middle of August and there wasn't a cloud in the sky as the wards of Lady Isabel strained for a look at their favorite subject. It had been an unusually dry and warm summer, and they were dressed in lighter-weight clothing, but that didn't mean it wasn't proper or fashionable. Quite the opposite, because Lady Isabel demanded it. Life at Axminster, since the Tatworth siege, had quickly settled down to normal, and even now the gatehouse was open and people were moving in and out as they went about their business. The difference these days was that the gatehouse was heavily manned and anyone coming in and out was thoroughly inspected.

The events from six weeks ago had not been forgotten.

Rickard Tatworth had been sent home shortly after his defeat and his punishment had been that his army was completely disbanded. Grayson had absorbed some of the Tatworth men and so had Hereford, until Tatworth was only left with thirty men to run his rather large castle. In addition, Curtis had ordered his men to search every corner and every chamber at Tatworth Castle, removing any weapons or anything that could be used as a weapon. They even took the knives out of the kitchens so the cook was left with only a couple of very dull knives to use in the course of her duties. All sharpening stones had also been removed, as had farming implements that had any kind of a blade on them. Anything that could be used in a fight had been stripped clean and Curtis had taken it all with him back to Lioncross Abbey Castle, seat of the Earl of Hereford and Worcester.

That left Lord Tatworth with nothing to defend himself with but also nothing to attack anyone with. Grayson had left about thirty of his own soldiers at Tatworth Castle to ensure that weapons were not made on the sly. The smithies were only allowed to shoe horses or help the wheelwrights in repairing wheels or anything else that required metal, but they were not allowed to fashion anything that could be used as armament. Stripped and dishonored, Rickard Tatworth was left a very unhappy man.

But it didn't end there.

He was disgraced among his allies, who were now ostracizing him. Tatworth had a few allies in the area, including St. Martin, and none of them responded to Rickard's summons or missives. When Rickard physically rode to a neighboring garrison to find out why, they would not admit him and told him to return home. He still couldn't get a straight answer as to why he was being treated like a leper, but he found out soon enough that it was because St. Martin had been telling everyone that he had been petty and foolish in his attack against Axminster Castle and Lady Isabel.

The tides had turned dramatically.

That had left Tatworth without support, which worked in Axminster's favor. It seemed that the man had been completely subdued, punished in a way that Lady Isabel approved of, so life had Axminster continued as it always had. Tradesmen and farmers still did business there, the training of the royal troops continued, and Lady Isabel continued to educate the young women entrusted to her care. Everything was back to normal. Now, it was those young women who were desperate for the sight of the man that had them all swooning since the day he arrived.

Douglas de Lohr.

Each young woman was quite convinced that she was the right match for Douglas. He was kind and chivalrous, and pleasant even when they made fools out of themselves trying to impress him. When he spoke, he had a deep, beautiful voice with a slight lisp that made the young women sigh with joy. At this moment, they were supposed to be praying in the tiny chapel of Axminster, but one of them had seen Douglas walk by on his way to the stable and now all of them were trying to peer through the three lancet windows that faced onto the central bailey, hoping for a glimpse of the knight who looked like a Viking god. The mere mention of his name sent female hearts aflutter.

All but one.

Mira was the only one actually in prayer, as they were all supposed to be. At least, she was kneeling before the small stone altar and trying to concentrate, but the chatter about Douglas had her distracted. Unable to continue her rosary, she sighed heavily and stood up, going to the window and pushing between a couple of the young women to see if she could possibly see what had them fluttering like birds.

She couldn't.

The entire situation was ridiculous.

"Do you want me to seek him out and settle this once and for all?" she asked with some sarcasm. "Do you want to know which lady he favors so you will stop this foolish behavior? We have been going through this for months and it is time to end it. Who is brave enough to know the truth?"

Nine hopeful yet fearful faces were gazing back at her. Astoria, Davina, Helen, Ines, Louisa, Marceline, Primrose, and Theodora. All of them from some of the finest families in England, all of them ranging from fourteen years of age to eighteen. Mira was the oldest of the group at twenty years and three, but she was a special case. She wasn't truly part of them, but then again, she was simply because amongst the throng was where Lady Isabel wanted her. Astoria, Davina, and Helen were the second oldest, all of them having seen eighteen years. They were women grown.

And they were looking for husbands.

Maybe one husband in particular.

"Well?" Mira demanded again. "Do you want me to settle this once and for all?"

"You cannot simply *ask* him," Astoria said as if it was a frightful suggestion. From the House of de Luzie, she brought a great fortune with her to a marriage. "What on earth will he think?"

Mira looked at the tall, rather plain young woman. "What do you think he thinks *now*?" she said. "Astoria, he knows that all of you watch every move he makes. The man cannot even eat in peace without someone offering to cut his meat for him—and right now, we are supposed to be in prayer, yet you are paying homage to a man who looks like a god among us. You are praying to Douglas!"

She made a sweeping motion with her hand toward the bailey where he was last seen. The young women began to look uncertain, even ashamed, as Astoria and Davina and Helen looked at each other with worried brows.

"She's right," Helen finally said. "We should be praying. If Lady Isabel catches us not following her instructions one more time, she will punish us."

Astoria was usually the leader of the group. She was headstrong and bossy and she thrived on telling the others what to do. In the early days of Douglas' presence at Axminster, she told the women that he would be her conquest. That hadn't happened yet, and she was increasingly embarrassed that he'd not fallen at her feet simply because she demanded it. These days, she tried to pretend that it didn't matter because there was a secondary target in Davyss de Winter, who was also quite handsome, but he was also young.

She wanted an older man.

But he, so far, didn't want her.

Astoria spent most of her time these days trying to save her pride.

"She will not punish us if we all swear that we spent this time praying, as she instructed," she said, looking at the anxious faces around her. "Shall we swear it?"

The girls started to nod, but Mira spoke up. "Swear to a lie in a chapel?" she said, incredulous. "That is sacrilege, Astoria. Shame on you for suggesting such a thing. But… if each one of you prays right now, however quickly, it shall not be a lie, shall it?"

That sent most of the girls stampeding to the altar and dropping to their knees as they began rapid-fire prayers. *Hail, Mary, full of grace…* Astoria and Helen remained by the windows with Mira just as Douglas began to pass by. Mira caught sight of him first.

"There he is," she said, gathering her skirts as she turned for the chapel door. "I am going to settle this so there will no longer be any question. I will demand to know who he finds favorable so everyone will stop wondering."

"You'll put in a good word for me?" Astoria said before she could stop herself. When Mira looked at her, surprised she should verbalize such a hope, Astoria tried to pretend she hadn't meant it. "What I mean to say is that if you happen to speak of me, you can tell him that I may or may not be interested in his suit. I've not yet decided."

Mira knew she didn't mean a word of it but nodded, heading to the chapel entry door and giving it a good yank to open it. The door was warped and tended to stick. Leaving the chapel, she headed out into the bailey in pursuit of Douglas.

He wasn't too far ahead of her.

Dust blew up in her face as she moved swiftly, getting the hem of her green silk dress dirty. She didn't like the heat, or the sun, so she shielded her eyes from the bright light as she kept her focus on the prize ahead. Douglas was stopped by a de Lohr soldier and engaged in a brief conversation, but he happened to catch a glimpse of Mira coming up behind him.

That always brought a smile to his lips.

She was wearing a gown the color of her eyes today, and it made her look even more ethereal than usual. When their gazes met, his smile broadened and he put his hands on his hips in a somewhat stern gesture.

"And what are you doing out of the chapel?" he demanded lightly. "This *is* your prayer time, is it not?"

Mira smiled in return. "How would you know that?"

"I know everything."

"Then do you know that every girl in that chapel is watching you from the windows and *not* praying?"

His smile faded as he looked over at the small, sturdy chapel. He could see figures in the windows, suddenly disappearing when they realized his attention was upon them.

He sighed heavily.

"Lady Isabel is going to punish them if they continue that," he said. "I do not want to be responsible for their pain."

Mira chuckled. "Then you can end all of this attention right away."

He frowned. "How?" he said. "I have been trying to do that since it started, Mira. I swear to you, if I find Ines or Primmy in the privy one more time, waiting for me to relieve myself just so they can spy on me, I am going to jump into the river and swim away for good. Do they not know how unseemly that is?"

Mira was in full-blown laughter by now. "They know," she said. "I have told you repeatedly that you must tell Lady Isabel. She will end that behavior very quickly."

He shrugged. "I know," he said. "But it seems cruel to do it. She is very strict with her wards, I have noticed."

"Then you are weak and soft and it serves you right if they never stop spying on you."

She wasn't serious and he knew it, so it was a struggle to maintain a frown without smiling. "That is a terrible thing to say to me," he said. "How hurtful."

"I doubt it."

His eyebrows flew up. "Is that so?" he said, nearly sneering at her. "Very well, then. If you are so smart, tell me how I can end this attention once and for all."

"That is simple," she said, lifting her hand to shield her eyes again. "All you have to do is declare which young woman you favor most and the rest will leave you alone. None of them would dare tread on another woman's territory. Especially of the male persuasion."

His smile faded, as did his jesting mood. "Are you serious?"

"I am afraid I am," she said. "I told them I would ask you which lady you favor. Astoria asked me to put in a good word for her."

He shook his head and turned away. "I am not going to declare anything," he said. "If you could simply ask them to leave me to my business, I would be grateful."

Mira began to follow him. "I cannot," she said. "All jesting aside, my lord, they are very serious about you."

"Then that is their misfortune. And I told you to call me Douglas."

That was true. He had. Mira took up pace beside him. "Now who is being cruel?" she asked. "These are fragile young women. You do not want to upset them."

He stopped and looked at her. "They are all far too young," he said. "Why do they not fixate on Davyss? He is more their age."

Mira shrugged. "Because they like the blond, godlike creature who strolls the grounds," she said, her eyes glimmering with mirth. "As the representative of the wards, I must ask you to come up with a pleasing answer that does not hurt their feelings, yet does not commit you to anything."

His gaze lingered on her for a moment. Truth be told, he was fairly smitten with Mira and had been since the day they'd met, but given the circumstances and the politics at Axminster, there was no possible way he was going to declare that the only young woman he was interested in was, in fact, her. But he wasn't here to find a wife and, frankly, he didn't need the headache. He was here to do a job and a job only. But every day that he saw her, his resolve weakened more and more. In moments like this, she would have done less damage had she taken a battering ram to him. That rock-solid de Lohr composure was weakening.

But he almost didn't care.

"Very well," he said, rolling his eyes. "Is that what this will take?"

She nodded. "I am afraid so," she said. "I know they have been quite a nuisance, but one word from you will end it."

"Do you truly believe that?"

"I hope so."

He scowled. "That does not sound very confident."

She shrugged. "I cannot promise anything with that group," she said. "But I believe they will stop."

He looked at her, lips twisted in thought. "Then you will have to help me."

"How?"

He gestured between the two of them. "Pretend you are madly in love with me and I will pretend I am madly in love with you," he said. "You are the only one I trust, Mira. Anyone else would take it seriously."

He'd addressed her informally on more than one occasion and she found it quite endearing. She liked Douglas, very much. He was humorous and animated at times, and she'd found him to be very wise. He was always right, about everything, and she had come to trust his judgment. Not that they had any real relationship outside of an occasional conversation—and, one time, he'd helped her track down several errant chickens when it was her turn to manage the kitchens—but still, she liked him. She didn't have a brother, so Douglas had shown her what it might have been like to have had one. Or any sibling, for that matter. Perhaps even a husband.

She considered him a friend.

It was a foolish dream to consider he would ever be anything more.

Still, his suggestion was a surprising one and, if she thought about it, a suggestion to be feared. She was astute enough to know that pretending she was in love with the man might give her a taste of what it would actually be like, and she wasn't sure that was a good idea. With Douglas, it would be so easy to hope for the real thing.

She didn't want to fall into that trap.

"That is your only plan?" she said, avoiding giving him an answer. "That is a weak attempt. Can you not come up with anything else?"

Douglas had to admit that her refusal to play along disappointed him. More than that, it hurt his feelings. *Imagine that! Me—with hurt feelings!* He almost laughed at himself but couldn't seem to manage it. Shrugging his big shoulders, he shook his head and turned away.

"I do not," he said. "I am sorry that pretending to be in love with me is such an appalling prospect. I did not mean to offend you."

He was starting to walk away again, and Mira followed. "You did not," she said. "Don't be silly. I simply meant that I do not think they will believe it."

"Why not?"

"Because you are Douglas de Lohr. I am no one of note."

He came to a stop and looked at her. "That is not true," he said. "You are Lady Misery Isabella Rosalie d'Avignon. Your family hails from Lincolnshire and your father was Lord Wygate of Wygate Castle. You are of noble birth."

Her brow furrowed. "Who told you that?"

He threw a thumb in the direction of the gatehouse, or keep, or both. "Le Kerque," he said. "He says your uncle was none other than Caius d'Avignon of Hawkstone Castle."

She nodded. "He was."

"He and my father were friends, you know."

She shook her head. "I did not," she said. "But I do not like le Kerque telling you about my background. That should come from me."

Douglas braced his big legs apart, folding his arms over his chest. "He wasn't gossiping if that concerns you," he said. "We met shortly after I was stationed here and he told me about everyone of note who lives here simply to orient me. I know about you, about Lady Astoria, Lady Helen, and the rest of them. Would you rather have me not give a lick about any of you and treat you all like dirt?"

"That is *not* what I meant."

"Then what *do* you mean?"

She sighed sharply. Douglas was a forthright man and when he was correct, which was always, he could get a bit confrontational when challenged. Not that it had ever really happened between them, but she'd seen it happen with others. Eric le Kerque was one. Eric had trained men unchallenged for several years, and when Douglas made a suggestion one day, a probably a correct suggestion on weapon management, Eric had pushed it aside and Douglas had taken offense. The castle was still talking about it. Eric had eventually backed down and the two of them got along well enough, but Douglas was clearly a man used to having his way in all things.

Truth was, so was Mira.

"I simply meant that if you were curious about me, then I would hope you would ask me directly," she said. "I will tell you everything you wish to know, so let me explain to you why no one would believe you could consider me a marital prospect."

Douglas cocked a blond eyebrow, an imperious gesture. "Go ahead," he said. "I am listening."

Mira cocked an eyebrow, too. "First of all, I am not an heiress," she said. "I am not anything. Everything went to my brother, Payne. Secondly, when I finished fostering with Lady Isabel, I returned home to Wygate only to discover that my mother had taken another husband who had a daughter a little younger than I, and she immediately became very hateful against me. She told my mother that I had threatened her and intimidated her, and my mother believed her. She sent me back to Lady Isabel. Have you not wondered why I'm still here at my age? It is because my mother's new husband did not want me around. So I am here."

"What did your brother have to say about it? He is lord of Wygate, is he not?"

"He is," she said. "But even he could see what a fuss that girl was making over me. He told me I could stay if I wanted to, but I chose to return to Axminster where I was happy."

"I see," he said. "But all of this still does not explain why you feel you are an undesirable marital prospect."

She looked at him as if he were daft. "Did you not just hear me?"

"I heard everything."

"Then it should be clear to you."

He shook his head. "The only thing clear to me is that you find me to be a disgusting creature you could never be in love with," he said. "I am sorry that I am so appalling, my lady."

She scowled. "You are ridiculous."

"Is that so?"

"It is," she insisted. "Douglas, you know you are the most handsome man at Axminster and, more than likely, the entire world, and the fact that you are making me tell you this when you already know it is only feeding your pride. That is shameful!"

"Is it?"

Mira was ready to explode at him when she caught him laughing. He started laughing so hard that he bent over, hands on his knees, and she was trying desperately to maintain her outrage.

"Stop laughing," she said, fighting off a smile. "Stop laughing this instant, Douglas de Lohr. Do you hear me?"

He did, but he suddenly went down on one knee in front of her and took her hands, holding them in his two big fists.

"I know those silly chickens are watching us from the chapel windows, so they now see that I am on my knee before you," he said, his blue eyes twinkling with mirth. "Please, Mira. Please pretend to love me. Please pretend to belong only to me so that gaggle of children will leave me alone and stop watching me piss. *Please!*"

He was being dramatic and hilarious and very sly. He was making it look as if he was proposing to her and, of course, she had no choice but to go along with it. Or so he thought. She tried to yank her hands from his grip.

"Let me go, you fool," she said, trying very hard not to laugh at him. "Douglas, I swear I will beat you if you do not let me go."

The more she pulled, the more he refused to let her go, but she managed to get one hand free. That caused him to yank on her, pulling her into an embrace right out in the middle of the central bailey for all to see. He was on his knees, holding her tightly, his face pressed into her belly, as she began slapping him around the head.

"Douglas!" she gasped. "Release me this instant!"

He was laughing so hard that he was crying, his face pushed into her soft, warm torso. It would have been extremely enticing had he not had to suffer through the sting of her slapping at his head and ears.

"I will not release you until you agree to pretend to love me," he said, muffled against her belly. "Agree or we stay like this forever."

Mira knew he meant it. Furious, but also caught up in the man's undeniable charm, she stopped hitting him and he immediately released her. He stood up, but he still had one of her hands.

"Now," he said in a low voice. "Do we have a bargain?"

She was desperately fighting off a grin as she shook her head at him. "You are an insufferable arse," she hissed. "I swear you deserve everything that is coming to you. I hope a thousand foolish maidens follow you around and spy on every aspect of your life. I hope you never have a moment's peace!"

His grin broke through. "As long as you tell everyone that we are madly in love, I do not care what curses you bring down upon me," he said. "Do we have a bargain?"

She was looking at him most hatefully. "If we must."

"We must," he said. "Now, smile. You are very happy that I have declared my intentions. Smile!"

He hissed the last word, and she produced a sneering grin that not even he believed. "How is that?" she asked.

He frowned. "Terrible," he said. "You look like you have a bellyache."

"I do, and its name is Douglas."

He started laughing. "Insult me all you wish and I do not care," he said. "We have a bargain and you had better live up to it."

"And if I do not?"

His laughter faded. "Even if you do not want to make the bargain, you have," he said, suddenly serious. "Your honor is at stake, my lady. That is the most important thing in the world. If there is even a small part of you that has any respect for me, live up to that bargain. Do not disappoint me."

He meant it. All jesting aside, even Mira could see that. She may not have liked what he'd managed to wrangle out of her, but her honor was important to her. She didn't want to lose a friend.

"I will not," she said. "I will be a sickly sweet as you want me to be where you are concerned."

He eyed her dubiously. "Make it believable, at least."

"I told you that I will not disappoint you. I meant it."

He nodded, a faint smile on his lips, before lifting her hand to kiss it. With a lingering glance, he headed off, back to the duties that were part of his day, as Mira stood there and watched him go.

Her heart was still beating wildly in her chest.

Letting out a pent-up sigh, she put her hand against her sternum as if to ease her racing heart. All jesting aside, the man had made her feel faint with his sweet kiss and charming ways. She realized she wouldn't have been disappointed if this farce they were about to perpetrate were real.

But it was only make-believe.

Perhaps that would come to be the biggest disappointment of all.

CHAPTER FIVE

HE'D BEEN A great knight, once.

Eric le Kerque had fought with the armies of Henry III as a younger man. He'd been to France, to Flanders, and a dozen other places during his years as an active fighting man. He loved to travel and loved being part the greater army because he felt as if he was truly a man of destiny. He was well respected and liked by his men, something that continued to this day as he trained royal troops. But one thing that had changed was how he viewed the world in general, battles included. That fearless knight who was courageous in battle had come to an end in a little skirmish outside of Paris.

The day when Eric had transformed into something different had started out just like any other day. It had been a cold winter, and he awoke that morning to frost on the ground and a faint dusting of snow falling from clouds the color of pewter. They had been preparing to lay siege to a small castle belonging to a French duc who had stolen property from Henry, and the king wanted it back. Eric had suited up that morning and prepared to fight, but as he was approaching the castle on horseback, a volley of arrows cut both him and his horse down.

The horse died and Eric didn't, yet the road to recovery was more difficult than he could have possibly imagined.

The arrow had cut into his torso and damaged nerves to his legs. Because the initial arrow strike hadn't killed him, they had every reason to believe that he was going to recover, but a poison had taken hold a few days after the strike and he'd been sick with that for months on end. The poison had weakened everything about him, and when it was all finished, he had no strength in his arms and his body as a whole was diminished. But he had worked very hard to regain his strength, as much as he was able, and because Henry liked him, he put him in charge of helping train royal troops. His assignment had been Axminster Castle.

That had been about ten years ago, and Eric was good at what he did. He was a good instructor and he had patience, which was important when dealing with raw troops. He taught them to ride, to walk in a column, and military ethics, but when it came to anything that had to do with weaponry, he would leave that to his sergeants.

He didn't want to be around it.

His fear of deadly objects had made him a somewhat ineffective knight when Tatworth attacked. He was good with tactics and defenses, but when it came to the actual fighting, he remained at the castle and in command while he sent his men out to fight. He didn't get involved in any of the allies or their meetings, while Isabel did. Because of this, he hadn't even met Douglas until two days after Tatworth surrendered. Isabel had told him about the allies stationing troops at Axminster, something he didn't agree with, so he'd sent word to Douglas that *he* was in command once again and allied help was no longer required. That had brought Curtis to the castle to explain, yet again, that they were going to station de Lohr troops there for the foreseeable future and that Douglas would be in command while Eric would continue with his duties.

Eric had no choice but to accept it.

That had been six weeks ago.

This afternoon, as his men were being trained by others, Eric made his way to the keep and slipped in through a door used by the servants. He made his way up to the top floor, up the narrow servant stairs, until he reached a chamber that faced the northwest. The top floor of Axminster's keep had six chambers, interconnected, but that meant doors could be locked from the staircases and no one could enter the maze of chambers. That was why Eric and Isabel had been meeting there for the past few years, pretending that lonely chamber overlooking the northwest was theirs and theirs alone.

Pretending it belonged only to them.

Here, he had waited for his love to come.

"My apologies for my lateness," Isabel said as she came through the door. She gestured toward the servant staircase. "Is that one locked?"

Eric had been sitting at the window, gazing at the activity below. "Aye," he said. "Lock the chamber door behind you, my dearest."

Isabel did. With a sigh of relief, she pulled off her wimple, letting he red hair tumble down her back. She set the wimple aside, scratching at her scalp as she made her way over to Eric. He smiled at her, opening an arm, and she leaned into him as she peered from the window.

"Do you see any of my ladies down there?" she asked.

He shook his head. "Not recently," he said. "But I did hear about Douglas and Lady Mira."

Isabel put her fingers to her forehead as if to ward off a headache. "Oh," she said. "*That.*"

"Aye, *that*. What are you going to do about it?"

Isabel shrugged. "What can I do?" she said. "Douglas is not under my command, so I cannot discipline him, but I told Mira she is not to allow that type of display ever again. Evidently, he has asked for her hand."

"Is that so?"

"I have been told."

Eric moved over so she could sit beside him on the stone window bench. "He really should have known better," he muttered. "He is a de Lohr. He knows about propriety. What he did was impetuous. And vulgar."

Isabel looked at him. "Do you think so?"

Eric shrugged. "Truthfully, I do not," he said. "All things considered, I suppose it was rather romantic, but not for all to see. He risks her reputation doing that."

Isabel rolled her eyes. "Reputation," she scoffed. "Pah. What he risks is nine other ladies weeping their hearts and out and becoming hysterical because he has declared for Mira. Primmy actually fainted."

Eric looked at her but eventually lost the battle against the smile that threatened. "Good Christ," he muttered. "They are a dramatic bunch."

"Dramatic and annoying," Isabel said. "The older ones aren't too bad, but Primmy and Marceline keep fainting, each one trying to be more dramatic than the other. They have declared their undying hatred for Douglas now."

Eric shook his head. "*They* hate him?" he said. "God's Bones, they have been awful to the man. Following him around like a puppy, fighting to see who sits next to him at sup, and then hiding in the privy while he takes a piss. If anyone should hate, it should be Douglas—on them."

Isabel was listening to him, amused. "Do you care?" she said. "The man has usurped you in your own castle. Why do you care how he is treated?"

Eric chuckled. "He did not usurp me," he said. "I've told you that. We have overcome our misunderstandings from the beginning of his post here. Truthfully, I rather like him. He and his knight—the one they call Wolfie—have been very helpful with the troops who are going through combat training now. I wish I had de Lohr and Wolfie all the time to help like that."

Isabel leaned against him, her head on his shoulder. "I am glad he has been of assistance," she said. "But I simply do not think we need him or his troops here any longer."

He kissed her on the forehead. "That is not your decision to make, my dearest."

She sighed again, sharply this time. "Why not?" she said. "This is my castle. I should be the one making all of the decisions, including military decisions."

He gave her a gentle squeeze. "I do not disagree with you," he said. "We were doing quite well until Tatworth came along and tried to steal you away from me. You never did tell de Lohr that you and Tatworth had been virtually betrothed until I foiled his plans, did you?"

Isabel shook her head. "Nay," she said. "He did not need to know that, though I believe Rickard told him. I am not sure if Douglas believed him, but it does not matter. I got the better man."

"A better man you will not marry."

Her expression tightened and she pushed herself off the bench, away from him. "Must you always bring that up?"

He watched her walk over to a table that held wine and fruit. "I do," he said. "You told me you would marry me when the time was right, but so far, that time has not come. I fear it never will."

She looked at him, pain in her expression. "Please do not say such things."

"Why not?" he said. "It is true. You have let your father and brother get into your head and into your heart. They told you that you must marry a man above your station, no matter what you feel for him, so that is what you wait for. A better man than me."

She closed her eyes and looked away. "That is not true," she said weakly. "It is simply that the death of my brother has put such a large burden on me. Everything is mine, Eric. The stress and strain, the finances, the relationship with the king… everything. I want to marry you when my heart and mind are lighter than they are now. If I marry you now, I feel as if I cannot focus on our marriage."

He looked at her, a gentle smile playing on his lips. "Those are excuses, and weak ones at that," he said softly. "I love you, Isabel de Kerrington. I have loved you since the moment I first gazed upon you. I want to marry you and I want you to bear my son before you grow too old to do such a thing. You have already seen forty years. You will not be fertile much longer, my dearest."

"Is that all you care about?" she said. "A son? If that is your greatest concern, then you must find someone else to marry, because I will not be a broodmare."

"That is not what I meant and you know it."

"Do I?" she shot back softly. Then she shook her head and waved him off. "I do not wish to discuss it now. I must decide what to do about Mira and Douglas. I feel as if I should have a word with him about the situation, Eric. Do you not agree?"

She was changing the subject, as she always did when it came to marriage. Disappointed yet again, Eric simply went along with it.

"Would you rather I speak to him?" he asked, sounding dejected. "It might be better coming from me."

Isabel could hear the defeat in his voice and it cut her, but she refused to give in to it. She knew what he was thinking. She understood his disappointment. But the truth was that he was right—he was a lesser knight from a lesser family. She was the heiress to Axminster. When she married him, it would become his. Was he strong enough for it? Certainly, Eric was a kind and generous man. She loved him dearly. But she was frankly concerned about his being the Earl of Axminster and all it entailed. He wasn't born into it like she was. He would be assuming it, stepping into her father's and brother's shoes. The very sad fact was that she wasn't sure he could administer the job. It might crush him.

And she didn't want to crush him.

But she also didn't want to lose him.

"Nay," she said after a moment. "It is my responsibility. Will you find him and send him to the solar? I will speak to him there."

Eric nodded but didn't move. When she turned to look at him curiously, he simply extended an arm to her. It was an invitation for her to return to her seat beside him, to return to his embrace. Even when he was hurt, or disappointed, he never fought with her. He was subservient to her because he knew, deep down, why she was reserved. He didn't want to be the Earl of Axminster, but if he married her, he would be. He wanted to marry the woman, not the title.

But she *was* the title.

And Isabel knew it. She knew everything. Without another word, she went to him, allowing him to pull her into an embrace, allowing his lips to claim hers. They had utter, complete privacy in the northwest chamber and had taken advantage of it numerous times in the past. This was why they met here, a place of deep and abiding memories, because it had been in this very chamber seven years ago that Eric had claimed Isabel's virginity. She'd given it to the man she loved, a simple knight with a heart of gold. She, too, had loved him the moment she first saw him, and she always would. But she didn't want to talk anymore.

She simply wanted to taste him.

Even as Eric kissed her furiously, Isabel's hands moved to his breeches, fumbling with the ties. When he realized what she was doing, he helped her. With the ties finally free, Isabel's warm hands snaked into his breeches and sought out his semi-flaccid manhood. With the first touch of her soft hands, he knew he was lost. He couldn't deny her.

He didn't want to be denied, either.

Due to the chill morning weather, and because he was susceptible to the cold, there were myriad clothes on Eric's body and Isabel helped him yank it off, unwilling and unable to wait. He was wearing a woolen tunic underneath everything, but it stopped at his hips, so he was unconstrained when Isabel yanked his breeches to his knees.

There was a powerful sense of urgency now, of a desire so fierce that they were overwhelmed with it. Eric lifted Isabel onto the stone bench of the window, pulling her legs apart and wedging himself between them. She threw her skirts back and wrapped her legs around his waist, taking gentle hold of his now-rigid phallus and guiding it into her warm, slick folds. Holding her tightly, Eric impaled her upon his manhood.

Isabel gasped with the pleasure of it, her arms going around him, her nails biting into his shoulders. Feeling the man within her fed her soul as air fed the lungs. Eric held her tightly, thrusting into her willing body. He couldn't get enough of her, driving into her as she whispered heated words in his ear. Isabel's hands found his bare buttocks, squeezing them, and he found it wildly arousing. With a few more thrusts, he quickly removed himself before he could spill into her body. Instead, he spilled on the floor. But fingers finished for her what his phallus couldn't, and he silenced her cries of passion with his mouth as she found her own release.

As their passion cooled, their kisses transformed from wild and passionate to soft and gentle. Eric tasted her deeply, his hands roaming as he gently suckled on her mouth, moving under her garment, which had been loosened, and up her torso to her breasts. He fondled her nipples as their kisses trailed off. Isabel tossed her head back, her eyes closed as Eric toyed with her breasts tenderly. He finally laid her back on the bench and pushed her skirts up all the way, kissing her belly, finally suckling gently on her breasts.

Isabel let him. She let him do what he wished to do as the day around them went on. They could hear the men in the bailey, distant horses, the chatter of birds. Moments like this were a window into a life they could have, a life of normalcy as husband and wife. Moments like this were when Isabel was her weakest against his argument of marriage. When he took her yet again, she was a willing participant. As the man thrust into her, she found herself wondering if he would let himself spill into her this time and she would conceive that son he'd spoken of. He was usually careful about that, but sometimes he surrendered to his passion and released himself as God intended. Perhaps this time it was all a ploy to impregnate her so she would be forced to marry him.

Perhaps that had been his plan all along.

That thought had her resisting a little, wanting to move out from under him and accuse him of such a thing, but he felt her movement, and that only made him hold her more tightly. She moved again but that made him hit just the right spot with her, and she felt her release beginning, unable to pull away. She would let him do what he was doing—and no matter what her paranoia was thinking, her body had surrendered to him.

Her man.

Her love.

The scolding of Douglas de Lohr was going to have to wait.

CHAPTER SIX

"IF THEY LOVE one another, then you should be happy for them… right?"

Helen was trying to comfort Astoria, who had been inconsolable since witnessing the man of her dreams declare for someone else. *Mira*, of all people.

Misery Isabella Rosalie d'Avignon.

Misery aptly described what Astoria was feeling.

The girls—all nine of them—were in the smaller ladies' solar that was reserved exclusively for them and their lessons. They weren't allowed in the large solar that had been used by the Earl of Axminster, and was currently used by Lady Isabel, nor were they allowed to wander the keep. Other than the two bedchambers they shared between them, the kitchen, and a few other chambers, they were limited to where they could go. The ladies' solar was their main, and favored, gathering chamber.

A room that was seeing its share of drama at the moment.

"She seduced him," Astoria wept. "Rather than allow him to make his choice, which was clearly meant to be me, she seduced him and forced his hand."

Helen and Davina, the older girls, passed glances at one

another. They both liked Mira—all of the girls did—so to hear Astoria speak so unkindly of her was distressing.

"Mira would not do such a thing," Davina said. She was the more outspoken between her and Helen, and she and Astoria had, at times, pulled one another's hair in rage. "Mira is not like that. Sir Douglas must have seduced her instead."

Astoria whirled to her, tears on her cheeks. "How can you say such a thing?" she said. "You know that I've not yet decided about him. He must have taken my indecision as… as a rejection, and Mira took advantage of it!"

She was trying desperately to salvage her reputation. All of the girls knew she wanted Douglas. All of the girls knew Douglas did not have an eye for her, but Astoria made it sound as if she had the control.

But Davina shook her head.

"Astoria, I am sorry if you are sad about Sir Douglas and Mira," she said. "But Sir Douglas never looked twice at you. He never looked twice at any of us."

Astoria was starting to turn red in the face. "Obviously, that is not true if he declared his love for Mira," she said. "He was looking at *somebody*."

"Just not you."

Astoria shrieked, flying off the chair she'd been sitting on, slapping her open palms in Davina's direction. But Davina moved out of her way, pushing her, and she stumbled into the table. She would have fallen had she not caught herself on a chair, but on the tabletop in front of her was a fork. Astoria picked it up and brandished it at Davina like a knife.

"How wicked of you to say such things," she said. "You are lying about everything and I will punish you!"

Davina stood her ground. She wasn't as tall as Astoria, but

she was a few pounds heavier. And she was stronger, which was why Astoria hadn't charged her right away.

She sighed sharply.

"Put that fork down or I will tell Lady Isabel that you threatened me," she said. "There are seven witnesses here who will tell the same story, so stop being ridiculous. You are simply angry and trying to blame me, and everyone else, for your troubles."

Astoria still had the fork in her hand, looking around at the fearful faces of the younger girls, but she knew one of them would crack if pressed to support Davina's story. Therefore, she opened her fingers and the fork clattered to the floor.

"You are without sympathy," she said to Davina as she wandered over to a carved bench with cushions near the window. "Mayhap your heart does not dream of greater things, Davina, but mine does. It dreams of being a de Lohr."

"Why not a de Winter?" Davina said, secretly relieved that Astoria hadn't charged her. "Davyss is quite handsome. And he is closer in age. Why not him?"

Astoria plopped down on the bench. "He is too hairy," she sniffed. "The hair on his head is shaggy and hair covers his arms and chest."

"Douglas has hair on his arms and chest."

"But it is blond!" Astoria insisted. "It is like a dusting of gold on him. My beautiful, golden Douglas is gone."

She lay back on one of the cushions and started to sniffle again. Davina looked at Helen and shook her head at Astoria's antics. With nothing more to say, Davina left the solar, heading for the kitchens because it was her turn this month to supervise the evening meals. Once she was gone, Astoria popped up from the bench and rushed to the door, shutting it and bolting it.

Then she turned to the surprised faces in the chamber.

"Douglas was *mine*," she declared. "Davina is simply too stupid to know what a man wishes. She never had a chance with him and that makes her jealous. Would you not agree?"

She was nodding emphatically, which forced the younger girls to nod along because they were afraid of her. Only Helen wasn't nodding, but Astoria didn't give up. She focused on the younger girls, a more vulnerable audience.

"I know Mira seduced him because I saw her," she said as if it was a great secret she'd been hiding. "I saw her in the stables with him, and she… she lifted her skirts to show him what was between her legs."

"Astoria!" Helen gasped. "You know that is not true! You—"

"I did!" Astoria said, shouting Helen down. "I saw it and you cannot say otherwise because you were not there. Mira is a seductress and a wicked woman, and if any of you speak to her, then you are wicked, too!"

She had the younger girls fairly terrified at this point. Ines, Louisa, Marceline, Primrose, Theodora were looking at each other in terror, and Primrose went so far as to faint so she wouldn't have to deal with Astoria. But Astoria went to the girl and yanked her up into a sitting position, shaking a finger at her.

"Listen to me and listen well," she hissed. "If you speak to Mira again, I shall send a missive to your parents and tell them that you consort with a woman of foul morals. She is intent on leading you astray!"

The younger girls lowered their heads in fear. Marceline started to weep. Only Helen was left standing in shock. But the truth was that she was afraid of Astoria, too, because the young woman would do exactly as she threatened. She would send a missive to the families of these girls and tell them how they were frolicking with a woman who lifted her skirts to knights. Astoria was low enough to do it, and no one wanted her venom focused on them.

Pleased that the younger girls were cowering to her demands, Astoria stood over them a moment simply to make sure no one had anything to say to her. They wouldn't and she knew it. She had the power over them and liked that feeling. When the knight she lusted after was out of her control, at least she could manipulate some of those around her.

But Helen was disgusted by it. Turning away, she went to find the embroidery she had been working on the day before. Lady Isabel expected her ladies to be productive, and every day they were expected to embroider or sew for a few hours. Just as she reached down to pick it up from where it had been neatly tucked away, Astoria came up behind her and smacked it out of her hand. Startled, Helen spun around and shoved Astoria back by the chest, hard enough to make her stumble.

"Do not push me," Helen growled. "Do not push me and do not touch me. You may be able to strike terror into the hearts of others, but I know you for what you are. Don't you dare push me again or I will tell Lady Isabel everything you have said."

Astoria righted herself, torn between threatening Helen and backing off. Helen wasn't usually so bold with her, but even Astoria had to admit that her behavior over the past several moments was beyond what she'd ever done before. But she was embarrassed and disappointed, a bad combination, and having little self-control, she was deteriorating into the petty world of vindictiveness. As she gazed at Helen, she could see that she didn't have the woman's support.

"Careful," she said after a moment. "I do not suppose your

widowed mother would like receiving a missive that her daughter surrounds herself with trollops."

Helen's eyes narrowed. "And I do not suppose that your father would like receiving a missive that his daughter is a wicked, vengeful bitch," she said in a low voice. "I told you not to push me. Leave me out of whatever foolishness you choose to engage in, Astoria. I do not want to be part of it."

With that, she bent over to pick up her needlework and sat down, her back to the wall as she faced Astoria. She didn't trust the woman not to charge her again, or worse. She watched Astoria as the young woman looked her over and then chuckled. It was a dirty sound. Turning away, Astoria went to find the piece she had been working on the day before, also, as the five younger girls continued to cower in the corner.

And that was the way she liked it.

CHAPTER SEVEN

"IF YOU CONTINUE to hold your sword like that, you will get your fingers chopped off," Jonathan said loudly. "Hold it this way—not with your fingers splayed toward the blade."

He held up his sword to demonstrate to the royal recruits that were in training at Axminster. It was late afternoon and the weather was good for the work they needed to do. Today, it was more advanced sword tactics, something Eric had curiously passed off to the two sergeants that served him, but the sergeants could only teach basic things.

Douglas and Jonathan had seen that fairly quickly.

With Eric's permission, they'd taken over teaching the recruits the finer points of handling swords and various weapons. Axminster had a well-stocked armory, so there were plenty of weapons to train with and the men took to it eagerly. Douglas and Jonathan had watched the first few days of the weapons training from the wall, noting that the sergeants seemed experienced with the more rudimentary weapons like the mace or the axe. They knew how to use a sword, but not like a knight did. Now the men were learning from elite knights and were quite excited about their lessons.

Even if those lessons were coming from an enormous and fairly terrifying warrior.

Jonathan was a knight's knight. Blackchurch trained, he was more at home in a battle than most and, as it turned out, was an excellent teacher as well. He didn't just tell them how to do it—he showed them. If a man didn't do it correctly, Jonathan would show him how to do it correctly until the man got the hang of it. The men seemed to take to his teaching style, and after the first week of training, Douglas backed off and let Jonathan take over completely because he seemed to have a knack for it.

It was yet another thing that Jonathan was good at.

Truth be told, Douglas had been wondering from the start why Grayson had left Jonathan behind. A knight of his value should not have been discounted it so easily, and that's what it seemed like to Douglas. The Earl of Norfolk had a quality knight in Jonathan de Wolfe, a man with training and the family connections, so a man like that should have been integral to the workings of an army like Norfolk's. The last Douglas had heard, Jonathan had been in command of Arundel's army, but the Axminster battle showed that he was taking orders from Grayson. Although Grayson and the House of de Winter were intertwined with Norfolk and Grayson was, in fact, an earl, it still seemed odd to Douglas.

He just couldn't understand why men of that caliber had been left behind.

Because the House of de Lohr was tightly allied with the House of de Wolfe, as Douglas' father and Jonathan's father had been the best of friends years ago, Douglas and Jonathan had known each other virtually since birth. Jonathan was older than Douglas was, but they had always gotten along. He was glad to have Jonathan with him during his time at Axminster, but something seemed off with the man. Douglas couldn't put his finger on it, but it was almost as if Jonathan was hiding something. That was the best way Douglas could describe it. On the surface, Jonathan was his usual self—humorous, dedicated, and principled—but there was something in his eyes that suggested there was turmoil just below the surface.

Douglas had been pondering that very thing for the past six weeks. Jonathan hadn't spoken of anything out of the ordinary and Douglas hadn't asked him, but he was curious. He supposed that if there was something Jonathan wanted to know, he would tell him.

Meanwhile, it was business as usual.

As the day began to wane, Douglas continued to watch Jonathan from the wall walk as the man continued the troop training in the central bailey, the one that stretched from the gatehouse to the inner bailey and the keep. It was an enormous stretch of dirt, grass, and outbuildings, and the wall that enclosed it was equally enormous. The wall walk at Axminster was so large, and so long, that it was nearly a half-mile all the way around it. As Douglas moved down the wall, alternately watching Jonathan on one side and the countryside on the other, he could see Eric and Isabel coming from the inner bailey. He lifted a hand to the pair, waving, and Eric lifted a hand in return.

Isabel, predictably, didn't.

Douglas moved to the heavy ladder that gave access down to the bailey. There were towers with stairs, but those were mostly at either end of the wall, so he took the rather treacherous ladder down to the central bailey to save time. Eric and Isabel were still several feet away, heading in his direction, as Douglas went to meet them. Off to his left, Jonathan had his back turned to both Douglas and Eric as he abruptly stopped the trainees from the exercise they were engaged in.

"Stop!" he shouted, holding up his hands. Then he moved to the soldier nearest him and pointed to the man. "You there. Why are you holding your blade like that?"

The soldier froze, looking at Jonathan in confusion. "M'lord?"

Jonathan went to the man. "Lift your hand, but do not move it," he said. "Show me how you are gripping that sword."

Still puzzled, the man lifted his hand with the sword in his grip. Jonathan grabbed him by the wrist and held it up for all to see.

"Do you see the way he is holding this?" he said to the group. "See how high his hand is on the hilt? He is going to break a wrist or worse with the first serious blow he delivers."

He made sure everyone could see it. As the group nodded, making sure they weren't holding their swords in that fashion, Jonathan let go of the soldier's arm.

"Who told you to hold a sword like that?" he asked.

The man was no longer puzzled, but now becoming increasingly mortified. "I have seen Sir Eric hold his weapon like this," he said nervously. "Is this not right?"

Jonathan shook his head. "Nay, it is not right," he said. "Only a fool would hold a sword like that. I cannot believe Sir Eric would hold his weapon this way. Are you certain?"

"Aye, m'lord."

"Then he was wrong," Jonathan said flatly. "I thought he did not teach weapons?"

"Not usually, m'lord," the soldier said. "But this time, the sergeants were ill. Sir Eric did what he could."

Jonathan simply shook his head as if Eric was the biggest

fool in the world as he adjusted the man's hand on the hilt. The problem was that Eric, now standing a few feet away with Douglas, had heard him. So had Isabel. Before Jonathan could say anything else that might slander Eric, Douglas cleared his throat loudly.

"Wolfie," he said. "We have visitors."

Jonathan turned around, seeing the very man he'd been speaking of right behind him, and by the look on Eric's face, Jonathan knew he had heard him. Rather than pretend he hadn't said what he had, he leaned into it.

He wanted to clear the air.

"Ah, le Kerque," he said. "Just the man we have been discussing. I must ask you something. Have you taught them to position their hands so high on the hilt? I can only imagine you were misunderstood, but I want to clarify."

There was something in Eric's eyes that suggested defeat. Defeat and humiliation. He looked at the soldiers around them, all of them looking at him, waiting for an answer. It was true that he'd heard the entire conversation between Jonathan and the soldier and clearly heard Jonathan call him a fool, but he wouldn't address it. He wasn't confrontational by nature and certainly not with a knight of de Wolfe's caliber.

If the man thought he was a fool, so be it.

"A bad habit I picked up over the years," he finally said. "I found I had more control that way. I know it is a bad position and it leaves the wrist exposed, but the sword I used had a guard on it to protect my fingers, so I was comfortable in doing so. Unfortunately, I seem to have passed my bad habit on to the soldiers."

Jonathan could see that Eric was embarrassed and he shook his head firmly. "Not at all," he said. "Now that you explain it to me, I understand why you showed them your technique."

"It is not much of a technique," Eric admitted. "I haven't been to…"

Jonathan wouldn't let him finish. He turned to the group of soldiers and held up a hand to silence their chatter. "Sir Eric has explained why he showed you how to hold the sword in such a manner," he said loudly. "I have heard his explanation and I accept it. Each man must be comfortable with their weapon and that is how he was comfortable with his, but I would suggest until you become adept with your sword that you hold it further down on the hilt. If you decide you'd rather hold it closer to the blade, eventually, then that is your choice."

He was trying to restore the respect for Eric that he had stripped away with his callous comment. The man he'd scolded initially for holding the blade poorly asked another question of him, and he went to the man, entering into a discussion about sword techniques. Douglas, who had been silent through the entire exchange, agreed with Jonathan completely. Eric's way *was* a foolish way. But he also knew that Jonathan was now trying to save the man's pride in the face of his men.

It was a complicated situation.

"Le Kerque," he said to Eric. "I was thinking about riding over to Tatworth and seeing how the situation was. Would you care to go with me? I could use your counsel."

Eric shook his head. "You are kind to ask, but I will remain here," he said. Smiling weakly, he dipped his head. "If you will excuse me, I have tasks that await."

He moved away before Douglas could say another word. As he watched the man walk off, he heard Isabel's low voice.

"I have a need to speak with you, Sir Douglas," she said. "Come with me."

She turned toward the keep. Feeling like he was about to have his bum slapped, Douglas followed. He remained a step or two behind her because she was walking quickly and he suspected she didn't want him to take pace beside her. The woman had a clipped manner at the best of times, and he thought this particular incident might have something to do with what they'd overheard from Jonathan. Lady Isabel didn't like her knight insulted and it had been clear from the beginning that she was protective of him. Douglas was coming to suspect there was more going on there that she didn't want anyone to know.

So he remained silent.

Isabel took him into the keep and into that lavish, two-storied solar that was so impressive. He entered the chamber and shut the door behind them, but he didn't move away from the panel. He remained there, legs braced apart, hands clasped behind his back, and waited.

It wasn't long in coming.

"I do not appreciate Sir Eric being demeaned to the very men he is training," Isabel said as she turned to him. "But I suspect that has been going on since you and de Wolfe began helping with the training. Showing how much better you are than Eric."

Douglas shook his head. "We are not better than Sir Eric, my lady."

"I heard that de Wolfe is Blackchurch trained."

"He is, my lady."

"And that gives him the right to glorify it over a mere knight who did not have that opportunity?"

"He is not glorifying it over anyone, my lady."

Isabel, who had been mostly pacing since entering the

chamber, came to a halt and glared at him. "I heard it with my own ears," she snapped. "De Wolfe called Eric a fool and I will tell you, quite plainly, that I will not stand for that. I will send you all back where you came from immediately if there is one more instance of that behavior. Am I making myself clear?"

Douglas nodded. "You are, my lady."

He didn't say anything more, mostly because he wanted her to have her complete say before he began to defend both himself and Jonathan, but given what they had just heard in the bailey, he really couldn't blame Isabel for her reaction.

"I never wanted you here to begin with," she said, growing more agitated. "With Tatworth subdued and his army disbanded, you are unnecessary. I do not even know why you are still here. Can you tell me that?"

Douglas made sure to look her in the eye as he spoke. "Because the situation is volatile, my lady," he said. "Tatworth's army has been disbanded, that is true, and he has allies who are currently ostracizing him."

"Then you are not needed!"

"But the situation could change," Douglas said evenly. "According to what I have been told, Tatworth has been tight with his allies for years. Generations of alliances. If he should convince them that he has been wronged, then they may decide to support him again and march on Axminster simply out of vengeance."

"But—"

"The situation is not stable, not at all," he said, cutting her off. "We are here, and remain here, to deter anyone from attacking Axminster purely out of a misplaced sense of revenge. My brother, and my father, have been long allied with your father and brother. They feel that this is what they would both want."

Isabel was so angry that she was twitching. "What about what *I* want?" she said. "I am the heiress. This is *my* castle."

"Then what do you want, my lady?"

"I want you out!"

"Because you feel that we have insulted le Kerque?"

"Because you disrupt everything," Isabel said. "Need I mention your display to Lady Mira earlier today?"

That brought Douglas some pause. He had been wondering when he would hear about that little action, and here it was. He cleared his throat softly.

"It was not what you think, my lady," he said quietly. "I realize my action was for all to see, but there was a reason behind it."

Isabel was nearly beside herself. "What on earth could that reason be?"

Douglas lifted a blond eyebrow. "Because your ladies, the ones you take great pains to mentor and teach, have decided I am a target for the most inappropriate attention," he said. "Two of them have even hid in the privy to watch me while I relieve myself. Is this the sort of behavior you let go unchecked?"

Isabel was shocked. She went from angrily twitching to taken aback very quickly. "Of course not," she said. "My ladies are the very model of decorum."

He shook his head. "In my experience, they are not," he said. "And I am not entirely sure their parents would think so, either, yet you've done nothing about it. You've let them harass me, spy on me, and God only knows what else that I do not know about. Therefore, I've had to take matters into my own hands."

Isabel was horrified. "What is that supposed to mean?"

Douglas was becoming irritated because she seemed too defensive, as if he was making things up. "It means that I convinced Lady Mira to pretend to be in love with me so that your ladies would back off and leave me alone," he said. "Lady Mira did not wish to do it, but I forced her into it. I would not have to if you had taught your ladies some discipline in the first place, so do not blame this on me. This is your folly, Lady Isabel. Not mine."

Isabel was absolutely stunned. Stunned and outraged and offended. He had insulted her, her teaching methods, and the very young women under her tutelage.

But the truth was that he was right.

Isabel had known that her ladies had taken a shine to Douglas. They had admired him and giggled about him. She had heard it. She also knew that their admiration of Douglas had distracted them from their tasks, because she had seen it from time to time and admonished them accordingly. But she didn't know about the spying in the privy. That was new to her. Or perhaps she had heard it but refused to believe it, or even let it take up space in her mind, because she knew her ladies were better behaved than that. *Axminster's Angels.* The finest families trusted her.

But de Lohr was from a fine family, too. Perhaps the finest in all of England.

And he didn't have a high opinion of her or her ladies.

I've had to take matters into my own hands.

If such a thing got around…

"Then you are telling me that what everyone saw was not a genuine gesture of romance?" she finally said.

Douglas shook his head. "Nay, my lady, it was not."

"You did it to discourage my ladies?"

"I did it so I could piss in peace."

That was a blunt way of putting it, shocking to a lady's ears, but Isabel had heard enough shocking things in this brief conversation. "I see," she said, noticeably subdued. "Then I apologize, Sir Douglas, for the measures you've had to go to in order for a little peace. You must understand, however, that my ladies are not used to strange knights in the castle and—"

"And that is your excuse for their lack of discipline?" he said, cutting her off again. "What happens when they go to a party or another household and see strange knights? Will you use that excuse when they follow the man around and annoy him into being cruel to them? How much understanding will you have when you are the one who is being paid to teach them discipline? It will be your fault, not theirs."

Isabel was becoming angry again. "As you have pointed out more than once, Sir Douglas," she said snappishly, "I will accept responsibility for their behavior and take great steps to ensure it does not happen again. But your very presence since you arrived at Axminster has disrupted everything."

He rolled his eyes. He couldn't help it. "So now you are back to blaming me again," he said. "Lady Isabel, I am here because I am ordered to be here. Not because I want to be here. I have other things I could be doing, more important things, but here I am, trying to prevent an aggressive neighbor from taking all of this away from you. Mayhap I should simply leave and take my men with me. Then you can fend for yourself, and when Tatworth's allies return and take your castle, you can tell everyone how that was my fault, too."

He hadn't raised his voice, but his message and words were clear. Isabel, usually so confident, had to admit that she understood his reasoning. And she was blaming him for everything simply because she didn't feel as if she needed, or wanted, any outside presence at Axminster.

"I would not blame you," she said. "You seem to think badly of me."

"Because you are blaming me for everything from le Kerque's damaged pride to your ladies' undisciplined behavior."

She knew that, but it was difficult to admit it. "I simply said that your presence was disruptive."

"And you live in denial," Douglas said. "The only thing disruptive about this place is you, because you throw a tantrum when things are not to your liking."

Her brow furrowed and she was about to lash out at him when she suddenly turned away, taking in a deep breath to keep what was left of her dwindling composure.

"No one has spoken like that to me in years," she muttered. "You remind me a great deal of my brother, Sir Douglas. He was the only one brave enough to tell me the truth about things, and I trusted him, but in this case, I do not know you and I do not trust you. Your words are disrespectful to say the least."

Douglas knew he'd overstepped, but she had pushed him in that direction. He was tired of being ignored by her, and when she wasn't ignoring him, she was treating him like an imposition.

"Mayhap they are, my lady," he said. "But you have been showing me great disrespect since the moment I arrived. You let your ladies treat me with the same disrespect, yet you expect me to show you honor and obedience. How can I when you have set the precedence on how we are to treat one another?"

She turned to look at him then. "Is that what I have done?"

"It is."

Isabel pondered that. Her mood swing, so prevalent since they entered the solar, seemed to be waning at the moment. She was cooling. Douglas wasn't entirely sure this was going to end pleasantly because she didn't seem the type able or willing to surrender her pride, so he was on his guard as she began to pace again. She seemed lost in thought more than agitation or anger.

Still, he was on his guard.

"Then we should settle this once and for all," she said. "I feel as if my request for assistance has opened the door to an invasion of another kind. An army of men is determined to keep my castle from Tatworth, but they don't seem to realize they have taken it over just as Tatworth intended to do."

"I am sorry you feel that way, my lady."

"If I were to ask you to leave now, would you?"

"The truth is that I cannot until I have clear instructions from my brother."

"Then I am, indeed, invaded. You were simply less violent about it."

She had a point. Sort of. Douglas lifted his big shoulders. "Then how do you propose we settle this?"

Isabel looked at him, pondering the answer to that question. She was quite calculated when she wanted to be, and she wanted these men out. She knew they were men of honor and intended to use that to her advantage.

We should settle this once and for all.

She intended to.

"I will make a bargain with you, Sir Douglas," she said. "Are you willing to listen?"

He sighed. "My lady, I cannot—"

"If you do not bargain with me, then I will be forced to send word to the king of your unlawful occupation of my castle," she said, interrupting him. "I do not think he will be pleased, and even if he allows you to remain, it will cause… problems. Especially when I tell him that you have been coercing my young woman into romantic situations."

She probably would. Douglas was beginning to curse Curtis for forcing him to remain at a post where he was so desperately unwanted. He could feel his irritation rise again but didn't give in to it. He was sick of arguing with her. Perhaps if he agreed to her bargain, she would shut the hell up and accept what had been dealt.

"It would be unkind, and untrue, to do so," he said in a low voice. "But if you wish to settle this once and for all, what is your proposal?"

Isabel's gaze lingered on him for a moment before trailing away, across the solar, until it came to rest on a table with a game board upon it. She indicated it.

"My father was a man with a sharp mind," she said, moving over to the table against the wall. When she came upon it, she reached down to pick up one of the many pieces on the game board. "He was a man of tactics, of great thought, and of victory. He taught me those aspects of *shatranj*, a game he enjoyed greatly. Do you know how to play?"

Douglas nodded. "It is called chess," he said. "My father learned to play it when he was on Richard's crusade in the Levant and has taught it to his sons. We all learned to play."

"Do you consider yourself an expert?"

"I am passable."

She looked at him. "Then let us play this game to settle this situation," she said. "If you win, I will no longer question your presence here. You can stay for as long as you wish and do whatever you deem necessary whilst you are here. But if I win, you will go. No questions, no argument. You will take your men and go."

Douglas had a feeling that was where she was going with this. He shook his head.

"I cannot leave without my brother's order," he said. "I have told you that."

"And I do not care about that," she said. "You will leave on my order and you will tell your brother that you did. This is *my* castle, Sir Douglas. If I do not want you here, then you will go."

He could hear that bristling determination in her voice again. It was clever—she couldn't physically make him leave and didn't have the manpower to force him out, so she was going to rely on a battle of wits. It was perfect, in truth, because he'd lied to her. He wasn't merely passable in his skill with this game.

He was an expert.

Perhaps if he agreed, she'd settle down… once and for all.

"Very well," he said. "If you wish to take your chances with this, then I am willing."

"Good," she said, now happy. Or, at the very least, eager. She rushed to the solar door and yanked it open, calling for a servant, whom she sent for wine. As the servant fled, she returned her focus to Douglas. "Please sit. I am eager to commence."

I would not be if I were you, he thought, but he dutifully took a seat at the table. The set was quite beautiful, with an elaborate board made from opalescent stone and pieces on one side carved from the same stone. The other side had pieces carved from darker stone. It was an elegant game, a man's game.

But Isabel wanted to dominate it.

Douglas would have liked to have toyed with her, but he honestly didn't have the patience. Isabel had been difficult from the start, and if she wanted to settle this, as she said, then he was going to settle it on his terms. He'd played chess enough with his father and brothers to know that he was one of the better players in his family, and he doubted Isabel could compete. Chess was a game of strategy—and since he was excellent with military strategy, and Isabel wasn't, he was confident he could end this quickly.

He was going to try.

"When was the last time you played, Sir Douglas?"

Isabel was positioning her pieces to make sure they were in the correct spots. Douglas was doing the same thing, picking them up one by one, blowing off the dust, and then setting them down again. They were both pretending that this was a casual affair when the truth couldn't have been more different.

The stakes were high.

"I was just trying to remember," he said, setting his last piece down. "Probably around Epiphany. My mother has an enormous feast that lasts about three days and all we do is eat and play."

"Sounds charming," Isabel said, sounding like she really meant it. "I have no family any longer. I have often regretted that."

"Did you play this game with your father?"

She nodded. "Often," she said. "He was very good."

"Did you win?"

She glanced at him. "As much as he would allow."

Douglas had his eyes on the board, already planning out his strategy. "I will not allow you to win if I can help it," he said. "I hope you are not expecting that."

"I am not, Sir Douglas. But I will not allow you to win, either, if I can help it."

"Then the rules are established."

"They are."

"Ladies may go first."

Isabel settled down, her gaze fixed on the board. The servant came and brought drink, handing Douglas a cup and extending one to Isabel, but she brushed the man off. He set her cup down and departed the solar, shutting the door behind him, but she never gave notice. She was focused on the board.

Finally, she moved.

Her first move was unspectacular. A pawn moved one space forward. Douglas was looking for a particular move that would open up her king, because he could end the game in about two moves if she were foolish enough to do that, but the pawn she moved was at the very end.

He moved the same piece on his side.

With the next move, Isabel moved to the other side and moved the third pawn in, which was exactly what Douglas wanted her to do. She moved it out two spaces.

He moved a pawn on the opposite side out two spaces as well, making way for the queen to move on a diagonal. But Isabel wasn't watching that. She was moving to the front line of his pawns to clear them away so she could get to his king, but Douglas was already ahead of her. With his move, and hers, he was able to move his queen on a diagonal so that the spaces between his queen and Isabel's king were wide open. When she realized this, her eyes widened because there was nowhere for her to go. Her king was fixed and she couldn't move any of her other pieces in to block Douglas' assault. Shocked, she looked up at him to see a knowing smile on his lips.

"Your king is in danger, my lady," he said quietly. "I believe he belongs to me."

As her mouth fell open in shock, Douglas moved his queen in to take Isabel's king. In less than four moves, he'd ended the game, and Isabel was nearly beside herself to see what he'd done. She had been focused on removing obstacles to his king while he had changed his strategy with every move she made.

Now he had her.

He'd won.

"That is not possible," she finally said, looking at the board. "Was I truly that stupid?"

Douglas let his grin break through. "Nay," he said. "You were simply focused on my king. I was focused on you."

She shook her head in disbelief. "And I fell like a foolish knave," she said. "I cannot believe it."

"I was fortunate."

Isabel couldn't argue with him. "You were sharp," she said, lifting her eyes to his. "Well done, Sir Douglas. It seems that I am to keep my mouth shut and let you do as you please."

She was folding, just like that. Somehow, that didn't make his victory very sweet. Had she fought him on it, Douglas would have taken the victory and gloated over it, but she wasn't fighting him. She was conceding, with honor. Truthfully, up until this moment, he wasn't sure she had any, but she did. She understood.

A seed of respect sprouted.

"Since this was over so quickly, I would not be opposed to playing a few more games," he said. "Mayhap the best out of five?"

That seemed to surprise her. "But you have already won."

He shrugged. "Mayhap I took advantage of a momentary

lapse in your strategy," he said, holding up his queen. "As a knight of honor, I would be agreeable to a few more games to settle this once and for all."

Isabel heard her words and a weak smile spread across her lips. "You do not have to."

He flashed her a smile, putting his queen back down again. "I know," he said. "But I want to be fair."

It was the first time they'd actually had a pleasant moment between them. He was smiling and so was she. Perspectives were shifting just a bit. An understanding was starting to happen. Perhaps Douglas wasn't as bad as Isabel had originally thought.

And perhaps Isabel wasn't such a shrew after all.

"Very well, Douglas," she said, addressing him informally because the situation called for it. "Let us see if I cannot do to you what you did to me. Five games, you say?"

"Whoever wins three first is the winner."

"Then be on your guard, knight. I am coming for you."

That made him laugh. Settling back with his wine, he actually enjoyed the rest of the games. In the end, he beat her soundly, three games to two, but the truth was that Isabel didn't much care. She understood a little bit more about Douglas de Lohr now.

And she wasn't upset about it in the least.

CHAPTER EIGHT

NO ONE WAS speaking to her.

With the exception of Davina and Helen, none of the ladies would speak to Mira, nor had they since yesterday. There was a pre-scheduled trip into the town of Axminster on this fine morning, part of their education on bartering and trade, and Mira chose to ride a palfrey rather than ride in the carriage with the rest of the ladies. If they were going to ignore her, then she wasn't going to give them the satisfaction of knowing how much it hurt her feelings.

She'd rather be alone.

It had started yesterday after Douglas' dazzling display of chivalry for all to see. As he'd told Mira, he did it so the young women who had been lusting after him would finally leave him alone. He'd done it to save his own skin, but what he didn't anticipate was how they would turn on Mira. Douglas' only hope was that he would be left alone, as he had bluntly put it to Isabel, so he could piss in peace. He had staked his claim on Mira and instead of respecting those boundaries, all of that unrequited lust focused on him had turned dark and ugly against Mira.

The feast the previous night was where it had started. At first, Davina was the only one who would speak to Mira, and she told her what had happened and how the Astoria had reacted to Douglas' gesture. Helen had joined them at one point and told more tales of Astoria being hysterical that Douglas had chosen Mira and how she had convinced the younger girls that they were not to speak to Mira. Using Astoria's logic, Mira had seduced Douglas and she was a trollop, and the younger women were convinced that they didn't want to associate with the trollop. Astoria threatened to tell their families if they did.

Because she shared a chamber with the older girls, Mira had to sleep a few feet away from Astoria that night.

She wished she had the courage to smother her with a pillow.

Rather than sit and sulk, she was angry. Mira was angry with Astoria and the girls, angry with Douglas that he'd pulled her into this. The entire ride into the town, which wasn't terribly far, he'd ridden at the head of the escort. He'd never looked at her once. But he'd helped her mount her palfrey back at Axminster Castle, and when he smiled at her, she'd turned her nose up at him.

Now, they were heading into the heart of Axminster's market district. The city had a license to hold a market every fifth day of the month and Mira had been here many times as a result. She was particularly good at bartering for goods, but she suspected Lady Isabel would do it this time. Isabel was on a palfrey of her own, up near the front where Douglas was, while Mira rode at the rear with about ten other soldiers—staying to the rear away from Douglas and the girls who were angry with her.

She didn't care in the least.

Not much, anyway.

Axminster's market was set up in an enormous square with dozens and dozens of stalls from farmers, craftsmen, and more. The dust of summer was kicked up once again as the party from the castle headed into the thick of the city. Douglas was directing the escort off to the side, where a big English oak provided shade for the horses, and the carriage had been pulled aside as well. Jonathan and Davyss, who had been riding in the rear near Mira, helped the ladies from the carriage while one of the soldiers helped her dismount.

But she waited.

She wanted to see how Isabel was going to organize the young women before she joined them. Davina kept waving her over, but she wouldn't go until she saw Douglas heading in her direction. Given that she didn't want to speak with him at all, she joined Davina and Helen, steering clear of Astoria and her little group. When Isabel joined them, Mira took a step and pretended to twist her ankle. She took on a noticeable limp until Isabel told her to stay with the carriage, which was exactly what she wanted. Watching Isabel and Eric, followed by Davyss and Jonathan, lead the young women away, she waited until they were completely gone before turning for the carriage.

Douglas was standing behind her.

"Oh!" Mira gasped because she'd nearly plowed into him. "You startled me."

Douglas' focused lingered on her, those sky-blue eyes appraising. "You and I must speak," he said quietly. Then he held out a hand to her. "Did you really hurt your ankle? Do you need assistance?"

Mira shook her head firmly. "If I did, I would not take it from you," she said. "You want to speak? Then let us speak. You have caused a great deal of trouble for me, Douglas de Lohr, and I am not happy about it."

He sighed. "I know," he said. "And I am very sorry for that. I had no way of knowing those that profess their undying love for me would turn their jealousy upon you."

"They have," she said. "Unintentional or not, I am not going to continue with this farce any longer. I must live with these girls, and if they are ostracizing me, I am useless to Lady Isabel."

"That is not true."

"It is," she snapped. "Douglas, I have nowhere else to go if Lady Isabel decides I am ineffective in my duties because all of the girls are jealous. I cannot go home because of the situation there with my stepfather and stepsister. I have told you about that."

She was venting on him and he knew it. Contritely, he stood there and took it. "I know," he said softly. "As I said, I am very sorry."

That wasn't good enough for Mira. She threw her arm in the direction of the marketplace, pointing. "Mayhap you are," she said. "But if you do not have a good plan to get me out of this mess with those girls, then I will take matters into my own hands. I must keep this position or I will be homeless and destitute."

He shook his head. "You will not be, I promise," he said quietly. "I will send you to Lioncross and you can serve my mother."

That threw some water on her fiery temper. "You... you *what*?" she said. "Send me to Lioncross?"

"Aye."

"But that's madness."

"Why?"

"Because I have no ties there," she said as if he were daft. "You would simply thrust me upon your mother and insist she permit me to serve her? She would tell you to jump in the lake."

He fought off a smile. "How would you know what she would say?" he said. "You do not know my mother."

"I know you, and that is all I need to know about anyone in your family," she said, rolling her eyes and moving away from him. "I am *not* going to be a burden on your mother, Douglas. You were generous to suggest it, but it will not work. Forget it."

He watched her as she climbed, agitated, into the carriage. After a moment's pause, he followed.

"Lady Mira, I am not sure what more I can say," he said. "I have apologized for misjudging the repercussions of my action. I have apologized that you must bear the brunt of it. I have offered to find you a position should Lady Isabel decide you are no longer suited to whatever it is you do for her, but you reject everything I say. Therefore, I will suggest one last thing and our agreement may be ended. When the ladies return from the market for the journey home, I give you permission to publicly humiliate me and tell me that you are not interested in me. You may do this in full view of the ladies. Since you need their support and admiration and you clearly do not want or need mine, that should put you back in their good graces. After that, I will not trouble you further."

Mira was surprised that he'd suggest such a thing. To humiliate an elite knight in public was most definitely a serious matter. Yesterday they'd made a bargain, and even she thought it might work. It wasn't his fault. But she was blaming him for her misery.

Misery.

That was her name, after all.

"Stop being such a martyr," she finally said, backing down a little. "We had a bargain and we are sticking to it, no matter how it has come back on me. It wasn't your fault. You did not do it deliberately."

Douglas felt a good deal of relief that she wasn't truly furious with him. He leaned against the carriage, his eyes twinkling at her.

"I really *am* sorry," he said quietly, a smile on his lips. "But my offer stands—if you must break our pretend engagement in front of them, I will understand."

They were fairly close together, her face about a foot from his. She looked at him, unable to be irritated in the face of his impish expression. He was so devilish that it was both endearing and irritating at the same time, and in spite of herself, she broke down in a grin.

"I should punish you by forcing you to marry me," she said. "That will teach you not to make bargains like this. You will have to explain it all to your parents, and I am certain they would be very angry with you for such a deception."

He shrugged. "Mayhap I will marry you anyway," he said. "I do not need to be forced into it. And my parents would be delighted."

She chuckled and sat back in the chair. "Of course they would," she said sarcastically. "Douglas de Lohr, the fifth son of the Earl of Hereford and Worcester, marrying a woman with a small dowry and no property. They would chain you up and beat you until you regained your senses."

He winced. "Ouch," he said. "That is too painful. Besides, my father is not the beating kind, nor is my mother. You will like them when you meet them."

She scowled. "Meet them?" she repeated. "I do not think the

earl and the countess and I travel in the same social circles."

"It does not matter," he said, moving away from the carriage, distracted by something down the avenue. "When you are my wife, we will all be of the same social standing."

Mira watched him, sensing that he was no longer jesting. He seemed quite serious and she didn't like it.

"Stop," she said quietly. "You go too far."

He took his gaze off whatever he was seeing down the avenue and looked at her. "Too far with what?"

"Stop talking like this marriage is real," she said. "I will pretend with you, but I am not going to act as if this is truly going to happen, so please stop speaking that way."

He cocked his head. "Don't you like me?"

"I like you very much."

"Enough to marry me?"

"I told you to stop it."

He grinned and shook his head. "Stop what?" he said. "I am serious, Mira. You need a husband and, as my mother has pointed out many times, I need a wife. What is wrong with me that you should not wish to marry me?"

She looked at him in shock. Shock that was quickly turning to frustration. "You're serious."

"I am."

Her eyes narrowed. "I told you that I am not a viable marriage prospect," she said. "Why on earth would you want to marry someone like me?"

His grin widened. "Because I like you," he said. "I liked you the moment I first saw you. I like your beautiful hair, your beautiful eyes. You are a small, fragile-looking woman but you are anything but fragile. I think you are stronger than I am in many ways. You are a rare bird, Lady Misery Isabella Rosalie d'Avignon. Pretending we are in love has made me want to be in love. Why not be in love with you?"

Her eyes widened. "Oh… Douglas," she breathed. "You cannot be serious."

"Why not?"

"Are you telling me that you've fallen for your own deception?"

He shook his head. "The only thing I've fallen for is you."

"What are you saying?"

He shrugged those big shoulders. "I suppose I should explain myself," he said. "I'm trying to make this seem like a normal and natural thing that we've both been expecting when the truth is that I cannot explain it at all. My father has always called me the wise one. He says I have an old soul. I do not act on whims and I do not make decisions that I will regret later. Every decision I make, no matter how small, is sound. The idea of marrying you… It has just come to me, that is true, but the more I think about it, the more I like the idea. I was attracted to you the moment I first met you and that feeling has only grown stronger."

Mira was sitting back against the carriage seat, looking at him in astonishment. In fact, she was rather leaning away from him as if afraid she was going to catch whatever madness had infected him. But she was also jolted by the possibility that he might actually be serious. He said he was. He was acting as if he was.

She was absolutely speechless.

"I do not know what to say to that," she finally said.

He was struggling not to feel embarrassed by a declaration of his intentions that seemed to come out of nowhere. As he'd told her, he hadn't planned it. He'd also told her that he didn't act on whims, but this certainly seemed like one. A reasonable whim. But one that felt *right.*

He endeavored not to feel vulnerable about it.

"You could start by telling me if there is any interest on your part," he said. "If being married to me, if being the mother to my sons, is of no interest to you, then you only need tell me once and I'll not ask again."

She just looked at him. Nothing seemed to be coming forth. She simply stared at him with those green eyes that were pale and bright, an unearthly color that seemed to burrow down deep into him. He hadn't even realized that until now.

Now, something was changing between them.

Something was happening.

When the wait became excessive, Douglas turned around and began to walk away. He couldn't stand there with her staring at him and not have the answer he wanted. He would have to accept the fact that her silence *was* the answer. All of this was happening too fast. It was too sudden. He'd made a fool out of himself and he was embarrassed. But he couldn't leave her alone in that carriage, so he was heading over to tell the soldiers who had remained to guard the horses to keep an eye on her when he heard her voice behind him.

"Douglas?"

By the time he stopped and turned around, she was nearly upon him. She had climbed out of the carriage and followed him. It was difficult not to be on his guard as he faced her.

"What is it?"

She was staring at him again, and he almost asked her the same question again, but she broke from whatever trance she was in. Somehow, she couldn't seem to stop staring at him, as if trying to figure out if this was all real. If he truly meant what he said. Even though he'd told her he was serious, she was having trouble grasping it.

Her expression was full of questions.

And perhaps a little fear.

"You must understand something," she said, her voice quivering. "I have never, in my life, heard those words where they pertained to me. I never imagined I would."

He was a little less embarrassed by her confession, but not by much. "And I never imagined I would say them," he said, folding his enormous arms over his chest and averting his gaze. "Contrary to what you might think, this was not easy for me."

"I believe it. How do you feel now that you have said it?"

He was still looking away, but he started to chuckle. "I am not certain yet," he said. "It all depends on how you intend to answer."

"Might I have time to think on it?"

He nodded. "Aye," he said, turning to look at her again. "I do not expect an answer today or tomorrow or even a month from now. It is an important question that should be taken seriously. But I would like to ask you one more."

"What is it?"

"Is there *anything* about me that you like, Mira?"

"There is everything about you that I like, Douglas."

He couldn't keep the grin off his face at her frank reply. There had been no hesitation. "Ah," he said, now feeling the least bit giddy. And nervous. "I see. Then… then that is a fine answer. I am satisfied."

Mira was starting to laugh because he seemed rather twitchy now that she'd eased his mind a little. "You had better take me into town and buy me something to eat," she told him. "And probably to drink. I think I need it."

"I think I do, too."

"Shall we go?"

"If I offer you my elbow, will you take it?"

Giving him a look of exaggerated exasperation, she grabbed his elbow and pulled him toward the main avenue. "Come along, my impetuous lad," she said. "We are going to eat well and we are going to speak more about this proposal you have given me."

"Before or after we get drunk?"

She grunted in response. "You are impossible."

He smiled down at her, his long blond hair draping over one eye. "I am *quite* possible, my lady," he said. "I intend to show you just how possible."

Grinning, Mira met his eye for a moment before looking away, unable to hold his gaze. Her breathing was coming in quick gasps and her heart was thumping strangely in her chest, all signs of madness, she was sure.

But a good kind of madness.

Something that had started off as a pretense had turned into something else.

CB

"AND THEN I am going to annex all of Norfolk. It should all be under one house, and that house will be de Winter. When I am the head of the house, it will be the most powerful in England."

Jonathan had been watching Douglas and Lady Mira in the distance as they skirted the market and headed toward the north side of the city, but he was listening to Davyss de Winter spout his plans of grandeur. Truthfully, almost since the moment Douglas had taken up residence at Axminster, young Davyss was lauding his plans for the de Winter empire when he came to power.

And what plans they were.

As the heirs to the Earldom of Radnor, the de Winter family owned practically all of Radnorshire, but they also had deep ties to Norfolk. Great swaths of the shire belonged to the House of de Warenne, the Lords of Surrey, and Davyss' mother was the sister of the current Earl of Surrey. Lady Katherine de Winter was more powerful that her brother and certainly more formidable. She had a son who thought just like her. A big, strapping, powerful, talented son who was a full-fledged knight at least two years before he should have been.

Jonathan had to grin at the ambitious Davyss.

"Who are you going to annex?" he asked. "Bigod's properties? If you try, you will not keep him as an ally."

Davyss knew that. He knew all of it, fundamentally, but he had a big ego and a big mouth. "Mayhap I will marry one of their ugly daughters," he said. "That would join our families, and when Bigod dies, I will step into his place."

"He has a nephew, Davyss," Jonathan said in a low voice. "And I take exception to your calling Bigod women ugly."

That brought Davyss pause. He and Jonathan had served together for some time and he'd known the man most of his life. He knew why Jonathan, an elite, Blackchurch-trained knight, was now languishing at Axminster when he should be out leading armies. Davyss' callous comment touched on that very thing.

"I did not mean all of them," he said. "Forgive me, Wolfie. That was a careless thing to say."

Jonathan waved him off, as if none of it mattered. "Go on," he said. "Finish telling me how you will make one great de Winter empire and force the end of the Bigod dynasty."

It was the first time since reaching the marketplace that Davyss had stopped talking. Or at least took a breath before he continued. His comment about Bigod women had slowed him down, and he was genuinely contrite about it. As Lady Isabel and her women stood over near a man who sold exotic fabrics from all over the world, Davyss and Jonathan were on guard several feet away. Eric had gone off, somewhere, so it was just the two of them.

Davyss' attention shifted from his boasting to Jonathan.

"I'm sure you are weary of listening to me boast," he said. "I've not had the chance to tell you how sorry I am that you ended up at Axminster. You know my father offered to speak to Bigod on your behalf. You do not have to stay here."

Jonathan held up a gloved hand to silence him. "I know," he said. "And I appreciate it. But it seems that we are at an end."

"Just because he thinks you seduced his niece?"

"I *did* seduce her."

"Because you're in love with the girl," Davyss said. "Everyone knows that."

Jonathan took a deep breath, trying to shake off the pain that the subject provoked. "It does not matter anymore," he said. "I was foolish to have pursued her. She was meant for someone else and I knew that from the start."

Davyss was watching him as he pretended not to care when the truth was that he cared a great deal. Jonathan and Lady Elizabeth Bigod was a subject of gossip up through the king's court, something that embarrassed his brother, the Earl of Wolverhampton, but the king had been surprisingly sympathetic.

Roger Bigod, however, was not.

"She was in a contract marriage with an old man," Davyss

pointed out with disgust. "Bigod wanted his niece to marry the Flemish warlord simply for the money and military support when the truth was that she would have been much better off with a de Wolfe."

"Davyss, please."

Davyss knew he should shut up, but the entire situation had him outraged. "Lady Elizabeth loved you, Wolfie," he said, slamming a gloved fist into an open palm. "She should have been allowed to marry the man she loved, but instead, Bigod tossed her into a ship and sent her across the sea to her betrothed when he discovered your affair, and he is punishing you by sending you to do menial work. It simply isn't fair."

"Fair or not, that is his decision."

Davyss couldn't understand why Jonathan was being so blasé about it. "You should go back to Warstone Castle and serve your brother," he said. "Mayhap that is where you belong, on the Welsh marches where you can be of better use instead of wasting away in Norfolk's arsenal."

Jonathan caught sight of Eric as the man headed toward them from the northern side of the city where he'd evidently been. "If you want to know the truth, I have already considered that," he said. "I might go home again. Or I might ask Douglas if I can accompany him back to Lioncross Abbey."

"Your brother would not be disappointed if you did not go home?"

Jonathan smiled thinly. "I take orders much better from others," he said. "No one likes to have your brother ordering you about, especially since we are twins and it is only by virtue of my birth order that I am not the earl."

Davyss could see his point. "I've never met your brother," he said. "Does he look like you?"

Jonathan shook his head. "Nay," he said. "We have the same coloring, but Robert is shorter than I am. He is a trained knight, but he was better at diplomacy like our father was. He was never a warrior."

"But your younger brother is."

"William is a god. You know that."

Davyss grinned. "I've not met him, either."

"Pray it is not in battle, for you, young de Winter, would lose."

Davyss chuckled, patting the gorgeous broadsword strapped to his side. *Lespada*, it was called, the hereditary weapon of every firstborn male in his family line. The sword was well over one hundred years old, but it looked new from the good care it had been given.

"Nothing can defeat Lespada," he said confidently. "Not even your great brother."

Jonathan lifted an eyebrow. "You think so, do you?" he said. "I would like to see that. Should I arrange it?"

Davyss looked away, pretending to be uninterested. Of course he wasn't willing to fight the great William de Wolfe. But it was easy to be brave when he was hundreds of miles away from the man. No chance of running into him.

Unless his brother arranged it.

"Why waste our time?" he said. "Look; there's le Kerque. I wonder where he went?"

Jonathan grinned at Davyss' change in subject. "I do not know," he said. "But I have a need to speak to him."

With Davyss standing guard as the women continued to barter, Jonathan made his way over to Eric, who was carrying a sack of something in his arms. He intercepted Eric before he could get to the women.

"Le Kerque," he said. "I wanted a moment to speak with you, but we've not had the chance since leaving the castle. Can you spare a moment?"

Eric nodded, shifting the sack in his arms. "Of course," he said. "What is it?"

Jonathan lowered his voice. "Yesterday when I was instructing the men," he said, "I was incredibly disrespectful to you, and I would like to apologize for that. I have no excuse other than I was frustrated at the time and let it show. It will not happen again."

Eric clearly hadn't been expecting the apology. After a moment, he smiled. "Unnecessary, de Wolfe," he said. "You were correct. I do hold my sword poorly."

"You hold it in a way that is comfortable to you. I should not judge that."

"You were right in instructing the men not to hold it that way."

"I am certain they would take sword instruction from you quite readily."

Eric's smile faded. "Nay," he said. "I do not teach that any longer. I have not in some time."

"May I ask why?" Jonathan asked. "Because of an old injury? I know you used to serve Henry, long ago."

"How did you know that?"

"I heard one of the men speaking about it."

Eric's gaze lingered on him for a moment as his mood began to sour. "Nay," he said. "No injury. I am certain a man like you, a Blackchurch knight, would not understand, but not all of us are as strong as you are. I was badly injured in battle years ago, and since then I cannot bear to pick up a sword. I have not fought in a battle since that time."

Jonathan frowned. "But you were part of the siege of Axminster," he said. "I saw you on the wall."

"Giving orders only," Eric said quietly. "I tell men what to do. I simply do not lead by example. That is why my sergeants give the men weapons training. If I try to pick up a sword, I break into a sweat. I am not proud of it, but it is the way of things. I'm sure you can imagine how humiliating it is to have you and de Lohr here, protecting a castle I should be more than capable of protecting."

Jonathan could see that they were on a sensitive subject so he simply shook his head. "We are simply here to help," he said. "I swear that we never intended to humiliate you."

Eric shrugged as if he didn't quite believe that. "It is what Hereford wanted, anyway," he said. "But your apology is noted. You did not have to do it. I did not expect you to."

"Why not?"

"Because why would a knight like you apologize to a knight like me? I am beneath such things."

Jonathan frowned, preparing to deny that statement, but Isabel caught sight of Eric and called to him. He quickly excused himself, going to Isabel, who took the sack from him. She peered into it and, delighted, began pulling out fat purple plums. She began handing them out to her ladies as Jonathan watched, realizing that le Kerque had been reduced to a figurehead, a messenger, a servant to Lady Isabel, and little else because of his fear of weapons. Jonathan had seen men like that before, men who had a brush with death and found the prospect of facing it again terrifying.

A sad situation, indeed.

Pondering that very thing, he slowly made his way back over to Davyss, wondering if he could possibly help le Kerque.

He planned to tell Douglas what the man had told him, and perhaps together they could figure something out. He had just reached Davyss, who was commenting on the fact that he, too, wanted one of those giant plums, when Eric was suddenly in their midst.

"Listen to me," he hissed. "Off to your left, near the intersection of the main road and another avenue that leads to the church, are several Tatworth men. I have already suggested to Lady Isabel that she start moving her women back to the escort."

Jonathan and Davyss immediately looked over at the indicated area. There were crowds of people all around, including merchants and their stalls, so it was difficult to get a clear field of vision. However, they could see a group of men standing near a corner, men who seemed to be having a lively conversation.

"That group over there?" Jonathan asked. "There are seven of them, I think."

"Aye," Eric said, spying the same men. "I recognize at least four of them. They usually escorted Rickard Tatworth on his visits to Axminster."

Jonathan could see that the men were armed. "They are not wearing Tatworth standards," he said. "Curtis disbanded the entire army. Half went with him and half with de Winter, so who are those men?"

"Knights," Eric said. He was clearly nervous. "Leominster may have taken the soldiers, but he clearly did not take the knights."

"Will they know Lady Isabel on sight?"

"They will."

"Damn," Jonathan growled. "Eric, you and Davyss move

her and the ladies quickly. There is no time to waste. Get them back to the escort and start moving out. Do not wait for me."

They were already moving, with Jonathan practically pushing Eric in the direction of the women. "Where are you going?" Eric asked.

"To find Douglas," Jonathan said. "He is wearing a de Lohr tunic, and if they see him, they might confront him."

"Isn't he back with the escort?" Eric asked.

Jonathan shook his head. "I saw him and Lady Mira head off toward the north, where the bakers are," he said, indicating the edge of the market because the escort was on the other side, tucked under the trees. "Go, now. Get back to the castle."

Davyss was already running up ahead where the women were scurrying back to the escort. Eric was on his heels, and Jonathan, keeping an eye on the Tatworth men, tried to stay lost in the crowd as he headed in the direction he'd seen Douglas and Mira go. He, too, was wearing a standard of the army that defeated Tatworth, so he was trying to stay hidden.

He had to find Douglas.

CHAPTER NINE

"YOU ARE A glutton."

Mira looked at Douglas with her eyebrows lifted, her eyes wide, and an expression bent on murder. They were sitting at a small, rough-hewn table, along with several other people, next to one of the larger bakeries on the street of the bakers.

But this conversation was just between the two of them.

"What did you just say to me?" she demanded.

He was trying very hard not to laugh. "You," he said slowly, "are a glutton."

"That's what I thought you said."

"It's true."

Her eyes narrowed. "You ate more than I did, Douglas de Lohr," she said. "You even ate that horrible stew that had all of the innards and eyeballs in it."

"It was delicious."

"It was disgusting!"

He did laugh then. They'd just come from the street of the bakers where two ovens, one enormous and one smaller, were blazing and smoking and creating some of the most marvelous baked goods. There were eleven bakers on the street—several smaller ones and then three or four larger ones. It was the larger ones who also prepared food, like fish pie or cheese tart or that terrible stew Mira had described.

It was called Garbage, and aptly so, because the contents came from the butchers on the next street and this particular vat of Garbage, in an enormous iron pot, had been cooking for almost a year. It was a continuous pot of stew. Every day, one of the bakers added water and another added more entrails or brains or chicken feet to it to keep it going. It was hot and cheap and nutritious and the broth alone, because it had been cooking so long, was rich and dark and salty. Douglas thought that Mira probably would have liked it had it not been for the chicken heads floating in it.

That alone meant she wouldn't touch it.

But she hadn't gone hungry. The street of the bakers, from one end to the other, offered a wide variety of foods. There was something for everybody. Mira had a fondness for eggs, so everything they hunted for had to have egg in it. Baked eggs, scrambled eggs, an omelet of eggs, and so on. Mira had been especially fond of a baked egg dish that had cream and cheese in it, and she'd stuffed herself silly with that and about a half a loaf of bread. Given that she was a rather tiny creature, Douglas found it humorous that she'd eaten so much.

Hence the glutton comment.

"Say what you will about the stew," he told her. "If you were half as brave as you thought you were, then you would try it."

Mira shook her head even before he finished his sentence. "Not me," she said. "But I do thank you for the feast. It was lovely."

He collected his purse, a leather pouch at his belt, and

weighed it in his hand. "I spent too much money on you," he teased. "I am poor, so we must go now."

Mira grinned. "You are a de Lohr, so I doubt you even know what being poor means."

"Do *you*?"

She shrugged, her smile fading. "Nay," she said honestly. "Not really. I have some money, money that I have earned from Lady Isabel, but I've never gone hungry. I've always had a roof over my head and I am determined to keep it."

She was referring to their earlier conversation about her being destitute if Lady Isabel decided she was no longer effective with the young wards. Douglas was well aware, but he didn't want to return to that particular subject.

"And you will remain well taken care of if I have anything to say about it," he said, glancing over his shoulder at a busy intersection where the street of the bakers intersected the avenue that led to the market. "Are you truly finished? Because if you are, we should return to the group. I am not entirely sure Lady Isabel would like you to be alone with me without an escort for so long."

Mira stood up, brushing crumbs off the traveling dress she wore. It was simple, brown in color, but she wore it like a goddess.

"You are correct," she said. Then she walked around the table and looked at him. "Douglas, I've decided something."

"What is that?"

"I am not going to let Astoria and the rest of the girls vex me," she said as they began to walk. "If they are petty and jealous, then that is their weakness. Not mine. If they continue to behave that way, I will tell them so."

He smiled. "I would expect nothing less from you."

They were heading toward the intersection now, moving through the crowds of people. Mira lifted her hand, shielding her eyes from the sun as she looked on ahead and the marketplace.

"Silly, foolish chickens," she said, disgruntled. "I'll show them what honor is. What character is. They'll not get the better of me."

Douglas could see the marketplace ahead, too. "I would not say they are entirely foolish," he said. "They do have an eye for me, after all. They have good taste."

She looked at him in exasperation. "God's Bones," she muttered. "You are not supposed to say that. I may say it, but not you."

"Why not?"

"Do you truly need your pride fed so badly?"

"If you are not going to flatter me, then I must flatter myself."

Mira broke down in snorts. "Poor man," she said. "It's not enough that nine other young women think you are handsome. You must hear it from me, too."

"That would help."

"Then I am concerned," she said, growing serious. "Is that enough? Should I go to the church and have the nuns tell you that also? What about the children playing down the avenue? Shall I have them sing your praises, too?"

He cocked an eyebrow at her. "Easy, lass," he said. "No need to get nasty."

She looked at him as if she had no idea what he meant. "I am only trying to bolster that great and fragile pride you have."

"Fragile?"

"It must be if you put such stock in only one woman's opinion."

He fought off a grin, scratching his forehead. "You certainly know how to put me in my place," he said. "I suppose I should be grateful."

She flashed a grin when he couldn't see it. "You should never put so much weight on one woman's opinion."

"I will do as I please, especially if it is the woman I have proposed marriage to."

They were coming to the middle of the intersection now, still moving through the crowd, but now avoiding cross-traffic. When a cart came too close, Douglas reached out and grasped Mira's arm, pulling her back to avoid being hit. They were about to continue when Jonathan abruptly appeared.

"Douglas," he said. "Good. I've found you."

Both Douglas and Mira looked at him. "So you have," he said. "We were just returning to the group. I hope Lady Isabel is not wondering where we went. Truly, we just went to find food. Nothing scandalous."

Jonathan shook his head. "Not that," he said. "Everyone is heading back to the escort quickly. It seems there are Tatworth men in town, and we are concerned they might start something."

Douglas went from relaxed man to professional knight in the blink of an eye. His expression tightened and he took on the look of a hunter. "Have they seen us?" he asked.

"Not yet."

"Where are they?"

Jonathan pointed off toward the southeast, where there was an entire row of two- and three-storied wattle and daub homes, neatly in a line.

"Over there," he said. "There is a group of about seven of

them. Eric recognized them, so we are hurrying everyone back to the castle."

Douglas couldn't really see who he was talking about because there were a lot of people in town on this day.

He frowned.

"What in the hell are they doing here?" he wondered aloud. "Axminster is not their town. They have no business being here."

"Unless they are scouting for Lord Tatworth, simply to get the lie of the land."

Douglas looked at him. "To see if we've let our guard down?"

"Possibly."

Douglas didn't like the sound of that. "Then we are going to find out what their business is," he said. "Come along."

Quickly, he and Jonathan escorted Mira back to the escort, where the ladies were just loading up into the carriage. Because Douglas wasn't certain what they might be facing, he separated eight soldiers out of the escort, and Davyss, to form the confrontation party. Eric would take the remainder of the soldiers and the women back to the castle. Even if Eric wouldn't wield a sword, the soldiers would and Eric was proficient at command.

The decision had been made.

But Lady Isabel wasn't so sure.

"Douglas," she said, "is there truly a need for this? If we leave them alone, won't they simply go away?"

Douglas knew she was concerned. She wanted to keep the peace. She'd been concerned for everything that had happened after her allies defeated Tamworth, including Tamworth's discipline. Now she didn't want his men confronted in a public place. But Douglas had his reasons.

"My lady, the simple fact is that they have no reason to be in Axminster," he said. "Unless they are shopping at the marketplace, which I strongly doubt, there is no reason to be here. This is not their village. I simply want to find out why they are here and reiterate that they are not welcome in Axminster."

Isabel was torn. "But why must you confront them? Can we not leave well enough alone?"

"Would you prefer I leave them to do whatever it is they are here to do and they end up harassing the citizens of Axminster?" he said. "My lady, they do not belong here. I am going to ensure that they understand that."

Isabel sighed heavily, looking to Mira, who nodded her head. "It is better this way, my lady," Mira said. "You do not want those men creating trouble."

Isabel still wasn't entirely in agreement, but she didn't argue. She turned and climbed back into the carriage as Mira turned to Douglas.

"What are you going to do?" she asked quietly.

Douglas' eyes glimmered. "Why?" he said. "Are you worried about me?"

She sneered. "Never," she said. "I hope they cut your head off."

He couldn't help the laughter. "You'll be sorry you said that if they do," he said. "You had better say a prayer that you have not cursed me."

Her smile broke through, letting him know that she had been jesting. "Aye, I would be very sorry if they did," she said. "May I remain here and wait for you?"

He shook his head and turned her for the palfrey she had ridden. "You may not," he said flatly. Once they reached the animal, he lifted her up onto the horse. "Return with the escort and wait for me there."

He started to turn away, but she reached out and grasped his arm. She ended up catching a handful of his long hair, and as he turned to look at her, his arm slipped from her grasp but his hair did not. He held it, fingering it, as she gazed into his eyes.

"Be careful, Douglas," she murmured. "Please."

There was a pull between them at that moment that was difficult to describe. Something liquid and powerful, like the currents of a river, pulling and pushing with unseen force. It was the very first time the jesting, the conflict, the denials had not been an obstacle between them and all they could feel was something warm and real.

It *was* real.

Douglas could feel the impact.

"I will," he said after a moment, taking her hand away from his hair and kissing it before letting it go. "Go back now. I will see you later."

Mira nodded, perhaps reluctantly, and gave her horse a little kick to move it forward. The escort was already moving away, but once she caught up to the carriage, the soldiers forming the escort closed in around her for protection.

That was all Douglas needed to see.

Trying to shake off the power of that moment between them, he turned to Jonathan, Davyss, and the eight soldiers left behind.

"We are going to pay the Tatworth men a little visit," he said, crooking his finger. "Follow me, but do not draw your weapon unless they draw or I give you a command. Clear?"

Ten heads nodded, though the knights knew that Davyss

would like nothing better than to feed Lespada some flesh and blood today. In fact, the young knight had his hand on the hilt and the weapon was already halfway out of the sheath. Jonathan had to push the weapon back down again, much to Davyss' displeasure.

But he understood.

Douglas had the Tatworth men in his sights as the group crossed the marketplace and headed toward the corner where the defeated enemy was located. As Douglas walked, he reached into the purse at his side, the same one with the coins, and pulled forth a strip of cloth. Gathering his hair back, for it was long enough to cover his chest and then some, he tied it up with the strip of cloth so it wouldn't get in the way if there was a fight. That was something he always did. He had his mother's hair, thick and beautiful, and she had never had the heart to cut his as a child. The master knights of Kenilworth, his trainers, had tried to force him to cut it but he wouldn't, so he'd gotten in the habit of tying it back so an enemy couldn't grab it and use it against him.

When the hair went back, Douglas meant business.

"You," he said loudly as he came upon the men that were still gathered on the corner. "Identify yourselves."

The seven men, who had been laughing and drinking since they were standing near a tavern, didn't react at first. They didn't realize that Douglas was talking to them. But one man noticed and, with fear on his face, tapped the man next to him and pointed. Very quickly, the men realized that a heavily armed knight was addressing them and was backed up by two more heavily armed knights and several soldiers. The man in the front, who had originally had his back to Douglas, turned around and appeared not to have any real concern with what he was facing.

He looked Douglas up and down.

"You first," he said.

His men burst into laughter, but it was nervous laughter. More than that, they were starting to back away. Before Douglas could reply, a small, thin man from the tavern next door suddenly darted out and pointed at the drinking Tatworth men.

"They stole from me!" he cried. "Those drinks are mine. They took them and would not pay!"

Douglas looked at the old, frightened man. "They've not paid at all?"

The man shook his head. He was dressed in broadcloth that was soaked and stained, and he had a rag that he'd been using to dry off his hands and would have looked like any other happy citizen, but his face was red with anger and he was pointing furiously to the collection of Tatworth men.

"They came into my tavern and demanded drink," he said. "I provided it and they've been steadily drinking since the nooning hour. But they came outside with their drink and have refused to pay me for any of it."

Douglas looked at the man who seemed to be in the lead. He was older, with bad skin and dirty blond hair.

"Is that true?" Douglas asked.

The man grinned, revealing big, yellowed teeth. "We're not done yet," he said. "We'll pay when we're done."

Douglas didn't believe him for a moment. "Pay the man."

"When we're done."

"Do it now or I'll take your money and do it for you, plus something extra for the man's trouble."

The threat of physical violence was quite real. The man in the lead looked Douglas over to try to determine if he was simply being a bully, or perhaps he was only bluffing, but somehow, he didn't think so. He snorted rudely, pointing to Douglas' de Lohr tunic.

"Hereford," he said. "I've seen that before."

"If you have, then you know I mean what I say. Pay the man now."

It took the man several long seconds to decide that was probably the best course of action for him and his men. There was a nearly even number of men on both sides, with the knight's group having a slight advantage, but more than that, the man in the lead knew that he and his friends were no match for three heavily armed knights.

That made his decision for him.

With another snort, this one of frustration and irritation, the man yanked his purse from a pocket and opened it, tossing coins onto the ground at the tavernkeeper's feet.

"There," he said. "Take your damnable money so the de Lohr dog will be satisfied."

Douglas cocked an eyebrow. "You have a big mouth for a man who is looking death in the face," he said. "Because you are clearly too stupid to realize that, let me tell you what sort of danger you are in. I am Douglas de Lohr, son of the Earl of Hereford and Worcester. My companion to my right, this enormous knight, is the brother to the Earl of Wolverton. He is a de Wolfe. He is also the brother to William de Wolfe, the greatest knight in the north of England. But mostly, this man is a Blackchurch-trained knight and he can kill each man standing with you without any help from me. The other knight is the heir to the House of de Winter. You know the de Winter war machine. He may be young, but I assure you, he is quite deadly."

The revelations pouring forth had the man in the lead standing up to take notice. His comrades were already trying to flee, but the de Lohr soldiers were stopping them. No one was going anywhere. The man tossed his drink aside and put up his hands in a supplicating gesture.

"We are causing no trouble," he said. "We've done no harm. Why do you harass us?"

"You tried to steal drink from the tavernkeep," Douglas pointed out. "You've yet to tell me who you are. How do I know you are not here to cause harm or create damage? If you do not tell me, I must assume the worst."

That caused the man to rethink his stance. "My name is Meriwether," he said. "I serve Rickard Tatworth."

"Ah," Douglas said. "Now we have an answer. And your friends? All Tatworth men?"

"Aye, my lord."

For the first time, Meriwether was starting to show Douglas some respect. Now that he'd tipped his hand and introduced all of the strength he brought to a fight, he seemed more willing to talk.

"What are you doing in Axminster?" Douglas asked.

Meriwether slowly produced a dagger he'd had tucked away. "Because I commissioned this from one of the smithies a few months ago," he said, making sure to hold it by the blade carefully. "I've come to town to pay for it."

"Did you actually pay for it?"

Meriwether snorted again. "The smithy is bigger and stronger than you are," he said. "Aye, I paid him. I had to unless I wanted my head smashed."

"But you sought to cheat the tavernkeep, who is *not* bigger and stronger than the smithy."

Meriwether lifted his shoulders in a noncommittal gesture. "I told you that I was going to pay him," he said. "I did."

Douglas gave him a disbelieving look, but before he could reply, it seemed like a gang of people came up behind him and, suddenly, a woman was flying at Meriwether with some kind of club in her hand. Before Douglas could intervene, she crowned Meriwether with it and an all-out brawl was sparked.

"He stole from me!" the woman was screaming as she hit him again before Douglas could grab her. "He stole from my stall! I want my things back!"

Punches were flying and people were rolling around in the dirt as some merchants descended on the men from Tatworth. Douglas, Jonathan, Davyss, and the rest of the soldiers were forced to jump in and start separating the combatants. Douglas narrowly avoided being hit in the head with the same club, which turned out to be not a club at all, but a stone pestle to grind grain.

And the woman's aim with it was true.

"Stop," he commanded, taking it from her as he pulled her away from the fighting. "Lady, you will control yourself. What's this about?"

"Him!" the woman shouted, pointing at Meriwether. "He came into my stall and scooped things up with his hands and then threatened me when I tried to stop him. I will stop him now!"

She pulled away from Douglas, heading again for Meriwether, who was just starting to come around, but the fight was dwindling by now and Douglas indicated for the woman to stand aside while he hauled a dazed Meriwether to his feet.

"It sounds as if you've been a naughty lad today," he said. Then he held out a hand, palm up. "Where is the merchandise you stole from this woman?"

Meriwether shook his head, trying to shake off the stars. He was going to deny knowing what Douglas was asking for when he caught sight of the woman with the pestle in her hand. He could also see that several other merchants that they'd stolen from that morning were pounding his comrades and taking back what had been stolen. Trinkets, soap, combs—they'd had their pick this morning, and no one had challenged them because they'd threatened everybody.

But now, there was safety in numbers. Seeing that the tavernkeep had gotten his money, the merchants descended. When Meriwether was too slow to respond, Douglas snapped his fingers.

"Come on," he said impatiently. "I don't have all day. Where is it?"

Realizing he was caught, Meriwether reached into the pockets of his tunic and began pulling things out, slapping them into Douglas' open palm. It was all jewelry, things for women, and Douglas looked at it in confusion.

"What's all this?" he asked. "Did you steal this for your wife?"

"I don't have a wife," Meriwether said, pulling out the last piece, a necklace. "But gifts like this can get me what I want in any town from Carlisle to Birmingham."

He lifted his eyebrows suggestively, and Douglas eyed the man he had little patience for. The woman was standing a few feet away, still screeching about her merchandise, so Douglas called her over to identify it. She could, of course, inspecting it for damage as she told Meriwether just what she thought of him.

The last thing Douglas handed her was a necklace with a

gold cross pendant. He glanced at it as he handed it over to her, but held it a moment longer to inspect it. It was a lovely piece, a delicate cross with semi-precious stones on it, and on the back he could see an inscription.

"*Meum arbitrium,*" he muttered. "My choice."

The woman plucked it out of his fingers. "Good," she said. "I was afraid this one was lost and I didn't want to lose it. 'Tis worth a good deal."

Douglas held his hand out for it. "Let me see it," he said. "What kind of stones are on it?"

The woman reluctantly handed it back to him. "Garnets," she said. "Amethyst and peridot. And the big pearl in the center of it."

The more Douglas looked at it, the more exquisite it became. "My choice?" he repeated. "What does that mean? What choice?"

The old woman was holding her hand out for it. "I purchased it from a nobleman who sold me his daughter's jewelry," she said. "The lass had taken the veil and had no more need for her finery. He said that he gave his daughter that necklace when she decided to take the veil, as a gift to commemorate the occasion, but she had to give her jewelry up when she went in the convent."

Douglas continued to look at the piece. "It could mean something else," he said after a moment. "For example, if a man were to give it to a woman, it could indicate that he chose her."

"Chose her for what?"

"His wife, of course."

The woman nodded. "True," she said. "May I have it back now?"

"How much do you want for it?"

The woman realized she might have a sale on her hands. "I bought it for six pounds," she said. "I'll take ten if you're serious. That necklace is solid gold, worth a great deal."

He nodded. "I can see that," he said. "I will give you seven pounds for it."

"Eight pounds and it is yours."

He handed it back over to her while he pulled out his purse. Eyeing her for a moment, he pulled out two gold coins, worth about seventy pence each. He put them in her palm and she smiled brightly at him, thrilled to have sold him such a fine piece.

"'Tis a pleasure doing business with you, my lord," she said. "My name is Magda. I own the stall with the red windows over on the street of the merchants. If you'd like to come by and see the rest of the things I bought from the nobleman's daughter, I'd be delighted to show you."

He carefully tucked the necklace into his purse and secured it back on his belt. "I might," he said. "Set the good pieces aside and I'll return in the next day or two. And if anyone ever comes to town again and steals from you, or harasses you or your fellow merchants, send word to Axminster Castle and I will come personally to dispense justice."

Magda was thrilled to hear that. "Thank you, my lord," she said. "What's your name?"

"De Lohr."

"De Lohr," she repeated thoughtfully. "Hereford?"

"Aye."

That was good enough for her. With a bold wink at him, she headed off with her merchandise and her pestle, talking the other merchants with her because they, too, had reclaimed their merchandise. When they were gone, heading back the way they'd come, Douglas turned to the Tatworth men.

"Now," he said in a low voice, "I do not want to see your faces in this town again. Tell Tatworth that his men are not welcome in Axminster and neither is he. If I catch you in town again, I'll throw you in the vault and keep you there. Is this in any way unclear?"

Meriwether nodded reluctantly. "Aye."

Douglas pointed a finger to the road that led out of town. "Go," he said. "And do not come back."

Meriwether gathered his dazed and bruised men, heading to the livery on the edge of town to collect their mounts. Douglas sent a few soldiers after them to make sure they left as ordered. That left Douglas, Jonathan, Davyss, and five soldiers remaining.

"Let get out of here, too," Douglas said, turning to Jonathan, to Davyss. "Back to Axminster for us."

Davyss and the soldiers broke away, heading back to the area where they'd left their horses, as Douglas and Jonathan brought up the rear.

"Did I see a welt on de Winter's eye?" Douglas asked.

Jonathan grinned. "He is going to have a beautiful black eye by tonight," he said. "But he is a true de Winter. The man is greatly at home in a fight."

Douglas grinned as they skirted the marketplace on their way to the horses. "He is eager, that is certain," he said. Then he glanced at Jonathan. "And you? No damage?"

Jonathan shook his head. "I hardly raised a sweat," he said. "What did you buy from that woman?"

"You saw that, did you?"

"I did. What was it?"

Douglas reached into his purse and carefully pulled out the

necklace, handing it to Jonathan, who inspected it closely.

"Exquisite," he said. Then he noticed the inscription on the back. "*Meum arbitrium*. My choice? My choice for what?"

"It evidently belonged to a young woman who took the veil," he said. "Her father gave her that to commemorate the moment, but she couldn't take it with her, so the merchant purchased it."

"Charming," Jonathan said, handing it back to him. "What are you going to do with it?"

"Give it to Lady Mira."

Jonathan looked at him then. There was a scowl on his brow. "I heard about the spectacle yesterday," he said. "When you knelt before her and declared your undying love."

Douglas fought off a grin. "Is that what I did?"

"Isn't it?"

"Nay," he said. "Not at all. It was a ruse to keep all of those silly women off my trail. If they know their quarry has been captured by someone else, then they should leave me alone. At least, that was the hope. Unfortunately, they've been making Mira's life miserable because of it. Jealous, petty women."

"So you're going to give the necklace to Mira and make it worse?"

Douglas shrugged. "I've decided that I *will* marry her," he said, looking at Jonathan's surprised expression. "I'm serious. I must marry, Wolfie. My mother has been harping on it for years, and I've finally found someone I can imagine spending my life with. Mira's a good lass. Beautiful, intelligent. My choice."

He was holding up the necklace as he said it, and Jonathan wasn't any less surprised by the declaration. In fact, he was a little apprehensive about it.

"Careful," he murmured. "An entanglement with a woman is how I ended up here, at Axminster. You must be careful how you handle this, Douglas."

"What do you mean?" Douglas said. "What does this have to do with you?"

Jonathan took a thoughtful breath. "Surely you have been wondering why de Winter ordered me to remain here."

"I assumed you would tell me when you were ready."

They'd reached the horses by this point. Davyss was already mounted, as were most of the soldiers, and the others were just now coming down the road in their direction, having seen off the Tatworth men. Jonathan took the reins of his horse before turning to Douglas.

"Lady Elizabeth Bigod is the niece of Roger, my liege," he said quietly. "I will not bore you with the details, but suffice it to say that Libby and I loved one another. But she was pledged to a Flemish warlord, an old bastard with more money than God and a big army. I will admit that we were planning on running off together to be married, far away where her uncle could not find us, but she was betrayed by one of her maids and our plans were discovered. Bigod put her on a ship to Flanders and that was the last I saw of her. He sent me to de Winter because he feels that he can no longer trust me, which is true. I did betray his trust, at least where Libby was concerned. All this to say that you must be careful when it comes to a woman. Sometimes… sometimes the unexpected happens. People get very odd when it comes to love."

Douglas was genuinely saddened to hear the tale. "I am sorry for you, lad," he said. "Why not go after her? If I loved a woman, nothing could stop me."

Jonathan was trying to be brave about a very touchy subject.

"You'd think so," he said. "You'd be wrong. She is already married, and even I cannot come between a husband and wife. Even if the wife should have been mine."

Douglas couldn't say much to that, mostly because he knew the man was right. "Then what will you do once we leave Axminster?" he asked. "Return to Grayson?"

Jonathan nodded. "Probably," he said. "I thought to return to my brother, too. Although Robert and I are like oil and water together, I know he will accept my fealty, so it is not as if I have nowhere to go. But I will admit that it has been a difficult few months."

He was smiling weakly, but Douglas could see the pain in his eyes. "I can only imagine, my friend," he said softly. "Why not come to Lioncross with me? My father would kill for the services of a knight like you. We could keep you very busy on the marches."

Jonathan's smile turned genuine. "I was thinking about that, to be truthful," he said. "It might be better than returning to Warstone, where Robert and I will butt heads over every little thing."

A smile crossed Douglas' lips. "Think about it, then," he said. "We'll speak more when you've had a chance to ponder it."

"I will do that."

By this time, the soldiers from the Tatworth departure had finally joined them and everyone mounted up. In short order, they were heading back to Axminster, tearing down the road as the sun began to wane. It had been an eventful day already and they were eager to return home.

None more eager than Douglas.

He had a certain young lady to see.

CHAPTER TEN

Axminster Castle

"SORRY TO APPEAR uninvited or unannounced, Lady Isabel, but I assumed that you would agree to entertain us for the night since my son fostered her a few years ago."

Isabel had been met in the central bailey by a large party she didn't recognize until the lord at the head of the party came to greet her. Then recognition hit.

She wasn't exactly thrilled to see him.

"Lord de Honiton," she said, forcing a smile. "It has been a long time since we last had the pleasure."

Lord Jerome de Honiton bowed graciously to her. A tall man with graying, dark hair, he smiled politely. "You are as lovely as ever, my lady," he said. "Raymond has often told me how much he misses his days at Axminster. He enjoyed it a great deal."

"Oh?" Isabel said, lifting a disbelieving eyebrow. "I seem to remember a lad who wrote to his father to complain every time he was disciplined, which was often."

Jerome laughed, as fathers who refused to believe their children were ever a problem do. "He was a curious boy who got into trouble," he said. "I have accepted that. I am not angry, of course. Your brother did what he thought was best. Raymond has not suffered."

As if on cue, the young man in question appeared. Coming away from an extremely expensive golden warhorse, Raymond de Honiton smiled at Isabel before bowing politely.

"Lady Isabel," he said in a lovely, deep voice. "It is an honor to see you again, my lady."

Isabel's gaze lingered on the young man who had caused unnecessary trouble during his years as a page. "Raymond," she greeted him evenly. "What finds you at Axminster today?"

Raymond looked at his father to explain. "Do you see that horse?" Jerome said, pointing to the flaxen-maned warhorse. "We have come from London, where we purchased that magnificent animal in celebration of Raymond's day of birth. We are simply traveling home, but it is another two days away, so we thought to rest here for the night. I hope it is not inconvenient."

Isabel shook her head. "It is not," she said. "How many in your party?"

"Myself and Raymond and about eighty soldiers," Jerome replied.

Isabel motioned to Eric, who had been standing several feet away. Raymond's days at Axminster had been before Eric's time, so he didn't know the young man or his father. When Eric came on her summons, she introduced him.

"Eric, this is Lord de Honiton and his son, Raymond, who was a page here for a few years before his father moved him to Kenilworth," she said. "Lord de Honiton, this is Sir Eric le Kerque. He will see to the settling of your men for the evening. Lord de Honiton, you may sleep in the keep, but Raymond will have to sleep in the knights' quarters."

Jerome didn't like that his son was being consigned to the outbuildings like a commoner. "May he not stay with me, my lady?" he asked.

But Isabel shook her head. "I have unwed ladies in the keep," she said. "It would not be proper. He may stay in the knights' quarters. It is quite comfortable."

Jerome understood. Sort of. Proprieties must be observed. But he still wasn't happy about it.

"Very well, my lady," he said reluctantly, looking at Raymond. "Just for the night, my son. You will be comfortable."

Raymond felt slighted. His expression said what his lips wouldn't. He had been a naughty boy those years ago, with delusions of grandeur as the son of Lord de Honiton. His family was a moderate military force in south Cumbria, but his mother had died at his birth and, as a result, his father had indulged his every whim. Raymond had grown up a spoiled lad, which meant when he came to Axminster, he had a harsh dose of reality because the de Kerringtons weren't afraid to discipline him.

He still remembered the shame.

Now, years after he left Axminster, he was still being relegated to second best. While his father could stay in the keep, he was being sent to the knights' quarters. As if he was just a common man. There was a large part of him that knew why he had been given those quarters, and propriety had everything to do with it, since there were several unwed maidens in the keep, but that did not ease his offense.

In his mind, he was being punished all over again.

"As you wish," he finally said, but his tone suggested he was unhappy. "May my horse at least have a good stall and good food this evening?"

Isabel could hear the same haughty tone from the same haughty young man she'd known those years ago. She hadn't liked him then and she was sure that she wasn't going to like him now. But she nodded, turning to Eric, who also nodded.

"Of course, my lord," Eric said. "Come with me and we shall find the best place for him. He's quite a magnificent beast."

Finally, he was being treated with some respect. Raymond headed off with Eric without another word to Isabel. Jerome smiled weakly at his son's rude departure.

"It has been a long day and difficult travel," he said. "I am afraid we may not be the most sociable guests."

Isabel was grateful that she was only going to have to endure one night of Raymond's return. "Understandable," she said. "Will you come with me, please? I will show you to your chamber. Tonight, we will feast and you may tell me of any news from London."

"With pleasure, my lady."

Plastering a forced smile on her face, Isabel led Jerome toward the keep, keeping up small talk on the weather and the local hunting when what she was really doing was counting the minutes until Raymond de Honiton was gone. Something told her the coming meal might not be so pleasant, considering the company.

Little did she know just how unpleasant.

ଓ

"REMOVE YOUR TRAVEL things and go about your chores," Mira said as she entered the chamber that the younger girls shared. "As you have seen in the bailey, visitors have arrived for the night and we must prepare. Ines and Primmy, the two of you will ensure the hall is clean and warm and ready to receive guests. Hurry along, now. There isn't much time."

Ines and Primrose were moving at lightning speed. They yanked off travel coats and rushed to don aprons. As that was going on, Mira turned to Louisa, Marceline, and Theodora.

"Louisa, seek Lady Isabel and offer your services with our guests," she said. "She may need you to guide the maids in preparing a chamber. Marcy and Theo, you will go to the kitchens and inform the cook. Tell her that Lady Isabel will want the good wine this evening, the wine that has been shipped from Burgundy last year. If the cook does not require your assistance, then go to the hall and help Ines and Primmy. Go, now."

The girls nodded, but no one spoke, which wasn't like them. They were usually full of chatter. They stripped off traveling coats and brushed hair quickly, preparing for work. It didn't really bother Mira that the girls weren't speaking to her, not after her conversation with Douglas—or at least if it did, she wasn't going to show it. With the younger ladies focused, she went next door to the chamber she shared with Astoria and Helen and Davina.

The three of them were in the chamber, removing their traveling clothing and brushing out the dust. While Helen and Davina looked at her and smiled, Astoria soundly ignored her. She was using a horsehair brush to clean the dust off her woolen traveling coat. Mira glanced at the woman, finally rolling her eyes to see that, yet again, Astoria was pretending she didn't exist. In this case, she truly didn't care. Astoria wasn't worth her attention. Therefore, she turned to Helen and Davina.

"You saw the visitors when we entered," she said. "Helen,

I've sent Marcy and Theo to the kitchens, but you had better go, too. Make sure the food is generously prepared."

Helen nodded. "Of course," she said. "Do we know who the visitors are?"

As Mira shook her head, Astoria piped up. "I do," she said. "I recognized them."

All three ladies turned to her. "Who?" Helen asked.

Astoria was carefully hanging her coat on a peg. "It's Raymond de Honiton," she said, turning to look at everyone but Mira. "I recognized him riding a big blond horse. He's grown up since he was last here, but I would not forget him."

Mira looked at her in shock. "Raymond?" she repeated. "Are you sure?"

Astoria still wouldn't look at her. "Of course I am sure," she snapped. "I am not stupid. I remember what Raymond looks like. So should you."

The problem was that Mira did. She well remembered Raymond de Honiton, a young man who had served as a page at Axminster a few years earlier. He had come as a boy, when Mira was still a young ward, and she remembered the young man who couldn't seem to understand why everyone wouldn't move to do his bidding. He would try to give orders and, when no one responded, throw a tantrum. That brought knightly beatings from lady Isabel's brother, but Raymond never seemed to learn his lesson. In fact, he spent five years at Axminster and hadn't seemed to learn anything in that time.

One of the things he never learned was that Mira was not interested in him.

Raymond was four years younger than Mira, but he was quite convinced that she was the woman for him. Even as a young lad, he'd followed her around, trying to woo her, and when that didn't work, he set about pinching her or grabbing her in inappropriate places. He was punished for it, repeatedly, but it didn't stop him. By the time he was sent to Kenilworth, his assault against her had grown bolder because he had grown bigger and stronger, which made the attacks increasingly frightening for Mira. She could only pray that in the seven years she hadn't seen him that his time at Kenilworth Castle had taught him that women didn't like to be groped or pinched, and that the knights of Kenilworth had managed to impart some manners on him.

"Of course I do," she said after a moment. "I simply didn't see him."

Astoria was focused on her now. "What are you going to do with Raymond here?" she said. "He was quite sweet on you. And now Douglas is here, too. Who will you give your attention to, I wonder?"

She was taunting her. Mira kept her composure when what she really wanted to was slap the woman across the face. She knew that Astoria was simply jealous, and the problem was that being kind and understanding about it wouldn't work with her. She lacked compassion or understanding herself. All Astoria was capable of were the very basic emotions—love, hate, and happiness. Because of it, she was about to get a harsh dose of reality.

Mira wasn't going to tolerate it.

"My attention and whom I give it to is none of your business," she said evenly. "I am very sorry if Douglas turned to me and not you. I am sorry if your feelings are hurt. But the lies you are telling the younger girls about me are petty and vile. I suggest you overcome whatever shortcomings you are feeling, because I did not cause them. I have not turned against you. But if you keep up this behavior, then I will turn against you and so will Lady Isabel. I don't suppose you want to be sent back to your drunken father and an uncle who likes to crawl into your bed at night—do you?"

Astoria was feeling cornered. "You're a seductress," she hissed. "Did you lift your skirts for Douglas? Is that what turned his head?"

Mira could see such hurt in the young woman's expression. She knew she should have been sympathetic, but she couldn't seem to manage it. Not when she knew there was nothing redeemable about Astoria. There never had been. She'd seen her turn against other girls and taken pleasure in it. Now she had turned against Mira. She was a bully.

And there was only one way to deal with a bully.

"Nay," Mira said, fixing the woman in the eye. "I did nothing of the sort. I didn't have to. It's simply that I'm prettier than you are. Why should he look at a sow like you when he can look at me and find more pleasure in it?"

Astoria's face turned bright red and she charged Mira with a shriek. Mira forgot her composure and lashed out, slapping Astoria when the woman raised her hands. That brought Helen and Davina, who got in between, separating them. Davina dragged Astoria away as Helen stood in front of Mira in case Astoria decided to charge again. But Astoria was hysterical, weeping with her hand to her cheek.

"She's going to tell Lady Isabel," Helen said with regret, looking at Mira. "But do not worry. Davina and I will tell Lady Isabel what we saw."

Mira wasn't the least sorry that she'd slapped Astoria. "She'd better learn to behave herself and accept the situation or there will be more where that came from," she said loudly so

Astoria would hear her. In truth, she was angry about the entire ridiculous circumstance and turned for the door. "I have things to attend to. So do you. I will see you later."

Helen nodded, watching her go with regret. The situation was, indeed, regrettable. She returned her attention to Davina and Astoria, catching Davina's eye and silently waving her away. Together, they departed the chamber, leaving Astoria sitting on her bed, nursing a stinging cheek and wounded pride.

Very wounded.

In that wound, something began to fester.

Mira wasn't going to have the last word in this, Astoria decided. What started out as mild jealousy had now turned into something darker. *I'll get her,* she thought. Douglas or no Douglas, now it was a situation between her and Mira. Of course Mira was prettier. She was beautiful. Everyone thought so. But no one thought that of Astoria. She was first made aware of that by none other than Raymond de Honiton himself several years ago, when Raymond had eyes for Mira and Astoria had eyes for Raymond. When she tried to press her affections, the boy actually called her ugly.

Now he was back.

And that gave Astoria an idea.

CHAPTER ELEVEN

HE WAS ON the hunt.

Not really a hunt, but Douglas was most definitely looking for Mira. Having arrived back at Axminster a short time earlier, he had been tied up helping Eric settle the escort of Lord de Honiton. Douglas had heard the name of de Honiton before but never had any direct dealings with the man. He knew he was a great supporter of the king, but little more than that. Douglas finished helping Eric settle the de Honiton troops and then went on his hunt for a certain young lady.

She wasn't hard to find.

With unexpected visitors at Axminster, Douglas suspected he'd find Mira preparing the great hall, and he was correct. She was there with some of the other girls, supervising the preparation of the hall. The advent of unexpected visitors had thrown the well-trained women into a frenzy. They wanted to make sure the hall was perfect for their visitors because nothing was more uplifting than a compliment on one's housekeeping skills. A happy visitor would spread the word of the lovely hospitality at Axminster, directly reflecting upon Lady Isabel and her wards.

Therefore, this was serious business.

Because there were so many women at Axminster, the great hall never really deteriorated into a men-only chamber. Douglas had been at many halls in his lifetime and, more often than not, they were a man's domain. The men gathered there, told their stories there, and shared meals and camaraderie. If they did it before battle, sometimes it was the very last time that friends would see each other in this lifetime. Therefore, some halls tended to be slovenly places with old rushes on the floor, smelling of old ale and old memories.

But not Axminster.

Axminster was clearly a woman's hall because the rushes were fresh, there were no dogs to be seen, and the floors were swept clean. And it wasn't a hard-packed earth floor, either. It was stone currently in the process of being scrubbed. There was a small army of servants and young ladies making sure the floor would be clean for Lady Isabel and her visitors.

And Mira was in the middle of it.

As Douglas stood at the door, he found himself watching every move she made. He thought that she was an ethereal, lovely creature at the best of times and now, in the midst of hard work, he realized she was the most beautiful woman he had ever seen. Douglas had grown up with a mother who was quite industrious, and his sisters had followed her lead. He had four sisters in total, all of them hard workers and brilliant women. He had grown up learning to admire a woman for her ingenuity and dedication, and as he watched Mira, he could see the same qualities in her that his mother and sisters had. Because of that, the feelings that he'd been experiencing for her were only growing stronger.

It was odd, really, for a man who had perpetually put off

any kind of marital suggestion from his parents. He wasn't exactly young anymore and knew, at some point, that he was going to have to find a wife. Even though he was the son of an earl, and a wealthy one at that, the truth was that he did not own any property. He didn't have a title like his brothers did and, being the fifth son, unless he married very well, there would be no title for him. His older brothers had married well and one of them had inherited an earldom through his wife. All of his older brothers had titles and property.

But Douglas didn't.

Truthfully, it didn't really bother him. He'd never had great aspirations for power for money or control. He was content serving his father and carrying out the man's orders, although that didn't mean he was a follower. Not at all. He was quite a leader, and he was well liked by his men, but he simply didn't have the ambition some men had—and when he married Mira, the possibility of his marrying for a title would be gone.

Considering the prize, it didn't matter to him.

Mira…

Thank God for her nickname because he honestly couldn't envision himself calling her by the name she'd been christened with. Frankly, he was surprised the priests even allowed such a thing, but her middle names were appropriate and that must have satisfied them. To name a set of twins Payne and Misery certainly reflected the mindset of the mother. A mindset that continued to be detrimental because the woman remarried and then banished her daughter based on her new husband's whims. He found that quite shocking, to be truthful, and quite terrible. Mira didn't deserve what she'd been given in life, at least not as far as a mother was concerned.

He hoped to change that.

He would give her an entirely new family that would love her and cherish her in the way it was meant to be. He already knew that his mother would love her and that she would blend in well with his sisters. Douglas' four older brothers were all married to women who were quite fine, and he thought that Mira would be a proud addition to the collection of de Lohr wives. In fact, that was how he felt about her.

Proud.

He was daydreaming about bringing Mira home to Lioncross Abbey when the very woman in question caught sight of him and paused in her sweeping to wave at him. She was near the hearth, sweeping out the ashes for the servants to collect, and as he went to her, Isabel and the rest of the young women entered the hall. A small army had arrived to help, and that included Astoria. When she realized Douglas was in the hall, she focused on him, but Douglas only had eyes for Mira.

"Well?" she said as he approached. "What happened with the Tatworth men?"

"What do you think happened?" he said, grinning. "I beat them within an inch of their lives and tossed them into the river."

She chuckled. "You did not."

"Are you calling me a liar?"

"I am."

He sneered at her, though it was lightly done. "If you do not apologize, I will not give you what I have brought," he said. "I'll give it to someone else and then you'll be sorry that you were so cruel to me."

She shook her head at him. "Poor lad," she said. "Hurt and insulted by a cruel woman."

"It is true. I'm going to tell everyone it is true."

"They'll think you a weak man, indeed, if you let me get the better of you."

His grin was back. "And I gladly submit to your whims, wishes, and words," he said. "Anything you want to say is fine by me. Even nice things."

He was flirting with her, and Mira could feel the flush in her cheeks because he was quite adorable when he did that. "Then I will have to think of some nice things to say," she said. "I could possibly tell you that you are quite handsome."

"Do you think so?"

"Conceivably."

"Tell me that you think so and I'll give you something for it."

She leaned the broom against the stone of the hearth and held out her hand. "Let me see what you've brought and I will determine what nice words it warrants."

She was clever. With a smirk tugging on the corners of his mouth, Douglas dug into the purse at his side and pulled forth the necklace. Carefully, he laid it in her open palm so that the cross was on the top, staring at her.

The smile immediately vanished from her face.

"Oh… Douglas," she gasped, picking up the cross to get a good look at it. "This is magnificent. Wherever did you find it?"

"A merchant in Axminster," he said. "There is a story behind the cross."

"What is it?"

He watched her as she inspected it. "Evidently, it belonged to a young woman who had decided to take the veil," he said. "Her father gave the cross to her as a token of her decision, but when she went to the cloister, she could not take it with her."

Mira turned the cross over to see the inscription on the

back. She held it up in the light to get a better look.

"*Meum arbitrium,*" she murmured. "My choice? That's a curious inscription."

"Not really," Douglas said. "Her choice was the cloister. The merchant said that the father gave it to her to celebrate her choice, but the more I think on it, I would wager he gave it to her to remind her what her choice was going to cost her—fine things, jewelry, her family, and possibly even a husband. I think he was reminding her of what she was going to leave behind."

Mira nodded as she turned the cross over again to admire the jewels on the front. "So it is a token with several meanings," she said. "What does it mean to you?"

He lifted his eyebrows. "That should be obvious," he said. "You are my choice."

She fought off a grin. "Did you give me this to brand me, then?"

"Of course I did," he said with muted sarcasm. "You will wear it every day and show everyone that you are *my* choice. Wear it like a flag, Mira, and wave it for all to see. You belong to me and I want everyone to know it."

She glanced up at him. "But I've not yet agreed."

That was true. She hadn't technically agreed to anything. Therefore, he sighed heavily, hands on hips in an unhappy gesture. "If you have not yet agreed, then give it back to me," he said. "I'll find someone else to give it to."

She was fighting off laughter now because he was close to pitching a fit. He was easy to taunt and they had a good rapport between them. In fact, she knew he wasn't serious, and he knew she wasn't serious. It was simply a formality for her to consent.

And they both knew it.

"You will *not* give it to anyone else," she said, putting it over her head and letting the necklace settle around her neck and chest. "I'll wave it like a flag, I promise. Why wouldn't I? You are my choice, too."

He cast her a sidelong glance, unable to keep the smile from his lips. "It is about time."

"You were from the start."

He turned to her fully, his smile breaking through. "I've been waiting my entire life to hear that."

"Then let it be said," she said, but quickly grew serious. "But you know that I bring nothing to this marriage but a small dowry. No lands, no titles. I am very sorry for that, truly. I must remind you because if you wish to change your mind, I would understand."

He shook his head before she even finished. "You are worth more than any title or any lands," he said. "I choose you for who you are, Mira, not for what you bring with you. And that's how it should be."

She was starting to flush again. "That is a sweet thing to say," she said. "I shall try to always live up to it."

Douglas reached out to take her hand with the intention of kissing it but caught sight of Isabel in his periphery and abandoned his plans. Until he was plain with Isabel about his intentions toward Mira—fully plain—he wasn't going to initiate any more public displays of affection. The first one he did had backfired spectacularly on Mira, so he wasn't going to risk it again.

Even if, this time, it was real.

"I know you will," he said softly. The clamor in the hall was growing louder as more cleaning was attended to, so he knew he needed to let her get back to her task. "I'll leave you to your work now. But I will see you tonight."

He winked at her as he turned around, but she stopped him.

"Wait," she said, grasping his arm to force him to pause. "There is something I must tell you about our visitors."

"What of them?"

She seemed reluctant to continue. "One of them used to be a page here," she said. "He was a young boy when he came and barely on the cusp of manhood when he left, but he used to be very… fond of me."

He didn't understand. "Fond?" he repeated. "He was your friend?"

She shook her head. "Nay," she said firmly. "Never a friend. He was a young boy who fancied me, and when I ignored him, he took to pinching my arse to get my attention. He was punished for it, but it did not stop him. Then he grew into a young man bigger and stronger than I was and he took to not only pinching my arse, but cornering me and trying to steal kisses. Frankly, he terrified me, but when he was sent to Kenilworth, my worries were over."

Douglas understood now, and that glimmer of warmth in his eye quickly changed to something hazardous. "And now he's back," he rumbled. "How long has he been gone?"

"About seven years. Time enough to mature, I hope."

"Or not," Douglas said. "Mayhap I should have a word with him."

Mira shook her head. "Do not," she said quietly. "Please. I am certain I mean nothing to him any longer and he has probably forgotten about everything, so let us leave it at that. But I wanted to tell you so you knew that I used to know him."

He patted her hand, still gripping his arm. "And I appreciate your honesty," he said. "But I will be keeping my eye on this man. What is his name?"

"Raymond de Honiton."

"Lord de Honiton's son?"

"Aye. Do you know them?"

Douglas shook his head. "I have only heard the name," he said, taking her hand off his arm but still holding it. "Swear to me that if he resumes his bad behavior you will tell me. Please, Mira."

"But—"

"It is important to me."

After a moment's hesitation, she nodded. "Very well," she said. "If it is important."

He nodded and, forgetting his pledge against public displays of affection, kissed her hand then quickly left the hall. Mira could sense something different in him, something tense and moody. Far different from the Douglas she had become acquainted with. But given that they had just declared their intent toward one another, she understood that he would be concerned with a man who used to harass her. If the situation were reversed, she would most certainly want to know.

Picking up the broom, she resumed her work.

ঔ

ACROSS THE HALL, Astoria had seen everything.

She'd been pretending not to notice or even care that Douglas was in the hall, but she couldn't help but watch the man. She'd had several infatuations in her young life and Douglas was no different. She was drawn to him, her thoughts only of him and the happy life they would have had together had Mira not come between them. She was so focused on him that she clearly saw when Douglas gave Mira something, which must've been a necklace, because she'd put it around her neck. That drove Astoria into fits of jealousy until Isabel snapped at her to continue the inventory on the fine pewter plates belonging to Axminster. Startled she'd been caught staring, she quickly turned back to her work.

But not for long.

Something was happening in the kitchen that required Isabel's attention, so the moment she departed through the servants' alcove, Astoria headed toward the hearth. Mira was bent over, sweeping out the last of the ashes from the corners while three servants worked with her to clean it all out. Mira had soot on her hands and forehead where she'd bumped it against the fire back, and the moment she emerged from the hearth and stood tall, brushing her hands off on her apron, Astoria was in front of her.

Mira eyed her.

"What do you want?" she asked.

The tone was decidedly unfriendly. Astoria was looking at Mira's neck, seeing a chain disappear under her bodice where she'd tucked the necklace away to keep it safe.

"What did Douglas give you?" she asked.

Mira had no time for her. "That is none of your affair."

"Tell me or I will tell Lady Isabel."

Mira focused on her then. "I do not care if you do," she said. "My business is my own and you would be well advised to stay out of it."

Mira wasn't being a pushover, which only seemed to inflame Astoria. She wanted the girls she bullied to cower and weep. But not Mira. Astoria knew she'd get slapped again if she got too close, so she made sure to stay out of arm's length.

"Did he give you a necklace to thank you for your favors?" she asked, sneering. "A gift for lifting your skirts?"

Mira had had enough. The servants were hearing this garbage, so she lifted her broom and whacked Astoria in the hip with the bristle end. Soot puffed up, getting on Astoria as she yelped.

"Go away, you liar," Mira snarled. "Get away from me."

Astoria was backed into a table by the broom and pushed it away. Mira brought it up again, this time aiming for her head, and clipped Astoria in the neck and face. Black soot puffed again, getting in her hair. Astoria screeched and kicked out, catching Mira in the knee with her foot, but Mira whacked her again with the broom. She did it twice, but in doing so, she came closer to Astoria, who was starting to slap out with both hands to fight back. One hand managed to grab Mira's left shoulder and part of her dress. Unfortunately, the chain was there and Astoria grabbed that as well. She meant to tear Mira's clothing but ended up breaking the chain instead. It came apart in her hand.

And Douglas saw all of it.

He'd come back into the great hall because he knew Isabel was there and wanted to ask her a question about security for the visitors. He hadn't seen Eric in the central bailey, so he sought out Isabel's advice, but instead he had walked into a fight. Mira was hitting Astoria with the business end of a broom while Astoria was slapping back at her. Concerned, he headed in their direction about the time Astoria got hold of the necklace and yanked. The chain came off in her hand while the cross pendant fell down through Mira's clothing. That was still trapped in her bodice, leaving Astoria standing there with a golden chain in her hand.

"*Stop!*" Douglas roared.

Both Astoria and Mira came to a shocked halt at the sound

of his loud and angry voice. They froze as he marched up on them, grabbing Astoria by the wrist and prying the golden chain out of her grip. Still holding on to her wrist, he glared at the young woman.

"What is the meaning of this?" he demanded, holding up the chain for her to see.

Astoria was terrified. "I… I did not mean to break it," she stammered. "But Mira… She attacked me!"

"I did no such thing!" Mira said, but she was so angry that Astoria broke the necklace that she kicked the girl, as hard as she could, in the thigh. "You attacked me first!"

Douglas put himself between the pair as Astoria began to weep. He still had hold of her wrist, but he handed the chain back to Mira, who was also beginning to weep. Before he could comfort her, however, he fixed on Astoria.

"I want you to listen to me and listen well," he said in a low voice. "Are you listening to me?"

Crying, Astoria nodded. "A-aye."

"Good," Douglas said. "Now, this rage against Mira is going to stop now. Do you understand me? You seem to think that there could have been some kind of romantic entanglement between you and me, and you hate Mira that she has disrupted your plans. Is that right?"

On the spot, Astoria was horrified. "I—I never said that!"

Douglas shook his head. "Nay, you did not, but ever since I have made my affections toward Mira known, you have gone out of your way to be cruel and vindictive to her," he said. "Now you have broken a gift I have given to her. I can only assume it is out of jealousy, so I want to make something very clear to you. Never, since the day I met you, have I had any inclination toward a romance with you. Ever. You are petty, small-minded, mean, and stupid. I have never said that to a woman in my life, but I will say it to you. Your ugliness on the inside leaves you ugly on the outside. You are jealous of a woman like Mira because you know you will never be like her, but that is your misfortune. It is not Mira's, nor is it mine. Your ugliness is of your own making. Am I making myself clear?"

Almost everyone in the hall was hearing this, Helen and Davina included. They were witnessing something that Astoria had needed for a very long time—a proper scolding. Douglas didn't raise his voice and he wasn't threatening, but the message was clear and Astoria was so horrified, so embarrassed, that she could hardly speak. All she could do was nod.

Barely.

But it was enough for Douglas.

"Excellent," he said. "I am telling you, quite plainly, to leave Mira alone. If you do not, then I will ensure you are sent away for good."

With that, he let go of her wrist and pointed to the other side of the hall. Astoria got the message, holding the wrist that he'd gripped and limping away, an exaggerated gesture because Mira had kicked her. As she moved back to the area where she'd been tending the plate, the other girls there moved away from her like she carried the plague. Everyone had heard the scolding, and no one moved to comfort her because she had deserved it. They all knew it. Douglas watched her return to her task before turning his attention to Mira.

She was holding the chain with tears on her cheeks, and he sighed sadly, reaching up to wipe the moisture from her face.

"No need to weep, love," he said softly. "I will have it fixed right away. It will be as good as new, I promise."

Mira sniffled. "She was so nasty," she said. "She asked me if it was a present for lifting my skirts to you."

He grunted with regret. "I am sorry," he said. "She is simply jealous. I've seen women like her before, and they always suffer greatly from their own foolishness. I would not worry over her any longer."

Mira continued to sniffle as she nodded her head and Douglas reached down, taking both of her hands and kissing them sweetly. When she looked up at him, he smiled to be of some comfort before finally taking the chain from her.

"Let me have the pendant," he said. "Where is it?"

Mira pointed to her waistline. "In my clothing, somewhere," she said. "I will keep it safe if you simply get the chain fixed."

"Very well," he said. "I will go first thing in the morning."

"Thank you."

He winked at her. "You are welcome," he said. "But I am sorry I have to do it."

"Me too."

"Will you be safe if I leave you now?"

He dipped his head in Astoria's direction, and Mira nodded. "Of course," she said, wiping away the last of her tears. "I have been dealing with that girl for a few years now. My trusty broom and I will keep her at bay."

He grinned but was precluded from replying when Isabel came back into the hall, shouting to the girls because they didn't appear to be working. Douglas caught sight of the woman, tracking her as she headed across the hall.

"Go back to work," he told Mira quietly. "I must speak to Lady Isabel."

Mira suspected why. She didn't stop him. She turned back to the hearth—but not before she saw Douglas intercept Isabel and begin a quiet but intense conversation. As she finished with the last of the hearth, she heard quite distinctly when Isabel went straight to Astoria and began to chastise her angrily. The sounds of Astoria weeping brought great relief.

Finally, the girl's reign of terror would be over.

Or so Mira thought.

CHAPTER TWELVE

"I HEAR YOU play chess, Douglas."

The question came from behind. Douglas was in the knights' quarters, bent over a basin of water with soap all over his face. He splashed the warm water all over his head and neck and face, standing up with it dripping off him to see Eric in the doorway.

"*I* play chess?" he said, blowing water out of his mouth as he reached for a towel. "Lady Isabel plays chess like a master. I barely escaped with my life, if you must know."

Eric chuckled, leaning against the doorjamb. He was already dressed and shaved, ready for tonight's feast. Douglas was running late, quickly washing up before the evening began, because Lady Isabel insisted on clean men at her table.

"I know very well," Eric said. "There have been several times when she has nearly taken everything from me in a heated game and stopped short of tossing my steaming carcass out into the bailey. Her competitive instinct is legendary."

"I know that now," Douglas said, drying off his face. "I shall not make the same mistake twice."

"Pity," Eric said. "She enjoyed the game. She only has me to play with, and I think she is bored with me."

Douglas refrained from commenting on that. The first thing that came to mind was *that is not what I've heard*, but he didn't say it. It was clear that there was something between Isabel and Eric simply based on body language, but as with everything else, if Eric wanted him to know, the man would tell him.

"Mayhap I would consider it if you act as my second," Douglas said, tossing the towel aside and hunting for a clean tunic. "I will never again enter the solar alone. I feel too vulnerable if Lady Isabel is in there."

Eric snorted. "Do not be troubled," he said. "She likes you. Speaking of liking, what happened in the hall earlier?"

"With what?"

"With the scolding you gave Astoria."

"Oh," Douglas said as he picked up a dark blue tunic. "That."

"Aye, *that*."

Douglas shrugged. "There is nothing much to tell," he said. "She has been harassing Mira because she feels that, somehow, Mira stole me away from her, and she broke a gift I'd given to the girl. I intervened."

Eric nodded in understanding. "She is going around telling everyone you called her stupid and ugly."

Douglas paused in pulling the tunic over his head. "You've heard this?"

"I have."

Douglas rolled his eyes and finished pulling the garment over his head. "I did say that, but there was much more to it," he said. "I told her that she was behaving stupidly and that made her ugly on the inside as well as the outside."

Eric fought off a grin at Astoria's dramatics. "I was sure

there was more to it when I heard what happened," he said. "If nothing else, you have been quite tactful since the day you arrived. You have never struck me as being the cruel sort, Douglas."

"My mother did not raise me to be."

Eric pushed himself off the doorjamb. "I did not think so," he said. "But I thought you should be aware."

Douglas straightened out his tunic, which clung to his magnificent torso. "Is anyone listening to her?"

"Not at all. They are telling her that she deserved it."

"She did."

Eric couldn't help it. He burst into soft laughter. "Of that, I am certain."

Douglas grinned as he picked up a comb and ran it through his hair. "Not to change the subject, but what do you know about de Honiton and his son?" he said. "I've heard the son fostered here for a few years."

Eric nodded. "It was before my arrival," he said. "Isabel tells me he was an undisciplined lad, spoiled, and his father refused to believe there was anything wrong with him."

Douglas set the comb down. "One of those, eh?"

"One of those."

Satisfied that his hair was properly combed, Douglas set the comb down and reached over to pick up his elaborate belt and scabbard, moving to strap them onto his waist. He wasn't going to wear any protection this evening, but he also wasn't going to enter a hall unarmed. That was something his father had taught him. Men drank and things happened, so it was always good to be armed.

"Mira told me that the lad behaved inappropriately toward her when they were both members of the de Kerrington household," he said. "Evidently, he had feelings for her that were not returned, so he resorted to pinching her in delicate places."

Eric was watching Douglas tie the leather straps of the scabbard onto his thigh to secure it. "I'd not heard that," he said. "In fact, I know nothing about the father or the son. But I suspect you are telling me this for a reason."

Finished with the ties, Douglas looked at him. "I am telling you this because Mira has agreed to permit me to court her," he said. "I would hope the de Honiton son has grown up and developed manners, but if he has not, I will defend her. I am simply warning you should it come to that."

Eric wasn't surprised to hear that. "I had heard about your dramatic proposal in the ward yesterday," he said. "So the rumors are true? You did declare your love?"

Douglas gave him a half-smile. "Not at that time," he said. "I did it to discourage the girls who were following me around. It was only a ruse at the time, but the situation has changed since yesterday."

"Now you are serious?"

"I am."

Eric nodded his approval. "Mira is a good girl," he said. "I have known her for years. She's so lovely that she looks like an angel amongst the heathens."

"I would agree with that. I noticed that about her, too."

"I'm sure you did," Eric said. He paused a moment before continuing. "I am not entirely sure I should mention this, as I do not wish to overstep, but I was here when she returned home and then came back again. She told you about her mother's new husband?"

Douglas nodded. "She did," he said. "She said the man's

daughter took exception to her, so the mother sent her back to Axminster."

"That is true," Eric said. "Lady Isabel was glad to have her back to help her with the young ladies, but I honestly cannot imagine anyone turning Mira away. She's a sweet lass. All this is to say that I hope she is not a whim for you. If you are not entirely certain how you feel about her, then break it off now. She does not deserve to be toyed with."

Douglas was studying him carefully. "You are protective of her."

Eric shrugged. "She has no one else," he said. "I suppose I've appointed myself her protector. A little, anyway. She does not know it and she would probably take a stick to me if she knew I felt that way, but I am asking you to be kind to her. She has a big heart and deserves to be happy."

Douglas smiled faintly. "That is as generous an endorsement as I have ever heard, de Kerque," he said. "I appreciate that you've assumed that role, though you were not asked. She did not tell me the two of you were close."

Eric shook his head. "We are not," he said. "But many years ago I had a little sister, and Mira reminds me of her greatly. Her name was Joanna and she was an angel. A sweet little thing."

Douglas was listening closely. "Am I to understand she is no longer with us?"

"Nay," Eric said softly. "Joanna drowned in the river near our home when she was about fifteen years of age. We're not quite sure what happened, but it seems that she was on the riverbank and somehow slipped in. My mother never recovered from it. You see, my father died about the time Joanna was born, and I was the man of the family. I protected Joanna from the moment she was born. I have never forgiven myself that I was not there to protect her from the river, so when I met Mira, and she reminded me so much of my sister, I suppose I appointed myself her secret supporter."

Douglas' smile broadened and he went to Eric, putting a big hand on the man's shoulder. "She could not have a better one," he said. "Let me assure you that she is not a whim for me. She something a good deal more, actually. I promise that I will do you, and Joanna, proud."

Eric smiled weakly. "That is all I ask," he said. "But now that you've told me about Raymond de Honiton, I will be watching him as well. I hope that is agreeable with you."

"Verily."

"Good," Eric said. Then he glanced over at the window to see that the sun was nearly all the way down. "We should go to the hall now. Lady Isabel will want us there to entertain her visitors."

Douglas swept his arm in the direction of the door. "After you, my lord."

It was a show of respect and Eric knew it. Feeling the least bit pleased, and also feeling some camaraderie with Douglas, he headed from the knights' quarters with Douglas on his heels.

CHAPTER THIRTEEN

THERE HE WAS.

Astoria had been waiting for him. Dressed in her finest, as Lady Isabel had asked of all of her ladies, she was standing near the hall entry with Davina and Helen and Primrose. The four of them were greeting the men as they entered and directing them to tables. The rest of the ladies were at the dais, making sure cups of wine were full and generally seeing to the management of the hall. Lady Isabel would not allow them to wander amongst the soldiers' tables, but they were allowed to be on the outskirts of the room and to dance with the men provided they kept a safe distance from them.

This evening, the rumor that Lord de Honiton's son was in attendance had been flying from mouth to mouth. Ines and Marceline, Primrose and Theodora were all atwitter about it. It seemed that the loss of Douglas de Lohr was quickly forgotten with the idea of fresh meat in their midst, so they were all quite eager for a glimpse of Raymond de Honiton.

But Astoria saw him first.

And she would put her plan into action.

Now, it was more than simply getting even with Mira. It

was more than punishing her for taking Douglas away. After Douglas told Lady Isabel about the broken necklace that afternoon, Astoria was going to get even with Douglas, too. It was clear that he'd been turned against her before she'd even had the chance to entice him, and that made him her enemy. The whole situation was veering out of her control and she was struggling to gain the upper hand on everything.

This was her chance.

Now, the very man who was going to unknowingly help her exact her petty revenge was in front of her. Without a word, she broke away from the group of young ladies and made her way to Raymond as he entered the hall. He stepped in, taking in the miasma of smoke and warmth and hum of conversation, and she blocked his path before dropping into a deep curtsy.

"My lord," she said. "I hope that you would remember me. I was here when you were a page at Axminster. My name is Astoria de Luzie."

Raymond was annoyed that the girl had nearly tripped him in her haste to introduce herself, and he looked at her impatiently.

"Nay, I do not remember you," he said. "Where is my father?"

That was a stab to Astoria's ego, but she pushed it aside. Instead, she pointed to the dais. "Over there," she said. "He is with Lady Isabel and Sir Eric and Sir Douglas. He is also with Lady Mira. Surely you remember her."

Suddenly, Raymond didn't appear so impatient. "D'Avignon?" he said. "Mira d'Avignon?"

"Aye, my lord."

"She's *still* here?"

"Aye, my lord," she said. "She is in the market for a husband these days, though she is rather old. And she remembers you, because I heard her say that she hopes for a dance with you tonight."

In a few short seconds, Raymond went from annoyed to interested. Years may have passed since he was last at Axminster, years of training and warfare, but other than getting bigger and stronger and more experienced as a warrior, he was still the same Raymond. The core of the lad that once was had never changed. Truthfully, he'd never even thought of the fair Mira d'Avignon when he arrived, assuming she'd long since moved on, so this bit of news was most surprising.

And encouraging.

Perhaps it would be a pleasant night after all.

"Is that so?" he said after a moment. "Is she still pretty?"

"Some say so, my lord."

"Good," he said, pushing past her. "I'll see for myself."

As he headed off toward the dais through the crowded hall, Astoria watched him go, a pleased expression on her face.

"What trouble are you up to?"

The question was whispered in her ear, and Astoria turned to see Helen beside her. As the woman eyed her suspiciously, Astoria's smile vanished.

"No trouble at all," she said. "But I remembered, long ago, that Raymond was rather fond of Mira. I thought he might like to see her again."

Helen scowled. "*Fond* of her?" she said. "I remember him pinching her and trying to force himself on her. Lady Isabel was going to send him away when his father mercifully sent him to Kenilworth. The man is an animal!"

Astoria shrugged. "That is of no concern to me," she said. "But it will be a concern to Mira. I wonder what Douglas will think of her when someone like Raymond shows her attention?"

"What do you mean by that?"

Astoria pretended to be uninterested in the entire conversation. "Nothing," she said. "Or everything. Mayhap he'll see Mira for the whore she is."

Helen grunted, shaking her head in disgust. "If you do not stop your harassment of Mira, not only will I tell Lady Isabel, but I will also tell Mira," she said. "I saw Douglas scold you today. You'll get far worse than that if you start something."

Astoria whirled on her, yanking the braid that was draped over her shoulder. "You'll do no such thing!"

Helen gasped at the pain of the tug, retaliating by stomping so hard on Astoria's toes that the woman howled in agony. That brought Davina running to separate them.

"Stop!" Davina hissed. "Stop or Lady Isabel will send you both out of here and punish you for embarrassing her in front of her visitors. Behave!"

Astoria was already limping away, removing herself from Helen and Davina, who were not on her side. But it didn't really matter anymore. She did what she'd set out to do.

The wheels were in motion.

The night was about to get interesting.

ଓ

CLAD IN A gown of green silk that was nearly the color of her eyes, Mira was combed and braided, her hair wound like a crown upon her head and the cross pendant from the necklace pinned to the bodice. Even if she couldn't wear it as a necklace at the moment, she still wanted to honor Douglas by wearing it, so she and Helen had pinned it carefully at the base of her neckline. It was in the same location it would have been had she worn the necklace. With some of Davina's rose perfume behind her ears and gently daubed on her hair, she presented a magnificent picture.

Funny how she'd never put a huge amount of stock in her appearance. Of course, she was always neatly dressed and clean, but doing anything elaborate was something she had never been particularly adept at. But tonight, it was different. In a few short days she had gone from an unattached woman to a lady with a suitor. That was new territory for her, but one that left her giddy with delight. In fact, Mira wasn't sure she could eat a bite tonight because her stomach was in knots, but not bad knots.

On the contrary.

She was very much looking forward to the feast.

The night at Axminster Castle had settled into a cool but brilliant evening. A smattering of stars brushed across the sky and night birds could be heard in the distance as the soldiers walked the walls with torches in hand, staying vigilant while a great feast went on in the glowing hall. Lord de Honiton had only brought about twenty men to the feast with him, leaving the rest out in the central bailey cooking their supper over an open fire, but the hall was packed with Axminster, de Lohr, and some de Winter men.

It was a full house.

Somehow, Mira couldn't remember an evening so beautiful. Food smelled better and the light and warmth from the hall was somehow brighter than it had ever been. She'd arrived early to ensure that the visitors were taken care of, but Lady Isabel was already there, so Mira simply made sure the dais was properly set.

She'd never met Lord de Honiton, and as she stood at the

edge of the table making sure everything was in order, she couldn't help but watch the man as he spoke to Isabel. He seemed happy, and congenial, and nothing like the son Mira remembered. Somehow, as the years passed, she had built Raymond up in her mind to be something akin to a monster. She honestly didn't remember much about him, only the apprehension she'd felt every single day as she went about her duties when he was around.

For quite some time, that had been a nightmare.

But it hadn't always been that way.

When Raymond was young, he hadn't been so bold. He was younger than Mira was, a little slip of a boy with a wild crown of dark hair and enormous brown eyes. He was almost angelic looking when he first came, but that quickly changed when his behavior began to come to light. He hadn't been there more than a few months before he decided Mira was meant for him.

That was when the assaults began.

At first, they had been benign. He was a young boy, so he didn't have the grasp of a more mature man when it came to wooing a woman. His attempts had amounted to nothing more than leaving her bunches of wilted field flowers or bringing her an egg or something of that nature. Mira had been polite at first, and that had been her mistake because he'd taken that as a sign of interest when there was none. His little gifts had gone on for a year or two, and her second mistake had been keeping any of them. She should have simply given them all back, but she didn't.

As he began to mature, the situation grew worse.

Mira remembered the first time he pinched her on the behind. She had been so startled that she hadn't reacted other than to yelp. He had grinned devilishly at her, thinking it was a game or perhaps even that she liked it, and her third mistake had been not stopping that behavior immediately. At first she simply ignored it, and when that didn't work, she politely told him to stop. He ignored the request and continued pinching her any chance he got. She finally had to tell Lady Isabel, who had to see it for herself before she took action. When the punishment began, that was when the situation turned positively ugly.

The pinching became vindictive. When that wasn't enough, he graduated to groping her at any opportunity. He would wait for her in the shadows of the keep, where the pages were not allowed, and when she walked by, he would reach out and grab any piece of flesh he could. Sometimes it was her stomach, sometimes just an arm. But there had been times, more than once, when he'd managed to get a handful of her breast. Lady Isabel, who hadn't been entirely pleased with having the boy around anyway, took the opportunity to force her brother to send word to Lord de Honiton with the threat that the lad would be sent home if he couldn't behave.

Lord de Honiton had ignored her. It was the worst it had ever been the last year Raymond was at Axminster. Mira hadn't told Douglas just how bad because, frankly, she was embarrassed that it had gotten so terrible. Raymond, who by this time had gotten quite big and was growing strong, would wait for the opportunity to grab her from behind. More than once, he had pulled her into an alcove and held her so tightly that she couldn't breathe while one hand wandered over her breasts and moved down between her legs. He never actually went under her skirts, but he would grope her through the fabric. The first time he'd done it, she screamed and Raymond was badly punished, but after that he grew smarter. He would grab her and try to put his hand over her mouth so she couldn't yell. She took to carrying a dagger with her everywhere she went and finally had cause to use it one night when he grabbed her in the hall and she stabbed him in the hand.

That was when Raymond was no longer allowed in the hall or the keep. Thankfully for all of them, his father sent an escort to Axminster about that time with the news that Raymond would be moving to Kenilworth Castle to be trained by the master knights. It had been quite fortuitous, and the timing could not have been better because Mira was quite certain that she was going to have to kill the man to keep him off her.

And then he was gone.

Nay, she hadn't told Douglas about any of that because, as she suspected, he was a man who was serious about the defense of women, and in particular any woman who meant something to him. Douglas was chivalrous to the bone, so she didn't tell him the depths of Raymond's debauchery because she thought Douglas might simply go after the man and kill him for those offenses he'd committed those years ago. She didn't want Raymond's death anymore, but she did want him to leave Axminster as quickly as he could.

But she had to get through the night first.

Still, Mira felt very safe with Douglas in the hall. He gave her the courage to attend, to be in the same room with a man who had assaulted her in the past. Quite truthfully, had Douglas not been there, she would not have even got into the hall at all. But he *was* there, and she knew that nothing bad could happen to her as long as he was around. Given that she'd only known him a total of six weeks, it was a remarkable and unique feeling.

But one she wholly embraced.

Douglas had shown up to the hall with Eric just as most of the men were arriving. In fact, Lord de Honiton arrived about the same time, and the three of them walked to the dais together. Lord de Honiton was friendly, and good conversation, and he settled down with Douglas and Eric at the head of the table as servants provided them with the fine Burgundy wine. Mira hadn't been able to take her eyes off Douglas since he arrived, as the man was clean and shaven, his long blond hair neatly combed and flowing free, and he wore a dark blue tunic that emphasized his muscular arms and chest.

Of course she couldn't take her eyes off him.

Why would she even want to?

But she didn't speak to him because he was entertaining Lady Isabel's guest and she didn't want to interrupt. She had been trained to be a perfectly good hostess, and in Lady Isabel's world, women were seen but not heard. Therefore, Mira remained mostly in the shadows, watching the head table as well as the room to ensure that everything was running smoothly.

Unfortunately, that had been a mistake.

"Lady Mira?"

Mira heard her name, turning just in time to see Raymond nearly upon her. Startled, she gasped and stepped away, feeling the familiar terror flooding back. Those years of being able to push it aside and eventually forget were gone in an instant as he smiled at her, his brown eyes glittering.

"I knew it was you," he said before she could answer. "I was told you were still here. I did not believe it, however. Surely some man would have married you by now. But here you are—and more beautiful than I remember."

That voice. It sent chills of terror through her. Mira backed up, trying to stay out of arm's length.

"W-welcome to Axminster, my lord," she said. Quickly, she

indicated the dais. "Your father is waiting for you. Lady Isabel has ordered the fine wine brought forth, so I hope it is to your liking."

She was moving away from him already, but he reached out and grasped her by the arm. In a panic, she yanked her arm free and whirled on him.

"Don't touch me," she spat. "If you do that again, I shall scream and bring the entire hall running."

He looked at her as he had no idea what she meant. "I was simply going to ask if you would sit with me," he said. "I'm told you've not forgotten me. I've certainly not forgotten you. Mayhap I can convince my father to stay another day or two while we come to know each other once again."

Mira's heart was beating painfully against her ribs, her throat tight with fear. "That will not be necessary, my lord," she said. "Please come with me."

"Mira?" Raymond asked pleadingly. "Whatever is the matter? What have I done?"

She stopped to look at him. Knowing that Douglas was only a scream away fed her bravery. *What have I done?* As if he didn't know. It was a question that brought rage because he sounded so innocent.

It inflamed her.

"How can you ask that question?" she said, her voice trembling. "I had hoped I was well rid of you, but here you are again. I'd hoped you would have at least matured during your years at Kenilworth, but still, you grab me when you should not. Mayhap you have learned nothing at all, so I will tell you plainly. I spent years being terrified of you."

He looked at her as if shocked. "What?" he said, incredulous. "What did I do to frighten you?"

Mira looked at him as if he was daft. "Grab me," she said. "Pinch me, fondle me, kiss me. You were horrid and incorrigible. I want you to go to the dais and sit down and leave me alone. We have no friendship to rekindle."

He wasn't as daft as he was pretending. He knew why she was behaving this way. A lazy smile spread over his lips. "I thought you'd forgotten all of that," he said. "It was just child's play."

"*Child's* play?"

"Of course," he said. "I was a young man. Young and foolish. Can you not understand that?"

Mira didn't believe for one moment that he'd changed. She could tell by looking at him that he was still the same Raymond. With nothing to say to him, she simply turned for the dais.

"If you will come with me, please," she said, struggling not to tremble, "I am obligated to show you Axminster hospitality."

She approached the head table, and Raymond remained where she left him for a brief moment before following. Mira avoided eye contact with him and made sure to stay several feet away as he sat down next to his father. A servant provided him with the special wine, and after that, Mira's job was done. She moved back into the shadows to observe and manage. But Raymond kept his eye on her.

It wasn't over as far as he was concerned.

None of it.

ଓ

"SOMETHING TERRIBLE IS going to happen tonight," Helen said.

She and Davina were still by the entry door to catch any stragglers who entered. Lady Isabel liked order, and if any more de Honiton men entered, she wanted to ensure they were properly directed.

So far, however, the entry doors remained closed and the hall was quite full. A layer of blue smoke hung up near the ceiling even though the fireplace had a chimney, but there was a crack somewhere that let the smoke out. The food was beginning to come from the kitchens, with great hunks of boiled beef placed on the tables along with slabs of bread, butter, and bowls of beans and carrots. For the dais, the servants brought forth roasted birds that had their feathers restored to create the illusion of living creatures.

In all, it was a glorious display, befitting Isabel's reputation.

Even at a moment's notice, she could produce the finest feast in all the land. While she joined those at the dais and her ladies were relegated to a table just below the head table, Helen and Davina were still near the entry. Helen's words echoed in Davina's ears.

"Why would you say that?" Davina wanted to know. "What is going to happen?"

Helen was watching Astoria, who was where she wasn't supposed to be—mingling with the soldiers. She had servants with her, and together, they were handing out food and ensuring the men had enough to eat and drink, but Helen knew it was a ruse.

"Astoria," she said simply. "She is up to something."

Davina caught sight of her, too, speaking to some of the soldiers as she handed them food. "She is going to get her ears boxed by Lady Isabel," she said. "She knows Isabel does not like us to mingle with the men."

Helen shook her head. "It is more than that," she said. "Did you see Raymond come in earlier?"

"Aye," Davina said. "I saw Astoria speaking to her."

Helen sighed heavily. "I heard what she said," she muttered. "She told him that Mira still spoke fondly of him and would like to dance with him."

Davina's eyes widened. "She said that?"

Helen nodded. "She is trying to cause trouble with Mira," she said. "But she is playing with fire by telling Raymond that. You remember what he used to do to Mira."

Davina nodded solemnly. "I do," she said. "Oh, I do. We must tell Lady Isabel right away."

Helen shook her head. "Astoria will only deny it," she said. "I fear that something must happen before her wicked scheme will be discovered and she can be disciplined without question. Astoria is out for blood. *Mira's* blood."

They continued to watch Astoria as she finished helping with the food, but that didn't stop her from remaining to chat with the men. A lone lutist began to play over near the hearth, a man who lived at Axminster and whose sole purpose was to play at mealtimes because Lady Isabel loved music. The man was old, but he was very good, and this was a steady job for him. Everyone at the castle knew him. But neither Davina nor Helen were paying attention to the music. They were watching Astoria, who was speaking to the men and, once or twice, pointed to the dais.

The warning bells were going off in Helen's head.

"Mayhap I should tell Mira," she said. "I think she should go to our chamber and stay there for the night. With Astoria on the loose, she should not be here."

Their focus inevitably moved to Mira at the dais. She had been seated between Lady Isabel and Eric because everyone had been served food and she could take the time to eat, but that had been short-lived. She was up again, managing the servants at the edge of the room. Davina had the same opinion as Helen did. They didn't trust Astoria—no one did—but other than what Helen had heard, they couldn't prove that Astoria *did* say it. As Helen said, she would only deny it.

Still...

"I do not know if we should," Helen said. "It may make things worse, and we will be blamed."

Davina grunted. "How?"

Helen pointed to the dais. "Because Lady Isabel has guests," she said. "She will never forgive us for causing trouble whilst she has guests."

Davina knew that. The experience that guests had at Axminster was paramount to Isabel, and two whining young women, complaining about another young woman, would not go over well. Even if there was a good reason behind it.

Heavily, she sighed.

The pendulum to warn Mira was now swinging in the other direction.

"Then all we can do is keep an eye on Astoria ourselves," Davina said. "If it looks as if she is going to harm Mira, then we will stop her."

Helen nodded firmly. "And do it so Lady Isabel does not notice and become angry with us."

Davina couldn't disagree. "Is there any way we can simply remove Astoria from the hall?" she said, half jesting and half not. "*She* is the problem, not Mira. Mayhap we can lock her in the vault and forget she is there."

Helen looked at her. "That may not be a terrible idea," she said. "What if we can lure her to the vault and lock the door?"

"Then she will cry to Lady Isabel and we would be punished."

"Not if we deny it," Helen said. "It would be our word against hers."

"Our word and the word of anyone who saw us drag her down to the vault," Davina pointed out. "Nay, Helen. I believe the thing to do is to watch Astoria and protect Mira if we can. Anything else will cause too much trouble and we will end up being punished—not Astoria."

Helen nodded in resignation. "We will take turns watching her, then," she said. "I told Mira I would help ensure that the kitchens continue to run smoothly, so I must go there for a while. Will you stay here?"

Davina had her eye on Astoria still speaking with the men. "I will not let her out of my sight."

Helen knew she meant it, too, but the situation was frustrating at best. When they should be practicing their chatelaine skills, they were forced to keep an eye on a woman who was intent on creating havoc. Maybe. The unpredictability was the worst part. Would she… or wouldn't she?

God help them, no one trusted Astoria.

At this point, it was a waiting game.

CHAPTER FOURTEEN

"DOUGLAS," ISABEL SAID. "It is very important that you allow me to redeem myself with a game of chess. I am certain you realize that no one bests me in my own home. Not even Eric, though he tries."

She was heavily into the wine this night, on her third cup that Douglas could see. He fought off a grin, not taking her too seriously.

"My lady, you are most formidable," he said. "But I was only able to best you by the grace of God. I should not like to test Him with another game and could not stand the shame if I lost, so mayhap it is best if we do not play again."

"Nonsense," Isabel said, slamming her empty cup to the table. "You *will* play with me again. You have a keen mind, and I admire that."

"Thank you, my lady."

She eyed him, sitting back in her chair as she dragged her gaze over him from top to bottom. "You are also a fine form of a man," he said. "Has anyone ever told you that?"

He couldn't help it then. His grin broke through. "You should see my brother, Myles," he said. "He is the one all of the women find attractive. Westley isn't so bad, either."

Isabel snorted. "So you are from a family of beautiful men," she said, seeing a servant with a pitcher and waving them over. "My family was never so fortunate. All of the men looked like old trees with the bark peeling off. My brother was so ugly he looked as if he'd been struck by lightning."

Douglas broke down into silent laughter, watching Eric do the same thing. Isabel's cup was full once more, and she took a big swallow before her attention turned to Jerome and his son at the end of the table.

"Raymond was always a fine-looking lad," she said to Jerome. "You only have one son?"

Jerome was fairly drunk, too, on the very strong wine. "One is enough," he said. "He is my only child. My wife, God rest her soul, could only manage one. But he is a proud son and I am content."

"I see," Isabel said, her gaze lingering on Raymond. "No marriage for him yet?"

Raymond shook his head but before he could answer, Jerome spoke. "We are very selective," he said. "The lady must come with a good dowry and property. There have been a few prospects, but there are better ones out there. Money and position are key."

"What about her character?" Douglas said. He'd been listening carefully. "It seems to me that a lady without good character is not worth the money and property she brings to a marriage."

Jerome looked at him. "What do you mean, Sir Douglas?"

"I mean simply that I would rather have a wife of good character, one I was compatible with, rather than a fool who simply brought money and property to a marriage," he said. "The last thing you want is a wife who shames you or reflects badly on the family. You want a wife to be proud of."

"True," Jerome said. "That is very true. But marriage is more about strengthening a family."

"I would rather be with someone I liked. Even loved."

Jerome snorted. "Marriage is not about love," he said. "That is a fool's dream."

"My parents love one another and my father is most certainly not a fool."

"Who is your father, then?"

"Don't you know?" Isabel spoke up. She was incredulous. "You mean to tell me you do not know who Douglas' father is? My God, man, the standards of the Earl of Hereford and Worcester are flying all over Axminster. Did you not see them?"

Jerome suspected he should have, but he honestly couldn't remember. "I do not suppose I was looking at any standards," he said. "I do apologize if I have said something offensive."

Isabel shook her head at the man's propensity for ignorance before lifting the cup to her lips and drinking. It was Douglas who answered.

"You've not said anything offensive," he said. "My father is Christopher de Lohr, the Earl of Hereford and Worcester. He is not a fool."

Jerome's eyes widened. "Good God, he is not," he said. "I did not know, Sir Douglas. Forgive me."

Douglas waved him off. "No need," he said. "I suppose we all have our different philosophies on marriage and women."

"I think women need to be tamed," Raymond said. He, too, was feeling his wine because it had been a long day and he was exhausted. "There isn't one woman out there who knows what she wants or what she needs. It is up to men to teach them."

Isabel eyed the man from across the table. "You think so, do you?" she said, a hint of hazard in her tone. "I think men are in for a lesson themselves if they think that."

Douglas banged his cup on the table a couple of times softly in agreement. "I think men could learn a thing or two from women," he said. "My mother is a great teacher. I do not think my brothers and I would be the men we are today without her. That being said, she had to learn such a skill because my father was already a very important man when they married. He told me that all they did was fight the first few months of their marriage. I think they both had to learn a thing or two before they settled down and fell in love. In any case, they have set a good example for my siblings and me."

"Then what you are looking for in a marriage is love, Sir Douglas?" Jerome said. "It would seem to me that the son of an earl would look for something more."

Douglas shrugged. "I want to be happy," he said. "I think that is a fair statement for all of us. We all want to be happy in a marriage. But we must each decide what that happiness is."

Jerome conceded the point. "Very true," he said. "And may each of us find what we are looking for."

He lifted his cup in a toast to that sentiment, and Douglas lifted his as well. As they both drank deeply, Isabel leaned in Douglas' direction.

"And have you found what you are looking for here at Axminster?" she asked quietly.

He didn't turn in her direction, but he smiled at her question. She knew he'd taken Mira away from the escort earlier that day. The woman wasn't stupid. He was coming to respect Isabel for more than simply being a strong, independent woman with the weight of an earldom on her shoulders. Her respected her for asking an honest question.

He wasn't going to lie to her.

"I suspect you know the answer," he said quietly.

"I do," she said. "But you told me yesterday that your public display was only for show."

Douglas shrugged. "That was not a lie," he said. "It *was* for show at the time."

"What has changed since then?"

He had to think on that. "I have," he finally said. "My eyes are open now."

Isabel chuckled. "I am surprised you would admit that," she said. "But that is good to know. And I approve."

He turned to look at her. "That means a great deal to me, my lady," he said. "I may have to dominate you in another game of chess to celebrate."

She hissed and sat back in her chair, eyeing him unhappily. "I challenge you to another game at the day and time of my choosing," she said. "But not tonight. My head is swimming and an infant could best me."

Douglas was still grinning. "Then that is the best time to play, because my head is swimming, too."

Isabel laughed. She didn't laugh often, and she had a pretty smile. Eric had moved over one chair next to her when Mira had vacated, so he was sitting next to her now, grinning because she was laughing. Douglas gestured to the two of them.

"Speaking of marriage," he said quietly. "When can I expect to attend *your* nuptials?"

Eric's smile faded and Isabel's laughter abruptly stopped. "Where on earth did you get the idea that Eric and I will wed?" she said, almost angrily. "Who told you such things?"

Douglas gave her a long look. "I have eyes," he said. "I believe Eric will make an excellent Earl of Axminster. He is well liked, he is bright, and he is experienced. Moreover, you have affection for the man, so it would be perfect for you both. You should consider it."

The smiles on both of them were gone. Isabel was looking at Douglas, her eyes shining with a thousand words that she would like to say on the subject, but she refrained. After a moment, she simply shook her head.

"This is not a subject to bring up in jest, Douglas," she said softly.

Douglas could see that he'd hit a nerve. Eric was staring at the floor and Isabel's good humor had been greatly subdued. He was usually more tactful than that, but he'd had enough wine that it had tipped his judgment a bit.

He backed down.

"My apologies," he said. "I simply meant that I am sure my father would like you both as strong allies. And… feelings and affection do not happen every day. They are precious when they do. If I have overstepped, I did not mean to. It's simply that I feel happiness is within my grasp these days, and I suppose I want everyone to be happy too. To take the chance before it passes by."

Isabel nodded but looked away, perhaps with too much on her mind. Eric's gaze came off the floor and he focused on Douglas.

"Mira is a good girl, as I said," he said quietly. "She will make you a fine wife, Douglas. I could not be happier for you both."

His comment seemed to bring Isabel around. "Let us speak about you and Mira, then," she said, changing the subject away from her and Eric and back onto Douglas and his interest in Mira. "I said that I approve, and I do, but I am still greatly curious. What has changed since yesterday, Douglas?"

She wielded his name like a club when it suited her. Imperiously. Demandingly. *Douglas!* She did it with focus and foresight, but in this case, she was drunk and repeating questions, so he simply shook his head.

"As I said, my eyes are open," he said. "Open to the possibilities, to a chance I should not pass up. To be perfectly truthful, I thought Lady Mira was quite beautiful when I first met her, but nothing beyond that. Then I came to know a delightful young woman and… Well, when things happened, they happened quickly."

"And now you really do wish to marry her?"

"Do you think her mother would give permission?"

Isabel rolled her eyes. "You will get your permission from me," she said. "Mira's mother does not care what becomes of her and cannot be bothered. She is a weak, joyless woman. How she managed to give birth to someone as strong and stalwart as Mira is a mystery."

"If I ask your permission, then, will you give it?"

It was a straight question. Isabel's eyes glimmered at him, so much so that she had the man's attention. They smiled at one another, him in anticipation and her because she wanted to draw it out. She liked taunting Douglas because, as she'd said, he reminded her of her brother. There was a strange sort of sibling association there. They were so focused on one another, in fact, that they failed to notice Raymond leave the dais.

He'd been too far away to hear most of the conversation, but it didn't interest him anyway. He'd finished his food and had a couple of cups of that strong wine, and quite frankly, his mind was elsewhere. While his father sat there with a cup in his hand and his eyes closed, listening to the distant strains of the lute, Raymond headed around the back of the raised platform, back into the shadows where the servants were.

Where Mira was.

He, too, was on the hunt.

CS

IT HAS BEEN a strange hour.

That was what Mira thought as she directed the servants to clean up some spilled drink in the middle of the hall before someone slipped on it, but it had been strange not for that reason. It had been strange because soldiers, men she had known for many years during her time at Axminster, were smiling and waving at her. She wasn't sure why, so she hesitantly waved back. But it was happening at the table near the hearth, and one man even pointed to the minstrel and made swirling motions with his hands—as if he was telling her, or asking her, to dance. Strange things, indeed. But her first real inkling that something was seriously amiss was when someone grasped her by the wrist.

"Come, Mira," Raymond said. "I'm told you wish to dance with me, so let's dance."

Instantly frightened, Mira dug her heels in. "I do not wish to dance," she said. "I am busy at the moment. Mayhap one of the other girls would like to."

Raymond continued to pull. "Do not be shy," he said. "There is no need, not now. You are a woman grown and I am a man grown. May we finally declare our interest? I have thought of you through the years, you know."

He hadn't, but it sounded good. But Mira's eyes widened in horror.

"Interest?" she repeated, aghast. "In *you*? There has never been a more untrue statement, Raymond. I do not know who told you such things, but it is not true."

He grinned leeringly. "You do not have to lie to me," he said. "I knew you had feelings for me years ago. How you would gasp when I touched you."

Mira tried to yank her hand from his grip. "I gasped because I was horrified and disgusted," she said, finally managing to pull free. "Did you not realize that? I do not like you, Raymond. I never have."

He paused, the smile fading from his face. "I do not know why you should be so cruel to me," he said. "I am admitting that I have always been fond of you. You do not need to be cutting in order to hide what you feel."

Mira took a few steps back, creating distance between them. "I am not hiding anything," she said. "Leave me alone, Raymond. Your attention is not welcome."

With that, she scooted off, back into the shadows, as he watched her with both irritation and confusion. He was debating whether or not to pursue her when someone walked up beside him.

"Is she taunting you, my lord?" Astoria asked. "That is her way. She is known to tease men."

Raymond frowned. "Either you are lying or she is enjoying treating me this way."

"As I said, she is known to tease men," Astoria said convincingly. "The chase makes it sweeter in the end, I suppose."

Raymond nodded as if he suddenly understood Mira's game. "I see," he said. "Then I suppose I shall continue the chase, but the rewards had better be damn sweet."

"I have heard she lifts her skirts to the right man."

He looked at her in shock. "Truly?" he said. "I would have

never expected it from Mira. She did not seem the type."

"Time changes people."

Raymond considered that. "I suppose," he said. Then he peered down his nose at Astoria as if looking the woman over. "Well? You seem to know so much about her. What do I do now?"

Astoria watched Mira over by the dais. "What do you want to do?"

Raymond raked his fingers through his hair irritably. "If I could only get her alone, we could speak," he said. "But the way she is now… She is working this hall like a servant. She will not focus on me."

Astoria thought on that a moment and an idea came to her. "Do you remember the passages and stairwells of Axminster's keep?"

He nodded. "I should," he said. "I spent enough time in them. Why?"

"Do you recall the servants' stairwell down to the storage vault?"

"The one with the small door outside?"

"The same," Astoria said. "If you go there and wait, I could send her to you and you would have all of the time and privacy you need."

Raymond looked at her. "Why should you be so eager to do this?" he asked. Then he eyed her for a moment. "I thought I did not know you, but I believe I was wrong. I think I do know you."

You called me ugly, once, Astoria thought, but she didn't say it. Instead, she tried to seem as innocent as possible.

"I am eager to do this because Mira is my friend and I want her to be happy," she said. "She has spoken of you often in the years you have been gone. This is a chance for me to help her. But only if you are agreeable, of course."

Raymond believed her. He had no reason not to. With a shrug, he turned for the hall entry. "Then send her to me," he said. "I will be waiting."

With that, he headed out of the hall, leaving Astoria thinking she was about to get even with Mira for every little insult, every little infraction the woman had ever committed against her. It couldn't have been easier. Now the trap was set.

She simply had to send the quarry to it.

CHAPTER FIFTEEN

THE NEXT PERSON who touched Mira's arm received a scream of terror.

Douglas had to grab on to her to keep her from bolting.

"What?" he asked, alarmed. "What did I do?"

When Mira realized who it was, she tried not to weep with relief. "Nothing," she assured him. "I am so sorry. Nothing at all. You… you simply startled me."

They were standing back behind the dais, behind an enormous wooden screen painted with woodlands scenes. Some famous Savoyard artist had been commissioned to paint it and it was an object of pride for Isabel, but right now, it blocked Douglas and Mira from a roomful of nosy eyes.

He peered at her closely.

"Does this have something to do with Raymond?" he asked.

She was trying to pretend that nothing was amiss. "Why would you ask that?"

"Because I saw you talking to him," Douglas said, lifting a blond eyebrow. "I saw him with his hand on your arm, and had it lasted a moment longer, I would have intervened and cut his hand off. You should be proud of the fact that I did not bolt over the table and charge the man the very moment I saw it. I thought I was giving you the opportunity to handle the situation but now I see that I was more than likely wrong. He rattled you."

Mira was trying very hard to pretend that absolutely nothing was out of the ordinary, but that simply wasn't the case. Raymond had rattled her no matter how hard she tried not to let him affect her.

He had.

The tears began to come.

"He said that someone told him I wished to dance with him," she said, breaking down. "He told me that he had not forgotten about me and he knew that I had not forgotten about him. He wanted to dance and talk and I told him to go away and leave me alone, for whoever told him such things about me was wrong."

Douglas had both hands on her arms, trying to be of some comfort. He'd never really seen Mira as vulnerable because she always came across so confident and strong, but at this moment, he could see that vulnerability that she tried so hard to hide.

It had his protective instincts surging.

"He told you that someone told him you wished to dance with him?" he asked. "Is it possible he mistook you for someone else? Who else did he know when he was at Axminster those years ago?"

Mira sniffled, trying not to openly weep. "He knew Astoria and Helen and Davina," she said, wiping at her eyes. "It is possible he mistook me for one of them, but who would tell him I wished to dance with him? That *anyone* wished to dance with him?"

Douglas shook his head, rubbing her arms gently. "I do not know, love."

Without an answer, she gestured in the direction of the hall. "And some of the soldiers are waving at me," she said, growing agitated. "Why are they waving at me? I feel as if everyone is looking at me and waving at me and I do not know why."

Douglas was trying to calm her down because her voice was rising. "Has anyone said anything to you?"

"Other than Raymond, they have not."

"No one has tried to engage you?"

"Just waving. And smiling."

"And smiling," he repeated, muttering as if it might help him understand what was going on. He'd been so swept up with Isabel and Eric that he hadn't even noticed, and he felt bad about that. But as he listened to her sniffle, a thought occurred to him.

A thought that might explain the odd behavior of the evening.

"I hesitate to bring this up, but you mentioned that Astoria knew Raymond those years ago," he said. "And, as we know, she has been working in the hall tonight."

Wiping at her nose, Mira looked up at him. "She has," she said. "Why?"

"Well… I was simply thinking aloud," he continued softly. "Thanks to me, we know she has a vendetta against you. Is it possible she told him that you wanted to dance with him to cause you trauma? Surely she knows how he tormented you when he lived here."

Mira sighed heavily. "She knows," she said. "If she wanted to truly punish me, using Raymond would be quite an opportunity to do it."

"Possibly."

"But what about the soldiers? Why are they all waving at me?"

Douglas shook his head. "I do not know," he said, his hands still on her arms, though now he was gently caressing her. "Mayhap Astoria told them to, knowing you would be confused by it. I do not know, but I can certainly find out."

Mira nodded, feeling more in confident in Douglas' arms. In fact, without even realizing he'd done it, he had managed to pull her into his arms and she was snuggled against his chest as he embraced her tightly. For a brief moment, Mira closed her eyes, inhaling his scent, feeling his warmth, and thinking that there was no better feeling on earth than this. She could hear his heart beating steadily in her left ear.

Thump, thump. Thump, thump.

She pressed herself against him, feeling his big arms tighten around her. It was an embrace that made her feel giddy and faint, but she didn't care. She'd be very happy to feel this way for the rest of her life.

"Douglas?" Jonathan appeared behind the screen, his hulking presence filling up the space. "I am sorry to interrupt, but I have need of you."

Startled, Mira pulled herself out of Douglas' arms, putting distance between them, as Douglas tried not to look disappointed.

He turned to Jonathan.

"What is it?" he asked.

Jonathan, who had volunteered for night duty on the wall, cocked an eyebrow. "A fight," he muttered. "A few de Lohr men against de Honiton men. You'd better come. A man was stabbed."

Douglas grunted. "Christ," he muttered. "Badly?"

"Bad enough."

"Does de Honiton know?"

"Nay," Jonathan said. "I want you to evaluate it first before we summon him."

Douglas nodded before quickly turning to Mira. "I want you to do something for me," he said. "Will you, please?"

She was still a little flushed from their embrace, but she nodded. "What is it?"

"Go to your chamber and lock yourself in," he said quietly, firmly. "I have something I need to tell you, but it will have to wait. And I do not want you in this hall without me if Raymond is grabbing for you or if soldiers are waving at you. Get up to your chamber and lock the door until I come for you."

Mira was torn. "But Lady Isabel will expect me to—"

He cut her off gently. "Lady Isabel will understand when I have explained it to her," he said. "I want you to go right away. This very moment. Go back through the kitchens and into the keep. Do not walk through the hall, but move along the edges, away from everyone. Will you do this?"

Mira was reluctant to grant his request but, after a moment, nodded in resignation. Douglas grasped one of her hands, kissed it, and headed off with Jonathan to where a man had evidently been stabbed. Mira followed him out from behind the screen, leaning against it as she watched him depart from the hall. All of that beautiful, long blond hair made him look like a god above men. She remembered the texture of it well, how it was both soft but strong.

Kind of like Douglas.

Soft but strong.

And oh so wonderful.

With a smile on her lips, she turned away, moving back behind the screen again and preparing to leave the hall as she'd promised him. She came around the other side of the screen where Isabel and Eric and Lord de Honiton were sitting. They were deep into the wine and Isabel was drunk. Mira could tell simply from the way the woman was moving. She knew her well enough to know how animated she became when she'd had too much drink. Raymond, however, had not rejoined his father, and Mira had no idea where he was. Perhaps it was better to leave the hall now while he was gone, as Douglas had requested, and remain there until Raymond and his father departed Axminster. She certainly didn't want to chance being grabbed by Raymond again.

With that in mind, she came away from the dais and moved to the wall on the northern side of the hall. The servants' alcove was at the far end with a small door in it, and beyond that, the kitchens. She was so lost in thoughts of Douglas and counting the minutes until Raymond departed on the morrow that she failed to realize that, once again, she was being hunted.

This time, by a most foolish and wicked hunter.

CS

IT WAS ONLY by pure luck that she was alone.

Ever since her conversation with Raymond, Astoria had been watching Mira on the far side of the hall. Mostly, Mira was behind the screen that stood behind the dais, but every so often she would emerge to make sure there was enough bread on the table or that the wine pitchers were filled. She was doing her duty as Lady Isabel expected her to and therefore wasn't paying attention to anything else in the room.

That meant Astoria had been able to watch Mira freely from

her vantage point near the entry door. The problem was not only in getting Mira alone, but in convincing her to go to the storage vault where Raymond was waiting. Considering Astoria and Mira had been fighting for a couple of days, she wasn't entirely sure that Mira would even talk to her, much less believe her when Astoria said she needed to go to the storage vault. The only way around that was to apologize profusely for her behavior and, in particular, for breaking the necklace. Astoria had to make her believe that she was genuinely remorseful. Mira wasn't the hard sort, so a heartfelt apology might get Astoria exactly what she needed.

Mira's compliance.

As Astoria cooked up a plot that would send Mira to the storage vault where Raymond was waiting, she was disheartened to see Douglas join Mira behind the painted screen. She could only imagine what was happening that she couldn't see, like tender kisses and sweet words, things that Douglas should be saying and doing to her. The more the seconds ticked away and the more Astoria was positive that Douglas was ravaging Mira with his mouth, the more jealous and hurt she became. But she comforted herself with the knowledge that Raymond would soon be doing the same thing to Mira because, once she entered the vault, Astoria intended to send word to Douglas to tell him where she was. Once the man happened upon her in Raymond's arms, he would see for himself what an unworthy woman Mira was.

She would be ruined.

And Douglas would be looking for comfort.

So Astoria hoped, anyway.

As she tried to figure out how to get Mira alone, Jonathan suddenly appeared in the entry. He startled Astoria because, quite frankly, she was afraid of the man. He was big and hairy and powerful and absolutely terrifying. But they made eye contact as soon as he came in through the door, and he headed straight in her direction.

She struggled not to cower.

"Lady Astoria," he greeted her in a rushed manner. "Where is Douglas?"

Astoria pointed to the dais. "There," she said. "Behind the screen."

Jonathan thanked her with a nod of his head and was gone, leaving Astoria a bit rattled. Jonathan always had that effect on her. She watched him disappear behind the screen and, not a minute later, reappear with Douglas on his heels. They both seemed to be in quite a hurry, heading for the hall entry. Astoria watched them disappear out into the torch-lit night, but it took several moments before she realized that with Douglas out in the bailey, Mira was now alone.

Alone!

Astoria turned to the dais only to see Mira standing next to the screen, her gaze on the hall entry. She appeared lost in thought, and it occurred to Astoria that she had been watching Douglas leave. The stab of jealousy to Astoria's heart seemed to spur her forward, and she headed toward the dais just as Mira came away from the screen and moved to the perimeter of the hall. Astoria was on one side of the hall while Mira was on the other, and Astoria had to cross through the middle of the room to get to her. Mira was so focused on the door that led to the kitchen and the kitchen yard that she failed to see Astoria coming up behind her.

"Mira," Astoria said, watching the woman flinch at the sound of her voice. "I must speak with you."

Mira came to a halt, apprehension and even anger in her expression. "What do you want?" she said, then quickly raised her hand. "Forget I asked. I do not care. I have nothing to say to you."

She turned to walk away, but Astoria followed. "I know," she said, trying to sound repentant. "I do not blame you. But what happened today… When I grabbed your necklace… Truly, I did not mean to break it."

That was actually the truth. She hadn't meant to, so she wasn't lying about it. But Mira cast her a long look.

"Save your breath," she said. "You mean to destroy anything you cannot have, so I will not soothe any guilt you are feeling by forgiving you for your cruel actions."

It was Astoria's instinct to flare up when confronted, so it was a genuine struggle for her not to argue. "I am not asking for you to soothe any guilt," she said. "I… I simply wanted to say that I am sorry I broke it. I am sorry I have behaved so poorly lately. I do not know why I do, only that I have had to fight and defend myself my entire life. I suppose it is in my nature to fight against, and for, everything that does not go my way. You happened to be caught up in it."

Up until this point, Mira had simply been walking, trying to get away from Astoria, but now they were at the small servants' door that led to the yard beyond and, subsequently, the kitchen. Mira shoved the door open but came to a pause, turning to look at Astoria.

"You are wasting your time on me," she said. "Astoria, you have always been petty and small-minded, but the way you have treated me over the past two days is unforgiveable."

"I know, Mira."

"You turned against me for no reason at all other than the

man you had your eye on happened to have his eye on me. That was not fair."

Astoria kept her head down, properly contrite. "I know," she said. "I am sorry. I only wanted to apologize to you for my behavior."

Mira didn't believe her for a moment. "How long have we known one another?" she said. "Ten years? More? A very long time, which means I know you well. I've seen your cruelty toward others and I know how vindictive you can be when you do not get your way. I also know that you do not suddenly change your mind and decide you've been behaving poorly, so whatever game you are playing with me, I urge you to stop. It will not work."

Astoria sighed heavily. "I am not playing a game," she said. "And we have known each other a long time. I have considered you my friend."

"Not lately you haven't."

Astoria kept her head lowered. "Jealousy does terrible things to a person," she said. "I cannot control it. I do not know why."

Mira could hear a hint of the girl she'd known all these years in those self-centered comments. There had been a time when Astoria was fun and lively, but that was before her friends all became women before her, becoming pretty and refined, while she grew very tall and remained plain. Realizing she was not the prettiest girl in the room had been a blow, and ever since then, her pettiness came forth quite easily.

Sometimes, Mira missed that friend she used to know.

But not tonight.

"Just… leave me alone," she finally said. "Mayhap with time I'll consider your words, but for now… just leave me alone."

"As you wish," Astoria said. "But I actually came to you on

another matter. I was afraid you would not speak to me if I did not apologize to you first."

"What matter?"

Astoria gestured toward the keep, where there was a fortified exterior door that led to the sublevels where they kept the stores. It was the exterior entrance for ease in taking provisions down to storage, while there was a larger door, and stairwell, that was located in the kitchens.

"I was sent to find you and tell you that there is trouble in the storeroom," she said. "I've been told to fetch you."

Mira frowned. "What trouble?"

Astoria shook her head. "I do not know," she said. "I think it is rot in the grain. It must be bad if you have been requested."

Mira looked confused. "Rot in the grain?" she repeated. "I was just down there earlier and saw no evidence of such a thing."

"Then you had better make sure."

Mira shrugged and stepped through the door. She had no reason to disbelieve Astoria because Mira handled the inventory at Axminster along with the cook, both of them making sure there were always plentiful supplies. Therefore, it wasn't an unreasonable suggestion or request from Astoria, who knew that very well. In fact, she watched Mira head over to the inner bailey, with the keep just a few feet away. Mira disappeared from view and Astoria gave her about a minute to get to the storage vault door.

After that, Astoria ran back into the hall. Spying Davyss de Winter seated near the dais, arm-wrestling a de Lohr soldier while men placed bets and cheered him on, she'd just found the vessel by which to deliver the devastating news to Douglas of Mira d'Avignon's wanton ways.

The last part of her plan was about to take place.

CHAPTER SIXTEEN

THE BEST THING about lying in wait for someone was the very fact they had no idea what was coming.

The element of surprise was on Raymond's side.

Knowing Mira would probably run if she saw him, he made sure to position himself in the shadows at the bottom of the staircase that led from the small service door. The vault was illuminated by several torches that were secured to the walls because servants were coming in and out due to the feast, and he went so far as to remove some of the torches so the area would be darker.

Less chance of his being seen.

As a child, he'd spent a good deal of time hiding in this storeroom, playing with his friends, so he knew the place well. With the exception of inventory being in different places, it had changed little over the years. It still smelled like damp earth and straw, which was spread over the bottom of the dirt to keep the moisture at bay. Truthfully, he found some comfort in that smell.

He was rather glad that he and his father had stopped at Axminster for the night.

Glad for many reasons, but the most prevalent was the opportunity to reacquaint himself with Mira. In spite of what he had been told, she didn't seem all that eager to see him, but he attributed that to the surprise of his appearance. Mira put up a good fight, but he felt that it was simply for show. He was sure it was all part of the chase. Most of all, however, was the information from Lady Astoria about Mira lifting her skirts for men these days. He always thought Mira had been a proper lady, but apparently things had changed. He found himself hoping she would lift her skirts for him.

There was no better place to lift them than down in a dark, shadowed vault.

So he waited.

Surprisingly, he didn't have to wait long. As he sat on a firm sack of what turned out to be carrots, he could hear the door above squeak open. Footsteps hit the stairs and he heard Mira call out.

"Athole?" she called. "Bets? Are you down here?"

There wasn't anyone down there and, fearful that she might turn to leave if she found the storeroom empty, Raymond spoke in a high-pitched voice.

"M'lady?" he said.

Hearing someone call, Mira headed down the stairs. "Bets, is that you?" she said. "What's this I hear about rot in the grain? We were just down here earlier and there was nothing that I saw. Where did you find it?"

She was coming closer. From where Raymond was sitting, he could see her feet and then the bottom of her dress. She came off the stairs and headed toward the area where the grain was stored.

Raymond was compelled to strike.

Bursting out of his hiding place, he grabbed Mira from behind, slapping his hand over her mouth and hauling her up against him. As she screamed and kicked and twisted, he managed to carry her back to the darkened corner where the grain was stored in big, covered barrels. All the way back he carried her, pushing her into a corner between the barrels so she was effectively trapped.

Only then did he set her on her feet.

"Do not scream," he growled in her ear. "If I uncover your mouth, you will not scream. I only want to speak with you and I did not wish to do it in a hall full of men where your attention was divided. Do you understand me? There is no need to scream."

Mira's response was to try to kick him, scratching with her sharp nails until he yelped and yanked his hand away. She was able to peal a brief scream before he slapped a hand over her mouth again and shoved her back against the wall.

Now they were facing one another.

"I told you *not* to scream," he rumbled. "Now I shall have to keep my hand over your mouth until you hear what I have to say."

That brought slapping and twisting from Mira. Raymond was trying not to get hit in the face as she lashed out at him and keep his hand over her mouth at the same time, so he was forced to shove her into the wall to still her while he trapped her flailing hands. She was awkwardly pressed against the stone now, the right side of her face being ground against the rough wall as he used his body weight to subdue her.

"Mira, *stop*," he muttered in her ear. "I am not entirely sure why you are fighting so much, but it stops now. Your dear friend Astoria was kind enough to tell me what you could not, so there is no need to struggle. It is unnecessary. I prefer my women obedient and compliant."

The right side of her face was becoming scratched as he pushed and she struggled. Mira couldn't speak because of his hand over her mouth, but her terror was evident. She was gasping and grunting, her entire body tense, and Raymond pressed closer to her.

"It has been a long time since we last saw one another," he said. "I tried to tell you that I was glad to see you in the hall, but you would not give me your attention. If you would only stop and listen, I am certain we can rekindle what has been lost over the years. I will not hurt you and I do not mean to frighten you, but you are fighting so much that I have no choice. Do you hear me? You are forcing me to hurt you, Mira."

Mira tried to let out a scream, muffled by his hand. He could feel something warm and wet on his fingers, and realized it was tears. Mira was weeping.

Bizarrely, he tried to hug her.

"No tears, lass," he whispered, kissing her ear. "There is no need. If you would stop struggling, this will be pleasant. We spent moments like this in the past, moments you only told me tonight that you did not find enjoyable, but I will change your mind. You will let me do that, won't you? Change your mind?"

Mira suddenly went limp in his arms, and Raymond thought she might have swooned. She turned into something boneless and sagging, and he was forced to adjust his grip on her, but just as he moved his hand from her mouth, she came to life and brought her knee up into his groin as hard as she could.

Raymond doubled over and Mira ran for the stairs.

Gasping in fright and panic, she put her foot on the bottom step but slipped on the slick stone in her haste. She fell forward, striking her temple on the stone step. Collapsing on the ground, dazed, Raymond recovered from her knee to his groin and, angry and in pain, stormed over to where she lay, grabbing her by the arm, dragging her back into the darkness.

The hunter had finally caught his prey.

☙

SOLDIER FIGHTS WERE often the messiest.

Douglas had walked into what looked like a bloodbath. Men with too much drink and too much time on their hands had turned a friendly evening meal into a wasteland of destruction. The central bailey had been where de Honiton set up his encampment, which happened to be the same place de Winter and de Lohr had set up theirs. The two armies were allies in theory and the evening meal had been shared by all. There had been a large fire with a spit over it, roasting half a cow. The men had eaten their share and gotten drunk on the cheap ale that Eric purchased for the army, and that had unfortunately set up a rather large brawl.

Now, there was blood everywhere.

Jonathan had been on the wall, monitoring the sentries and not paying a good deal of attention to the soldiers down in the bailey. He could hear them laughing and singing, and he assumed everyone was getting along just fine until they weren't. The fight had started between just a few men, but by the time he got down there, both armies were embroiled in a fistfight. Inevitably, men began to produce daggers and at least six men were slashed. One of them had been stabbed fairly seriously, and Douglas and Jonathan stood by and watched the de Winter surgeon try to save the man's life. It was a de Winter soldier who had been stabbed and all indications were that a de

Honiton man had done it. As the de Winter soldier bled out in the dark earth, Douglas and Jonathan went into command-and-control mode.

The two knights separated the men, sending all armies back to their respective camps. The sergeants of the de Honiton contingent were cooperative, and horrified at what had happened, and Douglas demanded they turn over the soldier who had committed the crime. Truthfully, there seemed to be some confusion over who had actually wielded the weapon because no one wanted to incriminate a comrade, but the sergeants were relentless in their questioning.

"You'd better send for Lord de Honiton," Jonathan said quietly, watching men jostle around in search of the killer. "He will not be pleased if we do not at least tell him what has happened."

Douglas nodded as he, too, watched the de Honiton sergeants roust their own men. "I know," he said. "But the man is drunk. He probably will not even realize what is going on here, so let us find the offending soldier before we send for him. We do not need the man trying to figure it all out."

Jonathan could see his point. "Mayhap not," he said. "But this is not ideal. No one wants this visit to end badly, especially with an ally."

"And you were up on the wall when all of this started?"

"Indeed, I was," Jonathan said. "The men seemed to be getting along splendidly until suddenly, they weren't."

"What started the fight?"

"Who knows?" Jonathan said with a shrug. "These things can start so easily, as you know. One moment, everyone is friendly and in the next, the daggers are coming out."

Douglas grunted in agreement. "I've seen it too many

times," he said. Before he could say another word, however, he caught sight of someone heading toward them from the direction of the great hall. The man came closer, illuminated by the torchlight, and Douglas realized who it was. "Here comes Davyss, probably to find out why we're both out here. I hope Lady Isabel is not looking for me."

Jonathan could see Davyss on the approach as well. "Why would she look for you?" he said. "Her eye is on Eric, not you."

Douglas shrugged. "She seems to have taken a liking to me," he said. "The woman was trying to challenge me to another chess game not ten minutes ago."

"She wants to be beaten again, does she?"

"On the contrary. She wants to beat *me*."

Jonathan grinned. "That is not the same woman who tried to convince us to leave after we first arrived."

"Nay, it is not."

Davyss was in their midst now, acknowledging Jonathan with a nod of the head, but his focus seemed to be on Douglas.

"A word, Douglas?" he said.

Douglas could immediately see that he seemed quite serious. Davyss was an intense man as it was, but there was something in those eyes that seemed… edgy. Douglas wasn't quite sure what it was, to be honest. All he knew was that Davyss seemed stiff, which was an odd state for him.

"Of course," Douglas said steadily. "What is it?"

Davyss glanced at Jonathan before replying, "Alone, if you will."

With a shrug, Douglas followed Davyss several paces away from Jonathan and the soldiers who were lingering about. When Davyss felt they were far enough away from prying ears, he turned to Douglas.

"I am not exactly sure how to tell you this, so I will just come out with it," he said quietly, scratching his shaggy head. "I have been sent here by Astoria."

Douglas' brow furrowed. "Astoria?" he repeated. "Why? What does she want?"

Davyss sighed sharply. "She wanted me to tell you that Mira has gone into the storage vault with young de Honiton," he said. "She said you should know."

That bit of information lit Douglas up. His eyes widened. "She… she *what*?" he nearly shouted. "She's in the storage vault with Raymond?"

Davyss nodded, watching Douglas nearly explode with the news. "Aye," he said, concerned. "She said you should know and—"

That was all Douglas needed to hear. Without another word, he bolted for the keep as fast as his legs would take him. Because he was running, Davyss started to run after him. Jonathan, who had been watching the continued search for the murderer, caught the movement out of the corner of his eye and turned to see Douglas and Davyss running at top speed toward Axminster's keep.

Jonathan took off after them. He had no idea why Douglas and Davyss were running, but he knew it couldn't be good.

The bloody night was about to get worse.

ଓ

SHE COULD FEEL him trying to lift her skirts.

Struggling to pull out of the daze from hitting her head on the stairs, Mira could feel someone trying to push her skirts up. It took her a moment to come around, but she remembered that her last conscious moments were of her running from

Raymond. She remembered the panic and the fear. All that man meant to her was panic and fear. She could smell the damp earth of the vault and it spurred her terror when she realized where she was. Even in the darkness, she could make out the outline of Raymond's face—the man was on top of her. He must have gained the upper hand somehow.

The feet, and hands, began to fly.

Mira burst into full consciousness with a roar, screaming and shouting so loudly that it reverberated off the stone walls. Raymond was saying something—she couldn't quite make it out, but it was something that suggested she calm herself or ease herself or the situation would not be pleasant for her. Mira didn't care if it was pleasant or not.

She was in survival mode.

Her knees were aiming for his belly and groin as he tried to hold them down. The fact that she was moving around so much made it difficult for him to try to lift her skirts. He was trying to keep her from hurting him again, so he tried to use his body weight to pin her down as he attempted to kiss her. Mira's hands came up and she poked him in the right eye as hard as she could.

Raymond howled.

He also fell off her and she was able to worm out from underneath him. Everything was about surviving this moment, and she fought like an animal. Raymond grabbed at her again as one hand covered his right eye, and she slapped his hands, scratching at him. He gave up trying to grab her arm and went for her skirts, taking hold and yanking. The movement sent Mira off balance, toppling into one of the wheat barrels.

The stone that held the wooden top on the barrel rolled off and onto the next barrel. The wooden top was completely jarred away, and Mira grabbed it, using it to beat Raymond. He only had one hand as it was because the other one was trying to protect his damaged eye, so he could do little more than hold an arm up to keep her from injuring him further. She was panicking and he was quickly growing enraged.

With a growl, he reached under her skirts and grabbed her by the ankle, yanking as hard as he could. Mira was pulled down to her knees, but she didn't fall completely. Raymond yanked again and she held on to the barrel for dear life, terrified of what would happen if he pulled her to the floor again.

And then she saw it.

The rock that had rolled off the barrel lid.

Raymond now had two hands. He couldn't see very well out of his right eye, but that didn't matter. He was going to get Mira on the ground and she was going to stay there. With both hands, he grabbed her by the lower legs and pulled as hard as she could. With a yelp, Mira ended up on the ground, but she hadn't fallen before she grabbed the rock. It was a heavy thing, but not too heavy for her to use. As Raymond rolled her onto her back and tried to smother her mouth with his, Mira lifted the rock with both hands and crowned the top of his head with as much strength as she could muster.

And then she did it again.

Raymond fell off her, onto the dirt of the vault, as Mira scrambled to her knees and hit him in the head again and again. She hit him in the face, in the throat, and the blood began to flow out of his mouth and nose. The rock was becoming bloody as she banged on him again and again and again, pounding him until he stopped squirming. Until he stopped trying to lift his hands to stop her. She smashed his face until it didn't look like Raymond anymore, until the bones broke and shattered and it all became one giant, bloodied mass of flesh.

But still, she pounded.

He was going to rise up. She knew he was going to rise up and wasn't sure she could stop him a second time, so she had to make sure he never got up again. Blood began to splatter, onto her face and arms and chest, but she still continued to beat Raymond. Those years of fear were flowing out of her, giving her the strength to end the terror once and for all. She simply wanted it to stop. She was so wrapped up in her life-or-death struggle that she didn't see Douglas or Davyss or Jonathan flying down the vault steps, rushing into the darkness only to find her beating Raymond to a bloody pulp with a rock. Sobbing and screaming, she lifted the rock until she could lift no more. Until she heard Douglas' soft voice behind her.

"Mira, sweetheart," he said gently. "Mira, please stop. He cannot hurt you anymore, I promise."

She wasn't even startled to hear his voice. Crouched over Raymond, she didn't even realize she was covered in blood until she happened to look at the rock in her hand to see that it was solid red.

But she had stopped.

Douglas knelt down beside her, shocked at what he was seeing, and carefully took the rock from her hand.

"Let me have it, sweetheart," he said softly. "That's a good lass. Mira… what happened? Can you tell me what happened?"

What *had* happened? Mira had to think about it. She'd been in such a blind rage of terror that she had to remember what, exactly, had happened. It didn't seem real, any of it.

Why was she even here?

What was happening?

"I… I do not know," she said, dazed. "Astoria said there was rot in the grain and I must see to it immediately. I came down here and… and he grabbed me. *Raymond* grabbed me. He told me not to scream because he wanted to talk to me, but he would not let me go. He had his hand over my mouth and I… I could not breathe."

She was pale, her eyes wide on Douglas, who was looking at her in genuine horror. As he held her attention, Jonathan moved around to her to see if Raymond was still alive. Douglas distinctly saw Jonathan shake his head to indicate that the man was, indeed, quite dead. As dead as he looked.

And Mira had killed him.

"'Tis all right, lass," Douglas murmured. "You are safe now. I am here. Sweetheart, did he hurt you? Is the blood yours?"

She looked down at herself as if only just noticing that she was covered in blood. Unsteadily, she shook her head.

"I do not know," she said. "I tried to run from him but I slipped on the steps and hit my head. It must have knocked me senseless for a time because when I awoke, Raymond was trying to lift my skirts. I could not let him, Douglas. I could not let him touch me."

"I know, love."

"He grabbed me and pulled me down to the ground. I had to protect myself."

"I understand," Douglas said steadily. "It was not your fault. But… but you said that Astoria told you to come down here?"

Mira blinked, struggling to remember that part of the conversation. "Aye," she said after a moment. "She told me that she was sorry she broke the necklace you gave me. Then she told me that I must go to the vault because rot had been found on the grain. When I came down, Raymond was here. He grabbed me and tried to smother me!"

She reached out and grabbed on to Douglas for safety as panic swept her again. He held her hand tightly, seeing madness and terror in her eyes. She'd been frightened so badly, and had evidently been knocked silly, so she wasn't thinking clearly. Not in the least. Very, very carefully, Douglas stood up and pulled her with him, swinging her into his arms because she couldn't seem to stand up.

"I have you now," he murmured, getting Raymond's blood on his arms and chest because it was rubbing off her. "I have you and I shall never let you go, not ever. I will protect you, Mira, I swear it."

Her arms were around his neck, her unsteady eyes gazing back at him. "What will you do with Raymond?" she asked. "He will tell his father to punish me!"

"You do not have to worry over him," Douglas assured her steadily. "He will not tell his father."

"Will you tell him what happened?"

"Aye… I will tell him."

"And Raymond will be punished?"

He hesitated to answer because, clearly, she didn't realize he was dead. "Aye, love," he said quietly. "I will punish him."

That seemed to bring her great relief. She buried her face in Douglas' shoulder and wept quietly. Douglas turned his head away from her, catching Jonathan's attention.

"Find Eric," he said. "Bring him here. Tell no one else. Do you understand?"

"Aye, Douglas."

"*Go.*"

Jonathan went on the run.

CHAPTER SEVENTEEN

"WHAT YOU DID got a man killed. Was that your intention?"

It was dawn after the feast that saw the death of Raymond de Honiton. It the dim solar of Axminster, where phantoms crawled in the shadows and the smell of smoke was heavy in the air, Isabel was questioning Astoria. The young woman was a weeping mess. She had been for hours. Tied up in a chair in the solar of Axminster, because she'd tried to run off twice, she was sobbing so hard that she'd swooned.

But Isabel wasn't in a forgiving mood.

"Tell me what your intention was," she said angrily, kicking the leg of the chair to rouse Astoria. "Your petty persecution of a woman who never did you any harm has ended in a man being killed. Is that what you hoped for? Someone's death? I can only imagine it was Mira's death from the way you manipulated both her and Raymond, but instead, Raymond is dead and Jerome de Honiton has declared war on us all."

Astoria burst into fresh tears. "I… I did not mean for anyone to be killed," she sobbed. "I only meant… I only…"

"Only *what*?"

"I only meant to discourage Douglas from Mira!"

"By sending her to the vault where Raymond was waiting for her?"

"Aye!"

"And then telling Davyss to send Douglas down there as well?"

"So he would catch them together and know that she was a trollop."

"And you hoped it would end their romance?"

"Aye! But that's all I wished for, I swear it!"

Isabel had a small broom in her hand, one used to sweep out the ashes from the hearth. She'd collected it as a weapon to use against Astoria, to punish her, and as Astoria admitted her crimes, she swatted Astoria about the head and neck with the broom. It didn't really hurt, but the bristles were dirty and prickly, and Astoria screamed as if she was being stabbed.

Isabel whacked her some more.

"You wicked, wicked creature," she said angrily. "Your scheming and lies have cost a man his life."

Astoria wailed. "I am sorry," she said. "I did not mean that it should."

Isabel stopped beating her for the moment, but it was difficult to show such restraint. She wanted to beat Astoria until her anger was satisfied, which might take years at this rate. But more than that, she felt disappointment. Extreme disappointment that the years Isabel had been mentoring Astoria had only taught her to be mean-spirited and vindictive.

She felt like a failure.

Some of that anger was directed at herself.

"But it did," she said. "It *did* cost a man his life. No matter what you intended, your actions had severe consequences. It is clear that you are no longer suited to remaining at Axminster and under my tutelage. You have learned nothing from me, Astoria. I am greatly shamed by you."

Astoria looked at her, eyes wide with fear. "What do you mean?" she said. "Are you sending me away?"

Isabel nodded. "Far away," she said. "I am sending you back to your father. Mayhap he can impress upon you the error of your ways, for certainly, you do not listen to me. You were a happy child when you came here, so I do not know what has turned you into this unsavory creature, but I no longer want you here. You are a bad influence on the younger girls, and they are still quite malleable. I must try to undo whatever you have done to them. Mira warned me about your influence and I should have listened more closely, for now your wicked ways have cost us dearly."

Astoria's face was pale with fear. "Please," she begged. "Please do not send me back to my father. *Please!*"

"I am going to send you back to him with a full accounting of what you have done. Let him deal with you, for I am finished."

Astoria dissolved into more tears. Tears and mucus rolled down her face, onto the top of her dress, which was covered with ash from the broom to create a sort of mud. Momentarily finished in her interrogation, Isabel went over to the solar door and pulled it open to find Eric, Douglas, and Jonathan standing there. They were gazing back at her with various expressions of concern.

Isabel pointed at Astoria.

"Jonathan, untie Lady Astoria and take her to the top floor," she commanded. "There is a small chamber, facing north, that is usually used by servants, but it has a heavy lock on the door.

Lock her up in that chamber. Keep the key and surrender it to no one save me or Eric. Do *not* give it to Douglas. Do you understand?"

Jonathan nodded as he pushed past her into the chamber. "Aye, Lady Isabel."

As Jonathan was taking his prisoner into custody, Isabel's gaze moved to Eric and Douglas.

"Both of you," she said, quieter now. "Inside."

She stood aside as Eric and Douglas quickly entered the chamber. Astoria caught sight of Douglas, however, and began to wail again.

"I am so very sorry, Douglas," she sobbed. "Please forgive me. I never meant for any of this to happen!"

Douglas wouldn't even look at her as Isabel answered in his place. "You are only sorry that you were caught in your heinous scheme," she said. "Had your plan worked out as you had hoped, you would not be sorry at all."

Jonathan had Astoria on her feet, dragging her toward the door. "I am truly sorry, I swear it," she wept. "I did not mean for anyone to die!"

Jonathan hauled her out of the room and they could hear her weeping fade away. Isabel closed the solar door and looked straight at Douglas.

"Are you sticking to your story, Douglas?" she asked. "That *you* killed Raymond de Honiton?"

Douglas, who had been looking at his feet as Jonathan removed Astoria, lifted his gaze to Isabel.

"Aye, my lady."

"Then why was Mira covered in his blood?"

"Because she got caught in the spray, my lady."

"And she had nothing to do with it?"

"I killed him, my lady."

Isabel knew it wasn't the truth. She had seen the mess in the vault and she had seen the rock. She'd also seen Mira covered with blood while Douglas had very little on him. But Douglas had confessed to the killing right away, even to the point of silencing Mira when she tried to speak about it. Mira was currently upstairs, sleeping from a potion the physic had given her because of the injuries sustained in Raymond's attack, while Douglas freely confessed the killing not only to Isabel, but to a distraught Jerome de Honiton.

A man who immediately declared war on the de Lohr empire.

Oh, Isabel knew why Douglas had confessed. God help her, she knew. He did it to protect Mira, to protect Axminster, and to focus de Honiton on the much larger de Lohr war machine rather than the weaker Axminster. He was a man of conviction, of chivalry, of nerves of steel to lie as he had. To look Jerome de Honiton in the face and take the blame for something he did not do took a man of steel, indeed. Isabel knew all of this and she loved him for it. As a sister would love a brother, as a friend would love a friend. But it broke her heart that he'd accepted blame.

There was a pitcher of wine over near the hearth, stale wine that had flecks of dust floating on the top of it. Isabel, who was still slightly drunk from the feast only hours earlier, picked up the wine vessel and drank out of the neck. Long gulps. Licking her lips, she set it back down again and made her way over to Douglas.

She moved in very close to him.

"You may tell everyone that you killed him, but I want to know the truth," she whispered with her wine-ladened breath.

"Tell me what truly happened, Douglas, and I will take it to my grave. But this is my castle. I deserve to know the truth."

Douglas' gaze lingered on her. Her left shoulder was against his left shoulder. She was facing one way and he was facing the other. But she was as close to him as she could possibly be without standing on him. It was an intimate gesture of concern, of supplication, and of trust. Douglas had refused to tell anyone the truth of what happened and sworn Jonathan and Davyss to secrecy. They would never betray him, he knew.

And he knew Isabel wouldn't either. It *was* her castle, after all.

But he had to make sure.

"Are you doubting my word?" he finally asked, his voice like the rumble of distant thunder.

Isabel didn't seem pleased that he'd evaded the question. "Look at the situation from my perspective," she said. "Mira has clearly been battered. She was covered with blood, indicative of a fight for her life. You, on the other hand, do not have a scratch on you. And you say you killed him? With a rock smashed into his head, which would have been messy to say the least? If Mira did not do it, why is she covered in gore? And if you did it, how did you stay so clean?"

"I am highly skilled."

"Enough that blood would not even stain you?"

"Possibly."

"And a man fighting for his life would not touch you in any way?"

"I am a superior warrior."

"I agree," Isabel said. "You *are* a superior warrior. But I will ask you a direct question and you will give me a truthful answer. If you do not, I will never believe anything you say ever again. Are we clear?"

"We are, my lady."

"Did you kill Raymond?"

He didn't reply right away. He was looking away, his jaw twitching faintly, before he made the effort to turn in her direction. Even then, he simply looked at her, hesitant to speak at all.

"Does it truly matter?" he asked.

"It does to me."

He hesitated, but only for a moment. "If you do not keep your promise, I will cut your tongue out."

Isabel believed him, but she looked at him with some surprise. "When have I ever broken your trust, Douglas?"

His blue-eyed gaze drilled into her for a moment as if to emphasize his threat before he finally answered. "He was dead when I arrived," he whispered. "I was too late to do anything. He attacked Mira and she fought back the only way she could, with the only weapon she could find. But know this—had she not killed him, I most certainly would have. Therefore, I will take the blame for it. She does not deserve to."

Isabel had known all along that would be his answer, but she was still startled by it. She nodded faintly, silently thanking him for the truth, but now she felt sick inside to realize what Mira had gone through that brought them to this very tense moment.

"My God," she breathed. "What terror Mira must have felt to have been forced to fight for her life like that."

Douglas grunted in agreement. "She should not have had to do it in the first place."

Isabel nodded. "I agree," she said. "And she probably would not have had to do it had Astoria not manipulated the situation the way she did. *She* is to blame, Douglas. Not Mira."

"I realize that."

"What do you want to do with her?"

Douglas shook his head, his guard going down just a little. He'd been in fight-or-flight mode since last night, since all of this happened, and now as the sun began to peek over the horizon, he could feel the tension draining out of his body. Perhaps it was because he'd confessed to Isabel, or perhaps it was because Mira was actually safe for the moment and he could relax. Just a little.

But that didn't mean any of them were safe.

On the contrary.

"My concern is with Mira and with Lord de Honiton," he said. "You are far more experienced in dealing with wicked young women than I am. I will leave Astoria's punishment to you, but to be honest, part of me wants to turn her over to de Honiton so he can punish the woman who caused his son's death. Let her face the reality of what her actions have brought."

Isabel shook her head. "He is not in his right mind," she said. "I fear he would kill her in his grief. Moreover, he does not want Astoria. He wants the person who killed his son, and since you have confessed to it, he wants you."

"He shall not have me," Douglas said, sinking into the nearest chair. "I will leave Jonathan and Davyss here, but I intend to take Mira and return to Lioncross Abbey to tell my father what has happened. De Honiton has threatened to march on Lioncross, so I think my father should be warned."

"How foolish would that be?" Eric spoke up. He'd been listening to the entire conversation and had something to say with this latest subject raised. "Lord de Honiton, I mean. How foolish would it be for him to march on Lioncross? Your father probably carries five times the men that de Honiton does. Hereford will wipe him from this earth."

Douglas conceded the point. "I do not think anyone has marched on Lioncross since Ajax de Velt brought his army south and my father thought he was in for a siege from the Dark Lord," he said. "That was long ago, before I was born. But the point is that no sane man marches on Lioncross. No sane man marches on my father."

Isabel looked at him. "And that is why you are taking the blame," she said. "To deter de Honiton from exacting vengeance on Axminster. If he knows he must move against Hereford, he will think twice."

Douglas simply cocked an eyebrow as if she had answered her own question. But he looked away after a moment, running a weary hand through his long, unbrushed locks.

"You have given me permission to court Mira," he said. "She belongs to me and I shall protect her at all costs. If that means taking the blame to protect her, then I will do it without hesitation."

Isabel couldn't very well argue with the man, not when she agreed with him. In fact, she felt protective over him because he was so protective over Mira. It was chivalry not often seen, but Douglas was determined to shield his lady from a situation she shouldn't have been part of in the first place.

The whole bloody situation was a mess.

"Very well," she said wearily. "But I would suggest you send a messenger to your father right away. Even if you intend to take Mira to Lioncross, it will not be immediate. The physic says she must rest for a few days at the very least, and your father must know what has happened as soon as possible."

Douglas nodded. "Agreed," he said. "But I intend to take

Mira away as soon as she is feeling better."

Isabel made her way to the nearest chair, lowering herself into it. Much like Douglas, the excitement and stress of the night was beginning to wear off, leaving exhaustion in its wake.

"Poor Mira," she muttered. "The woman fights for her life, and what will it bring her? Persecution and torment. If Jerome knew it was her, and why, it would not absolve her. If he took it to a magistrate, they would probably condemn her to death."

Douglas glanced at her. "My brother, Roi, is the magistrate for Hereford and Worcester," he said. "He also happens to be the king's chief justiciar. He is the head of the system of laws in the land, so I can promise you that nothing would come of any charges de Honiton tried to bring."

"If that is true, then why did you accept blame?"

"Because I do not want her to suffer for having to defend herself."

Isabel knew that. She wasn't trying to harass the man, only make him think a little about the implications of his actions. But she didn't push too hard because she knew he was already well aware.

This would be the end of it.

"I know," she said. "I do not know why I asked that question because I already know the answer. Douglas, go and see to Mira now. I have a need to speak with Eric alone."

Douglas didn't hesitate. He moved to quit the solar, but the moment he opened the door, he was faced with something that forced him to stop dead in his tracks.

Jerome de Honiton was standing in front of him.

And he did not look pleased.

CHAPTER EIGHTEEN

HE DIDN'T EVEN recognize him anymore.

Jerome had been sitting with his son in the vault, the same vault where Raymond had been killed hours earlier. He was staring at the man who had been his only family since the death of his wife. Staring at the tattered remnants of the life he'd known and facing the cloudy facets of a future he hadn't been expecting. Raymond had been dead for several hours and had turned into a gross caricature of what he used to be in life. A gross caricature of what Jerome's life had now become, something strange and misshapen.

This nightmare he found himself a part of.

A nightmare with no end in sight. The alcohol that Jerome had imbibed the night before had mostly worn off by the time the sun began to rise, but death was, in and of itself, a sobering experience. Now, he had a sober, shattered mind that reflected what had happened and what he needed to do.

His son had been murdered.

He wasn't leaving Axminster without satisfaction.

Raymond had attacked a young woman, he'd been told. The same young woman that had been Raymond's target during his years at Axminster. A young woman who had evidently played games with Raymond, telling others that she was eager to see him and then, when he made advances, she retreated. At least, that was part of what Jerome had heard, rumors once the news of Raymond's death had started to spread, but the truth was that both Raymond and the young lady he attacked had been manipulated by another young woman who evidently had a vendetta.

Truthfully, Jerome was in shock. He felt as if he wasn't living in the real world. He'd sat for hours staring at his son's body, dumbfounded by what had happened, but that daze had given way to anger—anger great enough to make threats of punishment against those responsible. Douglas de Lohr, the son of the Earl of Hereford and Worcester, had killed his son in defense of this young woman. It was complex and convoluted, but the one thing that wasn't complex or convoluted was the fact that Raymond had died.

It was the only thing that was crystal clear.

And Jerome was going to exact his pound of flesh.

He had been stewing on it for several hours. He had threatened to march on Lioncross Abbey Castle, seat of the Earl of Hereford in Worcester, but that was the grieving father talking. De Honiton had a decent-sized army, but it would be no match for Hereford's. Even he knew that. Therefore, armed conflict was not the answer.

But he knew what was.

He knew where the pound of flesh would come from.

Ultimately, the situation was Lady Isabel's fault. This was her castle and anything that happened here was her responsibility. As the sun rose over the bucolic Devon landscape, Jerome knew what he had to do. He knew what he *wanted* to do. He'd lost his son this night. Nothing could bring Raymond back, but those responsible were going to pay dearly.

That very price was on his mind as he made his way out of the vault and to the entry level of the keep. Lady Isabel's solar was just off the entry and he knew she, and her knights, had been there for quite some time. As far as Jerome was concerned, they were all afraid to face him, afraid to admit their failings. No one stopped him as he entered the keep and went to the solar door. He went to open it, but someone opened it from the inside and he abruptly found himself face to face with Douglas de Lohr.

He'd never felt more contempt for a man in his life.

"Get out of my way," he growled. "Where is Lady Isabel?"

"Here," Isabel said. Hearing the man's voice, she'd leapt out of her chair to face him. "Please come in, Lord de Honiton."

Douglas stood aside as de Honiton entered, but de Honiton couldn't help but ball a fist as he walked past the knight. He lifted his hand to strike Douglas in the face, but Douglas grabbed the man's hand purely out of reflex and nearly crushed it. Jerome cried out in pain as Douglas clamped down.

"Douglas, release him," Isabel commanded. "Please—let him go."

Douglas did, but he pushed at the same time, thrusting Jerome nearly halfway across the room.

"Consider that a warning, my lord," he said in a decidedly threatening tone.

And Jerome took it for a warning. He stumbled over a chair and ended up leaning over it as he pointed at Douglas.

"He has killed my son and now he threatens to kill me!" he said. "I do not know what animosity this man has against me, but I demand protection!"

Isabel went to Jerome as Eric went over to Douglas, not to protect Douglas but to prevent him from charging de Honiton if the situation grew physical.

Isabel was focused on the brittle man.

"Lord de Honiton, I assure you that Douglas has no vendetta against you," she said evenly. "But he will not allow you to strike him. You will behave civilly in my solar."

Jerome's expression cooled. He looked between Isabel and Douglas and even Eric, his gaze jerky, his body quivering.

"I see," he said after a moment. "My son is dead and all you can speak of is behaving civilly. Where is the outrage that my son was *un*civilly killed in your castle?"

Isabel could see a grieving father before her, but it seemed to her that there was more to it. Jerome seemed slightly off beyond the normal burden of grief. It was in his eyes, in his movements. There was no reason here, no balance.

Something told her to be on her guard.

"I have repeatedly conveyed my condolences for this unhappy situation," she said. "But I have also explained to you that your son was attacking a young woman—most brutally, I might add. What did you expect? That he would simply be allowed to do as he pleased and harm a young woman who was resisting his advances?"

Jerome's eyes widened. "A whore who teased him!"

"An innocent young woman who was wrongfully accused of such a thing," Isabel replied firmly. "I have told you that this situation was manipulated by another girl out of jealousy. Your son happened to be a tool she used and nothing more, but what she did not force him to do—what no one forced him to do—was brutally attack a young woman who had made it clear she wanted nothing to do with him."

Jerome began to look at all three of them again, his eyes darting from one to the next. He stood up from his position against the chair, backing away as he pointed to the occupants of the chamber.

"I may not be as powerful as de Lohr, but I have friends and allies, too," he said. "Mayhap I cannot raze Lioncross, but I can create such havoc as you cannot possibly imagine. I can have archers anywhere, striking at your fathers and brothers and children. I can send men to ravage your women and burn your villages. I can make it so that you are looking over your shoulder every day for the rest of your life, wondering when I am going to strike next and who shall be my next victim. *You* are responsible for this, Lady Isabel, and I swear upon my son's dead body that Axminster shall never be safe again. I will do these things unless I have satisfaction!"

He was shouting by the time he finished, shaking his finger at Douglas, at Eric, and even at Isabel. Douglas was preparing to launch a verbal assault against the man, but Isabel lifted her hand to him, indicating he keep still. She had been the mistress of Axminster for many years.

She was going to handle this.

"May I ask what satisfaction you require?" she asked.

Jerome's eyes fixed on her. "I am not a fool," he said. "I can demand you turn de Lohr over to me, but I know you will not. Even if you did, his father would get involved and my entire family line would be destroyed. But the truth is that my family line is *already* destroyed. Stolen away from me when de Lohr killed my son. He took away my lineage. I have no more. But I want more. That which I have lost must be replaced."

Isabel wasn't following his train of thought. "How can it be replaced?"

Jerome seemed to cool again. His face relaxed, or perhaps it simply morphed into an expression that was a harbinger of things to come. There was something flickering in his gaze.

Something unsavory.

Now, the lack of reason and balance would be revealed.

"The girl my son has allegedly attacked," he said. "Who is she?"

Isabel frowned. "Allegedly?" she repeated. "I will let you see her. You will see the bruises and cuts upon her person and the lump on her head the size of hen's egg. There was no *alleged* attack, my lord. Your son most definitely attacked her and there is proof."

"Who is the girl?"

"Why do you want to know?"

"Tell me and I will answer you."

"Answer me now and I will tell you."

Jerome stamped his foot violently. "You will tell me what I wish to know!"

Suddenly, Douglas was between Isabel and Jerome, his hulking presence filling up the air. "If you do not speak politely to the lady of the keep, I will throw you from the window," he growled. "Grief does not give you the right to command Lady Isabel."

Jerome was both frightened and enraged. "You will not make demands of me, de Lohr!" he shouted. "You are a murderer!"

"And your son was a motherless deformity with the moral values of a goat."

Jerome picked up the chair with the intention of throwing at Douglas, but Douglas yanked it out of the man's hands and tossed it aside, leaving no barrier between him and Jerome. If

Douglas charged, there was nothing to stop him. As Isabel swiftly grabbed Douglas' arm and tried to pull him back, Douglas jabbed a finger at Jerome.

"Do that again and you can join your son in hell," he snarled. "I will not warn you again."

Eric had to help Isabel pull Douglas away from the confrontation. He had both hands on Douglas, dragging him away, as Isabel faced Jerome.

"You are fortunate that I do not let Douglas loose on you," she said, her patience in the situation waning. "Tell me what you want and be done with it."

Jerome eyed Douglas furiously but wisely refrained from baiting the man. His focus turned to Isabel.

"I want the girl who had my son's attention," he said. "Raymond was of marriageable age. It is very possible he would have married her because he has been attracted to her since they were young. It is the same girl, is it not? I have forgotten her name over the years. Mary, I believe. In any case, because of her, my son is dead. I will marry her and she will give me another son to replace the one she took from me."

It was a horrifying suggestion. Isabel visibly gasped but didn't dare look at Douglas, fearful he might see her moment of shock and charge Jerome once and for all. If that happened, she knew she couldn't stop him.

She didn't want to.

Still, she held her ground.

"Impossible," she said. "That young woman is already spoken for."

That wasn't the answer Jerome wanted. "To whom?" he demanded. "Tell me this instant! If she… *Wait*. She is pledged, you say?"

"Aye."

"A man who would not have taken kindly to my son's advances?"

"No man would wish to see his intended preyed upon by another."

Jerome's attention moved to Douglas. "And she was defended by this man who killed my son on her behalf?" he said in a shocking bit of astute logic. "Then he was not killed because the lady was defending herself. He was killed in punishment for being attracted to her!"

As Douglas remained surprisingly emotionless, Isabel tried to divert Jerome's trail of logic. "What makes you say that?" she said. "She could be pledged to anyone in England. Douglas was… He would have defended any woman being attacked. That does not mean they are pledged."

"Untrue!" Jerome said, his eyes wide and wild as realization dawned. "A man only kills when emotion or fear are involved. De Lohr was not afraid of my son, so it must have been because he was protecting something important to him. Why else should he kill?"

"He killed because your son tried to kill a woman," Isabel said angrily. "He did the right and true thing. Had you raise your son properly, we would not be having this conversation!"

Jerome was back to being furious. "I want that girl," he said again. "Bring her to me or I will tear this place apart looking for her."

"Douglas and Eric and the knights in the hall will stop you."

"Then provide me with a suitable replacement or my campaign of terror against Axminster and all who live here will never end," he cried. "Give me another girl!"

"I will not give you any of my young women."

"You must!" Jerome demanded. "This is *your* fault, Lady Isabel. *Your* fault that my son is dead. Your fault that there is such turmoil. And do not think I didn't hear about Tatworth attacking Axminster those months ago. Of course I heard. All because of *you*. I will, therefore, say again—give me a woman to continue my family line because it is your obligation. Give me justice!"

His shouting had reverberated off the walls, now abruptly still except for his heavy breathing. Isabel was still staring at him, watching every move he made and knowing he meant every threat that had pealed out of his mouth. The problem was that he was right—this *was* her fault. All of it. Raymond's death had happened at Axminster, and as it was her domain, she was responsible.

That was the sickening truth.

If Jerome harassed Axminster, it would be her fault. If he attacked Lioncross, it would also be her fault. All roads led to Isabel, and the longer she thought on it, the more she knew that she, and only she, should be the one to make amends.

There was no other choice.

"Eric," she finally said. "Remove Douglas from the chamber. You go with him."

Eric, still holding on to Douglas, looked at her in concern. "My lady…"

"Please," she said. "Wait outside. If you hear violence, you may enter, but only in that instance. Otherwise, you will stay outside until I open the door."

Eric didn't want to go. He looked at Douglas, who was looking at him for direction. If Eric obeyed, Douglas would. If Eric didn't, then neither would Douglas. Neither one of them wanted to leave Isabel alone with Jerome, but ultimately, she was the Lady of Axminster. They were bound to obey her orders.

Especially Eric.

All he ever did was obey her orders.

"Very well," he said reluctantly. "But we shall be outside the door if needed."

Isabel simply waved them on. When both knights were through the door and the panel was shut, Isabel indicated for Jerome to sit in the nearest chair.

"Sit down," she said quietly. "I wish to speak to you about this and we will do it calmly, just the two of us, without any swords or enormous knights hanging about. Agreed?"

Jerome seemed to relax a little now that Douglas was out of the chamber. "As you wish," he said, claiming the chair. "But I will not change my mind. I must have justice, and the only way to accomplish that is for you to give me what I want so that I may have another son to continue my lineage. That is only fair."

Isabel sat down in a chair a few feet away. "I understand that you are grieving," she said. "What happened is a terrible shock. But don't you think your demands are hasty? Should you not have time to grieve before you make such a decision?"

Jerome shook his head. "Nay," he said. "I have been with Raymond since I was informed of his passing. He was my only child. If I am to admit it, he could be… difficult. You tried to purge him from Axminster because of his behavior. Kenilworth did the same."

"I did not know that."

Jerome sat back in his chair, vastly calmer than he had been. It was just him and Isabel, and truthfully, Jerome wasn't confrontational by nature. He had a more reasonable personality than his son had, and last night he'd been quite amiable. But he was struggling with something that had upended his entire world and was so grieved that he was behaving irrationally, but deep down, something else was happening with him.

It was time for truth.

Ugly as it was.

Maybe if he told the truth, Isabel would be more apt to do as he wished.

"I will admit this to no one else, my lady, and if you repeat it, I will deny it," he said. "But my son was not very likable. He was my son and I love him because he is my son, but sometimes, I did not like him. You were around him for years. You saw how he was."

Isabel's eyebrows rose. "Something you had denied to me," she said. "When I wrote you about his behavior, you told me it was untrue."

He nodded. "At the time, I believed it," he said. "When Raymond left for Axminster, he did not have the naughty streak in him that you said he had. I assumed you were lying. But the master knights of Kenilworth had the same report, only worse."

"Then they confirmed what I had been trying to tell you."

Jerome nodded. Then his eyes unexpectedly filled with tears. "A father does not want to believe the worst about his son," he said. "But he had gambling debts. And there were at least two young women he had forced himself upon. One conceived a child she later gave birth to and surrendered to a peasant family. I paid her family a great amount of money for her troubles."

Isabel wasn't entirely shocked to hear this, given her experience with Raymond. "You said your lineage had died out," she said. "What about this child?"

"It is a girl. I do not want a girl."

That explained it, a little. "I see," she said. "So you want to marry again and have another son?"

He nodded. "As callous as this will sound, I do," he said. "I will mourn Raymond. I will mourn the son I failed, because surely, I failed him or he would not have been the way he was. Don't you see, Lady Isabel? This is another chance for me. In this tragedy, God has given me another chance to have a son who will honor the de Honiton name."

Isabel thought that it was a strange way to deal with grief. Lost one son, then make another. The new son would ease the grief of the one lost. She'd seen that happen with widows—marrying again to ease the ache of losing a husband—but she'd never seen it done with children.

Still… Jerome seemed entirely serious.

"If that is true, then you will have to find a wife elsewhere," Isabel said after a moment. "I cannot, and will not, provide you with one of the young ladies in my charge."

Jerome looked at her. "And I meant what I said," he said calmly. "If you do not give me one of them, I will do as I must. You will not know a moment's peace. Nor will de Lohr. I do not care if his father is more powerful than God. I will make it so he is hunted and hounded every day for the rest of his life. And Axminster will never be safe. Not you, not your wards, nor your vassals. It will be my life's work to see you ruined."

He said it as if discussing nothing more important than the weather. Isabel couldn't imagine that he was bluffing. He seemed quite sane and, in his own words, his lineage was finished. He had nothing to lose by harassing Axminster. The implications were great because if he carried through on his threat, she had everything to lose.

At this moment, noble families paid well for their daughters to be educated by Lady Isabel. It was considered prestigious. But if Axminster was not a peaceful place, courtesy of de Honiton and his grudge, then families would choose not to send their daughters there. Not if they knew the girls would be in danger. That would reflect poorly on Isabel and, eventually, she would lose what was a lucrative source of income. Her reputation would be in tatters. All because Raymond de Honiton couldn't control himself. Therefore, she had some horrific choices to make.

Give Jerome what he wanted… or face ruin.

He wanted Mira. Isabel knew that wasn't going to happen. That left Davina, Helen, or even Astoria because they were of marriageable age, but she didn't have the authority to promise them to Jerome. The girls all had families who had that power. The only power Isabel had was over Mira or…

God help her.

There was one other.

It was all she had left to bargain with.

"Then I will make a proposal," she said. "You have asked for a girl under my guardianship, but I cannot give this to you because although I am their guardian, their families alone have the authority to broker a marriage. I do not have that power. What I do have, however, is the power to offer you the Earldom of Axminster in exchange for peace. I am not beyond childbearing age and this could be a business arrangement and nothing more. Moreover, it would unite Axminster and de Honiton and create a large empire. Life at Axminster can continue as it has, with me at the helm, and you may live at de Honiton and continue your life as it is. As your wife, I will bear children for you and, God willing, a son. A son with de Kerrington blood who will inherit Axminster from you. This is a powerful offer I give you, Jerome. Consider it."

Jerome's eyes widened. "Axminster?" he repeated. "You… *you* will marry me and give me Axminster?"

"Axminster will go to our children."

He blinked, startled, as if he still couldn't believe the offer. He looked her over, from her feet to the top of her wimpled head, and began to nod.

"A striking offer, my lady," he said. "You are a handsome woman, to be sure. A reasonable woman. But how old are you?"

That was a question Isabel didn't like to be asked, but she supposed he had a right to know.

"I have seen forty years," she said. "As I said, my childbearing days are not over, but the older I become, the more they wane. If we are to marry and have a son together, it must be soon. But surely a wife of my experience and wealth will be much better than a silly young girl. You want a wife with wisdom, do you not?"

For the first time since he entered the solar, Jerome's mood seemed to improve. He was no longer shouting or demanding. His features weren't tight with grief and rage. He seemed… pleased. His expression lightened as he realized what a truly generous offer she was giving him.

"Your wisdom is unmatched, my lady," he said. "You do not have to extol your virtues, for I am aware of them. And your offer is quite astonishing. I would be a fool to decline."

"And you will leave Axminster in peace?"

"I will leave everyone in peace if your offer is true."

That was all Isabel needed to hear. "It is true," she said. "I will have my clerk draw up a contract, but you will let me announce it, please. I do ask for that privilege."

"You may have it."

Silence fell between them, a strange sort of void. Jerome was feeing some joy at being the next Earl of Axminster while Isabel was feeling lost and empty.

Dead inside.

But she did what she had to do.

"Then let us make arrangements to send Raymond home for burial," she said, trying to focus on what needed to be done and not the sense of regret that was trying to sweep her. "We may be married once he has been put to rest, if that is acceptable to you."

Jerome nodded, sensing that the conversation was over for now. He couldn't help but notice that Isabel didn't seem entirely thrilled by something she'd proposed, but he knew why she'd done it. She wanted peace at Axminster, and sometimes peace was made in such ways.

He didn't feel guilty in the least.

"It is acceptable," he said, rising from the chair. "You have made a wise decision this day, my lady. It will ensure that both of our families continue, since you are the last of your line as well. The de Kerrington name and the de Honiton name will create a family of wealth and power. You should be proud."

Isabel could hear the gloat in his voice and it made her sick to her stomach. It was a wise decision for him, but it was the only choice for her.

She had no idea what she was going to tell Eric.

"We shall see," she said. "You may go now, my lord. Make your arrangements. And remember that you are not to announce our agreement until I do."

With a nod of his head, Jerome went to the solar door and opened it to find four knights standing outside in various positions around the entry. Four sets of eyes turned to him as he exited, but Jerome didn't give them another look.

All except for Douglas.

He focused on Douglas and, at the risk of breaking his word to Isabel, went to the man. For a moment, he simply looked at him, this blond brute who had killed his son. But, perhaps in hindsight, Raymond's death was the catalyst for bigger and better things.

He tried to focus on the positive.

"You should be grateful," he muttered to Douglas. "She paid for your sins."

With that, he turned and left the keep, leaving Douglas standing there with his brow furrowed, wondering what in the hell he meant. Greatly concerned, he went to the solar door only to see Isabel sitting by the window, sobbing into her hand.

Whatever it was… it must have cost her greatly.

"My God," Douglas breathed. "What did she do?"

Eric was standing beside him, pale and distressed at the sight of his love in tears. If she was weeping and Jerome was calm, it must have been something serious, indeed.

"Go," Eric said to Douglas. "Go and see to Mira. I will see to Isabel."

He started to push past Douglas, but Douglas wouldn't let him go so easily. "Should I remain here in case you have need of me?" he asked. "Mira is sleeping. There is nothing I can do for her now. But Lady Isabel…"

Eric shook his head. "Nay, Douglas," he said. "You are a good friend, but I will see to Isabel now. I will send word if I have need of you."

"Are you sure?"

"I am. Go to Mira now."

With that, he closed the door in Douglas' face, leaving him

puzzled as well as apprehensive. One of the strongest women he'd ever known was weeping, broken, and he wanted to know why. He wanted to know why Jerome had made that comment to him.

She paid for your sins.

God help him, the more he thought about it, the more apprehensive he became.

CHAPTER NINETEEN

MIRA WASN'T SURE when she realized that she was awake, but it had something to do with the birds outside her window being extremely loud. They were so loud that she rolled onto her side and put her hand over her ear, but it didn't help. Her sleep-fogged mind struggled against consciousness until she finally had to give up.

The birds won.

Rolling onto her back, she found herself staring up at the ceiling of the chamber she shared with Helen and Davina and Astoria, only a quick perusal of the chamber showed that the girls weren't there. But someone else was.

Douglas was standing over by the window.

When their eyes met, he smiled.

"Did they wake you?" he asked, pointing to the eaves outside of the window. "I have been standing here for quite some time trying to convince them to quiet down, but they refused. I am sorry."

Mira smiled faintly. "It was a lovely thing to awaken to," she said, rubbing her eyes. "What are you doing here, alone with me? Does Isabel know?"

"Not to worry. She knows."

"How long have I been asleep?"

"Since last night," he said. "It is almost the nooning hour now. The physic gave you something to sleep last night."

"Why?"

"Because you needed it."

Mira's smile faded. She took a deep breath, heaving a heavy sigh. "It was not a dream, was it?"

"What, love?"

"Raymond."

Douglas came away from the window, making his way to the bed and taking her hand to kiss it. "It was not a dream," he said softly.

Mira gazed at him a moment before gently removing her hand from his grip and holding both of her hands up to look at them. They were battered, with scabs, and she flexed her sore fingers gingerly.

"What did you do to him?" she asked, lowering her hands to look at him.

Douglas shook his head. "What do you mean?"

"Did you punish him?"

He didn't answer her right away. In fact, he thought that was an odd question, so he cocked his head curiously.

"What do you remember about your struggle with Raymond?" he asked.

Mira drew in a long, pensive breath. "I came down the stairs after Astoria told me that there was rot in some of the grain," she said, fighting through the cobwebs. "I thought I heard the servants in the vault. Someone called my name, I think. But when I went down to investigate, Raymond was waiting for me. He grabbed me and we fought."

Douglas nodded, reaching out to take her battered hand again. "Is that all?"

Mira tried to think very hard. "I… I do not know," she said. "I feel like it was all a dream. I was fighting him. I tried to run. I was still fighting him and then I heard your voice. But I do not remember much more. That is why I asked if you punished him."

Considering she'd taken a serious blow to the head, he wasn't surprised that she didn't remember all of the details, but what he was fixated on was the fact that she didn't seem to remember Raymond was dead or that she had been the one to smash his brains in with a rock. Perhaps it was her mind's way of dealing with such a violent event, but in any case, the fact remained that she didn't seem to remember what happened. He thought not to tell her at all, but inevitably, someone would mention it.

He wanted her to hear it from him.

"Raymond is dead, love," he said quietly. "You fought him and he tried to kill you. He did not survive his attack against you."

Mira stared at him for a long time. From her expression, he knew she was trying to remember everything. He could almost see her thoughts and memories in her eyes. But it was clear that some things simply weren't coming easily to her, and she reached out, grasping him with her other hand.

"God's Bones," she whispered. "Did you kill him, then? Is that why I heard your voice?"

"He will not rise up against you ever again."

She took it to mean that he'd killed Raymond, and a tear trickled down her right temple. "Are you in trouble now?" she asked. "I never meant to cause you such trouble, Douglas, believe me."

He squeezed her hands. "I am not in trouble," he said. "You are not in trouble. Raymond is dead and he is no longer a threat."

That didn't ease her, and more tears started to come. "But his father is here," she said. "He surely must be… Douglas, what will his father do to you for killing his son?"

She was becoming distraught, and he sat down on the bed, her hands against his lips as he spoke. "Listen to me," he said softly but firmly. "Mira, you will not worry over anything because there will be no retribution. You were attacked. Raymond died because he attacked you and for no other reason than that. You did nothing wrong. Do you understand me?"

She was sniffling, her eyes watery. "A-aye," she said. "But… I remember that he was following me during the feast, too. He told me that he had heard I wished to dance with him. Do you recall that I told you that?"

"I recall."

"He seemed so insistent."

Another thing that Douglas was compelled to tell her simply so she would not be so confused by it. The truth would cause her some distress, but it was something she could at least reconcile. Therefore, he decided to be honest with her where Astoria was concerned. Given the situation, she was going to find out eventually.

"He was insistent because Astoria was telling him lies," he said. "In fact, Astoria manipulated the entire situation. She was the one who told you to go to the vault, was she not?"

Mira nodded. "She was."

"Because she had created the situation," he said. "She was trying to force you into Raymond's arms, which I was to discover so that I would cast you aside. She was the one orchestrating the entire thing to punish you for the fact that you have my attention."

Mira's tears seemed to be fading as a shocked expression took hold. The pieces of the puzzle were coming together in her muddled mind as she began to understand the extent of Astoria's involvement.

"Is *that* what happened?" she said incredulously. "God's Bones… I knew she was trying to harass me, but I can honestly say that it goes beyond what I thought she was capable of."

Douglas wasn't hard-pressed to agree. "I have seen things like this from much more important and mature people, men playing games that shape nations, but nothing like what Astoria attempted," he said. "She was trying very hard to separate us."

"And she pulled Raymond into her scheme."

"Exactly," Douglas said. "I suppose we will never know if he would have attacked you without Astoria's prompting. Mayhap he would have, mayhap not, but her lies pushed him into it. I wish we'd known that from the beginning. Mayhap we could have prevented what happened in the end."

Mira pondered her last memories of Raymond, remembering the smell of earth in the vault and the terror in her heart but little more than that. "I cannot be glad for his death, though I will admit I am relieved," she said. "So many years of harassment have ended, Douglas. It seems too good to be true to never have to worry about him again."

"His reign of terror, where it concerns you, has come to an end."

She gazed at him for a few moments before a smile spread across her lips. "For that peace of mind, I will thank you," she said, squeezing his hands. "I've never had a champion before."

He smiled in return. "Not only a champion, my lady," he said. "A husband."

"And you know this for certain?"

"Lady Isabel has given me permission to court you," he said. "She said that your mother would not care, so she gave her permission. I was going to tell you the good news last night before the evening got away from us. I will, therefore, tell you now. I have permission to court you."

Her smile was huge. "Are you sure you want to, given the madness of last night?" she asked. "If you have changed your mind, I would understand."

He shook his head. "I will not change my mind," he said. "You are, and always will be, my choice."

My choice.

The words from the pendant. Suddenly, Mira's smile vanished and she sat up quickly, looking around in a panic.

"The pendant," she said. "I was wearing it when Raymond… Where is it?"

He held her arms to prevent her from pitching herself right out of the bed. "It is safe," he assured her. "When I brought you up here after the fight, I took it off your bodice and tucked it away in the wardrobe. It is quite safe."

Mira was visibly relieved as she turned to him. "Thank you," she said sincerely. "I could not bear it if something happened to it."

It was a heartfelt sentiment. He could feel it. He was holding her hands but he let them go, reaching up to stroke the side of her head. He just wanted to touch her. Her blonde hair was like velvet in his hands, soft and warm and glorious. He tried very hard not to think about this petite, beautiful woman in a fight for her life against a man who was intent on brutalizing her.

That made him want to kill all over again.

"Nothing is going to happen to it," he murmured. "Or you. You have me now and I will see that you are always safe and warm and protected, Mira. I promise."

Mira leaned into his hand, her green eyes glittering at him. "It seems like a dream," she said. "I have never been courted before."

"And I have never courted before."

"Do you know what to do?"

He shrugged, his eyes glimmering with mirth. "I think so," he said. "I have four older brothers who have courted women. I have learned something."

"Is that so?" she said, interested. "What have you learned?"

He thought on that question. "Peter is the eldest," he said. "From him, I learned persistence. The man was very persistent when he courted Liora. Curtis is the second eldest and he married a Welsh princess. Do you know how they met?"

"How?"

"She tried to kill him in battle."

Her eyebrows lifted in surprise. "And he married her?"

Douglas chuckled. "He did and he is very happy," he said. "From him, I have learned patience. Women require great patience."

Mira waggled her eyebrows. "I think some require more than others," she said. "I hope I do not tax yours overly."

"You haven't yet," he said, grinning. "Where was I? Oh, and Roi is the brother who is a king's chief justiciar. He is quite scholarly, but also an excellent knight. His story is a little sad, in fact. The woman he married was meant for his eldest son. When Beckett was killed, Roi married Diara in his stead, and I swear to you I have never seen him more content. From him, I learned acceptance. Sometimes you must accept what life brings you."

"And it has brought you to me?"

He chuckled. "Something like that," he said. "Myles is the fourth brother, the one I am closest to. He is a glorious stud of a man, much pursued, and he fancied himself in love with a woman who, in fact, was no good for him. That pushed him into the arms of a bookish, beautiful woman whom he had no interest in, or so he thought. But Veronica is the best thing that could have happened to him, so from Myles, I have learned that what you want in life is not always what will make you happy."

She was watching his face as he spoke. "Does that apply to you?" she asked. "Wanting something in life that has slipped away from you?"

He shook his head. "Nay," he said. "Nothing that mattered, although I will say that out of all of my brothers, Myles and Westley and I seem to be the most pursued by women. I suppose we all look somewhat alike with the hair and the big build. Women seem to find it pleasing."

Mira started to laugh. "God's Bones, man, are you so humble?" she said. "Douglas, you are positively gorgeous. Surely you know that."

He looked at her rather coyly, part of his hair hanging down over one eye, which made him look impish. "If you say so, then it must be true."

Mira rolled her eyes because she could see that he was toying with her. "Spare me the false modesty," she said, reaching out to playfully pinch him. "You are a man among men, and if you ever cut your hair, I will disown you. I find it wholly attractive."

He grinned, flashing his teeth. "You needn't worry," he said.

"My hair has never been cut and never will be."

"Why not?"

"Because my mother never had the heart to cut it as a child and I got used to it that way," he said. "It has become part of my identity. As strange as it sounds, I do not think I would know myself if I did not have it."

Mira inspected his hair, running her fingers through it, feeling its strength in her hands. "Odd how things define us," she said. "Mayhap not to other people, but to us."

He closed his eyes, relishing the feel of her fondling his hair. "What defines you?"

She stopped grooming his hair and thought on it. "This," she finally said, turning her head and pointing to a little freckle on the edge of her chin. "See this? Strangely enough, my brother has one, too. In the same place."

"That is strange."

She nodded. "With everything that has happened in my life, with my mother virtually disowning me or even the harassment by Raymond, this little freckle ties me to someone I will always be part of," she said. "My twin brother. He will always be Payne and I will always be Misery. No matter what, I have him and he has me."

She resumed stroking his hair, and he watched her face as she did so. "You've not spoken much about your brother," he said. "Is he good to you?"

She nodded. "Verily," she said. "Where do you think the dowry is coming from? Payne inherited my father's lands and title and has always been kind and generous with me. When my mother sent me back to Axminster, he is the one who escorted me. He wanted to make sure I was well settled and had a good position. He knows I am happy here and he is content with that."

Douglas found himself wrapping his arms around her as she continued to stroke his hair, feeling her sweetness against him, dipping his head down to kiss her bare shoulder gently.

"I suppose I should ask him for permission to court you," he said. "He is technically the head of your family, is he not? I am not entirely sure I can accept Lady Isabel's permission because she made it sound as if your mother had the final word on your future."

His warm, soft kiss to her bare shoulder brought her movements to a halt. It was the naughtiest, most decadent thing that had ever happened to her, and her heart began to race. He caught her looking at him with a startled expression.

"What?" he asked. "What is it?"

The startled expression transformed into something of a smirk. "You should not have kissed me," she said. "In fact, you should not be alone with me in here. You know that."

He lowered his gaze but didn't move away. "Do you want me to leave?" he said. "I will if you want me to."

She reached up, pushing a long strand of hair that was hanging over his eyes back behind his shoulder. "I did not say that," she said. "But we should, at the very least, have a chaperone."

"Why?" he said, eyeing her. "Are you afraid of what I might do?"

She bit off a smile. "What *are* you going to do?"

"If you keep touching my hair, I just might have to touch something of yours."

"You can if you wish."

He looked at her fully then. He studied her face for a moment before lifting both hands and cupping her head between them. His thumbs brushed her cheeks, his fingers found their way into her hair, and before he realized it, he had pulled her to him and his mouth was slanting gently over hers. Every so gently. He was acutely aware that she was battered and bruised from the day before, but that wasn't going to stop him from kissing her.

He was desperate to do it.

Mira had never been kissed before, at least not like this. Raymond's childish attempts those years ago had been the only time she'd ever come close, and since he filled her with revulsion, that had been her predominant opinion of kissing in general. Sloppy, rushed, and unwelcome. But this…

This was not unwelcome.

The moment Douglas put his mouth against hers, she felt a jolt. His touch was warm and soft, but there was an undercurrent of… something. She wasn't sure what it was, but it felt as if lightning was coursing through his lips and bolting into hers. It was thrilling to say the least. For the first few moments, she kept her eyes open, looking at him because he was so close to her. She could see his eyelashes and eyebrows, the pores on his skin. Then she inhaled through her nose and his scent filled her. Something musky and salty and delicious.

That was when her eyes finally closed.

Now, her other senses were experiencing Douglas in a way her eyes couldn't.

Mira felt like flotsam in the sea, being pushed around by wave after wave of Douglas' strength. He suckled her lips, first the top, then the bottom, and managed to pull her mouth open when he did that so his tongue could stage an invasion. Mira's arms were around his neck, holding him fast, as he tasted her deeply. She let him, experiencing every movement, every sensation, with the greatest of curiosity. When he finally pulled away, he was breathing as heavily as she was.

For a moment, they simply stared at one another until Mira broke the spell.

"What… what did you do?" she said breathlessly.

He grinned, his lips red from his onslaught. "I think that should be quite obvious."

Mira struggled to regain her wits. "That… that was a *kiss*?" she said. "I've never known a kiss like that before."

He cocked a blond eyebrow. "Well and good that you haven't," he said. "Did you at least like it?"

She nodded eagerly. "Will you do it again?"

His mouth was on hers before she even got the last word out. His powerful arms went around her and she wrapped her arms around his neck, holding him so tightly that she was nearly strangling him. His hair got wrapped up in her grip and he finally had to ease up because she had trapped him with her vise of an embrace. He started laughing, pulling his hair out from underneath her arms, from her hands, and even from her mouth. It was everywhere. Mira laughed along with him, smoothing his hair down because she'd mussed it so badly.

"Are you done now?" she asked.

"Done with what?"

"Kissing me?"

His laughter grew. "Never," he said. "But if I keep going, we may… Well, I do not want to be caught in a compromising position. Lady Isabel might box my ears."

Mira grunted. "You'll be fortunate if that is all she does," she said. "But… it would be worth it, wouldn't it?"

Grinning, he cupped he back of her head, leaning over to kiss her again in a most tender gesture. Mira groaned softly, throwing her arms around his head and knocking him sideways in the process. She ended up pushing him into her and his teeth cut her lip. He realized it almost immediately because he could taste blood.

"Christ," he muttered, stopping his onslaught and holding her chin in his hand so he could get a look. "Let me see what I've done. I'm so sorry, love. I did not mean to."

He was looking at her lower inside lip even as she answered. "It was my fault," she said. "I'm not very good at this."

There was only a tiny speck of blood where he'd shoved a tooth into her gum, and he leaned down to kiss it. "You are excellent," he said. "But we will become more coordinated with practice. Enough so that I don't bite your lip or knock you silly."

Mira giggled. "I would not mind, I assure you," she said. Reaching up, she stroked his beautiful hair again. "It would be pain most pleasurable."

He chuckled, too. In fact, he couldn't seem to stop smiling or laughing. Everything about this moment made him want to smile and shout it to the world, to experience a joy he'd never known before. He wanted more of it, but he was also very conscious of the fact that Mira was bruised and battered from yesterday, so he didn't want to pile onto that. Better to let the woman rest and heal before he ravaged her again.

But he honestly wasn't sure he could wait that long.

"This is not supposed to be a game of pain or battering," he said. "This is supposed to be something passionate and tender, as much as two people can be, but I appreciate your sentiment. And your confidence. In any case, I think we have pushed the limits of propriety as far as we can, because I keep waiting for the chamber door to open and Lady Isabel standing in the doorway with a club that has my name on it. Therefore, may I summon a servant to help you dress?"

Mira's smile faded. "If I must."

"What's wrong?"

She shrugged, averting her gaze. "It is nothing, truly."

"Do you not trust me enough to tell me?"

She looked at him. "Of course I do," she said. "I simply do not want to sound silly with petty complaints."

"Let me be the judge of whether or not they are petty," he said. "I hope you feel that you can always tell me anything and I will never judge you. I will help you if I can."

Her smile returned. "That is very kind," she said. "I suppose… I suppose I was thinking that I do not want to leave this moment in time between us and face the world. When it is just the two of us, I feel very safe and happy. It's something I've never felt before."

"Nor I," he said. "I should not like to leave this moment, either, but the truth is that we must for now. But moments like this will come again."

"Then I shall look forward to that," she said. "It shall keep me fortified for what is to come."

"Meaning?"

She gestured toward the door. "Meaning I am not looking forward to facing what is outside that door," she said. "I am sure Lady Isabel wishes to speak with me about the incident involving Raymond. I can only tell her what I told you, but I know she'll want to hear it. Speaking of it again is reliving it, and I am not looking forward to that."

He cupped her face with one hand, kissing her on the cheek before he stood up. "I wish I could make this all go away for you," he said. "I will be with you when she questions you if you would like."

"I would, thank you."

He smiled at her, encouragingly, and she nodded as if to acknowledge that she could face whatever she needed to as long as he was by her side. Strange how a woman, so independent and used to being alone, now found herself swept up in this glorious creature who had declared his intention to court her. To marry her. God, how she could so easily give herself over to Douglas and blend in with him until there were no lines between her and him. Until they were one mass, one mind, one thought, one body.

Oh… to be *so* happy.

It was finally within her reach.

"I'll send a servant up to you then," Douglas said as he moved for the door. "I will wait for you down in the solar. I must speak to Lady Isabel anyway, so come when you are ready."

Mira nodded. "I will," she said. "And Douglas?"

He paused at the door, hand on the latch. "What is it?"

"Thank you."

With a wink, he was gone. Mira sat there a moment, an enormous smile on her face, before tossing off the coverlet and leaping from bed.

Oh… to be so happy!

CHAPTER TWENTY

"I CANNOT LET her do this," Douglas said strongly. "Let her break the betrothal. I will have my father send two thousand men to Axminster, permanently. An army of that size will keep de Honiton at bay. Eric, are you listening to me?"

After leaving Mira to dress, Douglas had come down to the solar because he wanted to know what had transpired between Jerome and Isabel. Why the woman had been left in a flood of tears. Unfortunately, he found out quickly enough.

It was worse than he could have imagined.

"I am listening to you," Eric said, no spark of life in his tone. After what Isabel had told him, the man was dead inside. "But Isabel has made the decision she feels best for Axminster. We cannot contest it."

Douglas' mouth was hanging open in shock and outrage. He looked at Isabel, still over by the window, though she wasn't weeping as she had been earlier. She was simply sitting there, still as stone.

All of the life had gone out of her, too.

"Isabel," Douglas said pleadingly. "You do not have to do this. I realize you are trying to appease Jerome, but this is not the way."

She sighed heavily before moving her red-eyed gaze to Douglas. "Douglas, I want you to listen to me and listen carefully," she said. "I am only going to say this one time, and once I say it, you are not allowed to argue with me. You are not allowed to make other suggestions. If you do, I will beat you within an inch of your life and send you and your army home. Do you understand me?"

Douglas was ready to explode but knew she was serious. He knew she was hurting and he honestly wasn't trying to make it worse, but he didn't believe this was the end. He couldn't accept it. Still, he nodded his head in answer to her question and turned away, pacing the floor in an agitated manner as Isabel rose unsteadily to her feet.

"Good," she said. "I want to be very clear about this, Douglas. As you are accepting blame for Mira's actions, I am accepting the blame for you. You are protecting the woman who will be your wife, and while that is admirable, I am making it so Jerome will be appeased and no one, including you and Mira, will every have to worry about him again."

Douglas couldn't keep his mouth shut at her path to martyrdom. "But—"

She jabbed a finger at him. "Silence," she hissed. "I am not finished. Now, is this a simple thing for me to do? It is not. It is a business arrangement and it is an arrangement for peace, and if you argue with me, you are diminishing my sacrifice. You are showing a lack of faith in my decision. Would you dare show such a lack of respect for me?"

Douglas, pale and upset, nonetheless remained stoic. He shook his head in surrender. "Nay, Lady Isabel."

"Do you think I do not know my own mind?

"Nay, Lady Isabel."

She nodded briefly. "You have answered as you should," she said. "I will marry de Honiton and he will have his son, God willing. He will also be the Earl of Axminster and our children will be the heirs. That is the way it is going to be. As for Eric… I would ask a favor of you, Douglas."

"Anything, my lady."

She glanced at Eric, but only briefly. Any longer and her resolve might weaken, so it was only a quick glance. It was clear that whatever time they'd spent alone in the solar had been a time of great anguish for them both, hashing out something that could not, would not, be changed.

And that was Isabel's choice.

"Will you take Eric with you to Lioncross Abbey?" she said, her voice beginning to crack. "He deserves a place of honor among great knights. He does not need to remain at Axminster and watch the results of my decision. I could not do that to him."

That was the most painful thing Douglas had ever heard. He'd become fond of both Isabel and Eric, and knowing they loved one another made this situation all the more tragic. After a moment, he nodded.

"If that is your wish, my lady," he said. "My father will make room for him. He will be honored."

Isabel forced a smile before turning to Eric. "Did you hear that?" she said. "Hereford will be honored to have you in his stable of knights. It is the prestige you deserve, Eric."

As always, Eric didn't argue with her. He simply nodded, a slight gesture, but said nothing. One could literally hear the man's heart breaking, shattering like the most fragile glass into pieces that could never be whole again. Knowing that was probably all she would get out of him, Isabel returned her attention to Douglas.

"Thank you," she said. "My heart is at ease. Now, if you will excuse me, I will retire for a time. It has been an… eventful day."

Douglas moved to the chamber door to open it for her. A gesture of respect, of chivalry. She smiled weakly as she approached the door, touched by his actions, but he stopped her before she could go through.

"My lady," he said, reaching down to take her hand. "What you have done… It is the greatest sacrifice I have ever heard of. It was something you did not have to do, which makes it all the greater. I shall never forget it. Or you. You have my undying respect."

He lifted her hand and kissed it gently, drawing a genuine smile from Isabel. "We did not start out as friends, you and I," she said. "But I now consider you a close one. I've told you that you remind me of my brother, so mayhap that is why I have a soft spot for you, Douglas de Lohr. I hope I am always worthy of your respect."

He smiled in return. "I have no doubt," he said. "But before you depart, Mira is dressing. I assumed you would want to speak with her. What shall I tell her when she comes downstairs?"

Isabel's smile faded. "Tell her nothing," she said. "She has suffered far more than any of us. This matter has been put to rest as far as I am concerned, so let us not linger over it. What's done is done. There is no going back."

"Aye, my lady."

He was still holding Isabel's hand, and she gave him a squeeze before letting go, moving wearily toward the stairs that led to the upper floors. Douglas watched her go before retreating back into the solar, where Eric was still sitting like a soulless man.

Empty and still.

Douglas was greatly concerned for him.

"And you?" he asked quietly. "How can I help you, Eric? Is there anything I can do?"

Eric didn't react at first. He continued to sit there, staring off into space, but after a few moments, he drew in a deep breath.

"I have been sitting here thinking on how I can salvage this," he said quietly. "Isabel is sacrificing everything for a situation that would have never occurred had de Honiton not decided to stay the night."

Douglas planted his bottom on the end of Isabel's big, heavy table and folded his arms over his chest. "Had we had any visions into the future, we would have denied him entry," he said. Then he hissed sharply and hung his head. "Had his fool for a son only kept control of himself. Had Astoria only kept her mouth shut. We could do this for the rest of the day, Eric. Many things led to this moment."

"I know," Eric said. "You should know that while you were upstairs with Mira, Isabel ordered Jonathan to take Astoria into the village and secure her a room for the night. We are sending her home with an escort on the morrow. Home to a father who ignores her and an uncle who lusts after her. I would like to say that I am sorry for that, but I am not. The woman was bred by swine and she returns to swine. Fate has a way of punishing people who deserve it."

Douglas grunted. "I suppose that will be punishment enough for her."

"Did you have something else in mind?"

Douglas shook his head. "Nay," he said. "She is beneath my contempt. I'll not waste another moment thinking of her."

"That is the way I feel about it. She has not only changed your life, but she has changed mine."

"More unintended consequences of her petty vengeance."

"Exactly."

They fell silent for a moment, hearing the bustle of the inner bailey wafting in through the windows. It sounded like just another normal day outside, while inside, lives were changing and hearts were breaking. Douglas' thoughts began to turn to Mira. He was looking forward to seeing her come through the solar door, but also wondering how he was going to tell her about Isabel's bargain. He knew she would be greatly distressed by it. As he pondered how to couch the terrible news, Eric suddenly stood up from the chair he'd been seated on.

"If I tell you something and ask you to keep it secret, will you do me that honor?" he asked.

Douglas watched him as he walked over to one of the lancet windows. "You know I will."

Eric drew in a long, pensive breath, gazing out over the inner bailey and the gatehouse. Beyond that was the central bailey, cluttered with shelters that had been established by the visiting armies.

"Douglas, there is only one solution to all of this," he said. "I am going to challenge Jerome to a fight. If he wins, he takes everything. If I win, he departs and never returns."

Douglas felt sorry for the man. It was a very simplistic plan in a complicated situation. "If you do that, you will be undermining Isabel's bargain," he said. "Please do not take offense, but I do not think it is a good idea."

Eric looked at him. "You don't?"

"Nay."

"Then what would you do?"

Douglas shrugged, coming off the table and moving over to where Eric was standing. "If we are speaking theoretically," he said, "the most logical thing is to eliminate de Honiton. With no Jerome, there is no bargain."

"Is that what you would have done had he demanded to marry Mira?"

"I would have killed him where he stood. I wanted to, believe me."

"That's what I want to do."

"What?"

"Kill him."

Douglas understood. God help him, he understood completely. The trouble was that Eric hadn't held a sword in years and would more than likely get himself killed trying to rid himself of Jerome. But the truth was that he was a man in love with a woman who had to bargain with the devil and was now pledged to him simply to keep the peace. It wasn't fair, any of it, and Eric was trying to think of a way out of it.

A way that wouldn't shame Isabel or get himself killed.

Had Douglas been in his situation, it would have been different. Douglas was a knight, born and bred for battle. He had killed his share of men, but always men who were a defined enemy. Douglas was a man who valued life and valued those he loved greatly. That meant he was a man with a soul and a conscience, and as much as he didn't have a problem killing a man who was a threat or an enemy, he didn't condone outright murder.

This coming from a man whose brothers, and father, were

involved in the Executioner Knights.

The Executioner Knights were a sect of assassins and spies, men who worked for the good of England any way they had to. Originally, William Marshal, the first Earl of Pembroke, had organized the guild to help him in his behind-the-scenes struggles with, and for, the crown, and he had kept the group a secret. The Executioner Knights helped him keep the kingdom solvent against foreign threats and, in the case of King John, even a king who sometimes was the enemy of his own people. Christopher, Peter, Roi, and Myles were all Executioner Knights. They had done some very unsavory things. Even Curtis had been involved from time to time, but Christopher had purposely kept Douglas and Westley away from the Executioner Knights. They had been small children during the time of his heavy involvement, and as his sons grew older, perhaps he was only willing to lend the guild just a few of his sons.

But Douglas and Westley had been kept out of it.

That never bothered Douglas until now. He wished he had the assassin instinct like his father and brothers and even his brother-in-law, husband to his eldest sister, Christin. Alexander de Sherrington was the greatest assassin the world had ever seen. Douglas was coming to wish he'd had some of the training that Alexander had, because if he did, he would have taken care of Eric's problem easily. Even though he didn't have the training, however, he know someone who did.

Right under his nose.

But he would have to think carefully about unleashing that kind of power.

"I understand," he said after a moment. "But you cannot challenge him. That is out of the question."

Eric knew that. The once-skilled knight was only a clumsy has-been these days. Ashamed, and defeated, he returned his attention to the window. "Then it is over," he said. "Isabel will bear the children of another man and I will have to live with that for the rest of my life."

Douglas stood beside him, also looking out over the bailey. "There are other ways of handling this situation that don't involve a challenge," he said quietly. "If you want to spare Isabel a marriage to Jerome, then you must be clever about it."

Eric looked at him. "What do you mean?"

Douglas shrugged. "Accidents, for example," he said. "Accidents happen all of the time. I am not advocating that you put him in front of a team of wild horses, but think of it this way… Something far subtler would be equally effective."

He had Eric's interest. "Like what?"

Douglas pondered the question for a moment. "For example, if you were to take him on a tour of what will be his new property," he said. "If he is to be the next Earl of Axminster, then he must inspect his domain. Take him to the wall because the view is better from there. There is a section of the parapet that is low, barely to a man's knees, and it would be nothing at all to give de Honiton an 'accidental' shove that sends him over the wall and to his death below."

Eric's eyes widened. "Do you think it will work?"

Douglas shrugged. "I think if Jerome goes to the wall, anything can happen."

A soft knock on the solar door interrupted them and they turned to see Mira entering. Dressed in a simple gown the color of heather and with her blonde hair neatly braided, she looked worlds better than she had last night. Other than a big bruise on her clavicle and scabbed hands, the signs of last night's struggle were minimal.

To Douglas, she looked like an angel.

"My lords," she said, dipping into a practiced curtsy. "I've come to see Lady Isabel, but I see she is not here."

Smiling at her, Douglas came away from the wall. "Nay, she is not, my lady," he said. "She has gone to rest. She did not sleep all night."

Mira was gazing at Douglas with the same expression he had—giddy and sweet. It was clear how enamored the two were with one another. "Then I am glad she has finally gone to bed," she said. "I suppose I should see to the young women and to tonight's meal, then. I can make myself useful until Lady Isabel awakens."

"The young women are in their small solar, I believe," Eric said. "I saw them there earlier. Davina and Helen were with them."

That left the obvious question. "And Astoria?" Mira asked. "Where is she?"

"Gone," Eric said simply. "She has been sent home. You need not worry about her ever again, my lady. She has gone home."

That brought obvious relief to Mira. "I see," she said, struggling not to shout for joy. "In that case, mayhap things will go back to normal around here. I will join Davina and Helen and the other young women. Thank you, Sir Eric."

With a lingering smile at Douglas, she departed the chamber and headed off to find Isabel's wards. Douglas watched her go, fixating his gaze on the shapely curve of her torso, before turning to Eric.

"Now," he said in a low voice. "Where were we?"

Eric's exhausted face reflected the new determination he

was feeling. "I do not know where de Honiton is, but I will find him and invite him to the battlements to introduce him to Axminster," he said. "It is a good plan, Douglas. When de Honiton is on the wall, I will do what needs to be done."

"Would you like me to help you?"

Eric appreciated the offer greatly, but he put his hand on Douglas' arm. "This is my fight, Douglas," he muttered. "You have given me the idea, but I will see it through. It is my love he is trying to take. I will be the one to stop him."

Douglas wasn't in agreement. "This is my fight, too," he said. "Isabel made the sacrifice to keep de Honiton from harassing me and my family. She said it herself. I am part of this whether or not you want me to be, so I will meet you on the battlements. Though I do not readily advocate what we are about to do, in this case, I will make an exception. De Honiton deserves all of this with his threats. What he and his vile son have done has affected all of us."

Eric nodded reluctantly. "Very well," he said. "If you feel strongly about it."

"I do," Douglas said. "I will not let him get away with this. Isabel does not deserve it."

Eric smiled weakly. "Did you think you would have such an opinion six weeks ago when you first came to Axminster?"

Douglas snorted. "I was ready to be done with the lot of you," he said, quickly sobering. "But not now. Now we are friends. We are bonded by that, until the end."

Eric was clearly touched. "Thank you, Douglas," he said, grasping the man's arm for a quick squeeze. "I am grateful."

With that, he headed out of the solar to find Jerome just as Jonathan was coming into the keep with Davyss in tow. The two of them eyed Eric as the man stormed past them and out of the keep, but they headed straight for Douglas.

"What is going on, Douglas?" Jonathan asked, clearly upset. "Why is de Honiton going around telling the Axminster soldiers that he is to be their new lord?"

Douglas rolled his eyes. "Christ," he muttered. "Is he truly saying that?"

"He is."

Douglas pointed to the solar. "Go inside," he said. "You are just the man I want to see."

Jonathan charged into the solar, followed by Davyss and finally Douglas. It was Douglas who shut the door as Jonathan went to the wine pitcher, draining what was left of it.

"It seems that we have a problem," Douglas said. "What I tell you now does not leave this chamber. Is that clear?"

Jonathan nodded, wiping his mouth with the back of his hand as Davyss went over to the pitcher with the futile hope of seeing if anything was left.

Douglas was focused on Jonathan.

"I will make this brief," he said in a low voice. "De Honiton has backed Isabel into a corner with his threats."

Jonathan frowned. "What threats?"

Douglas grunted in exasperation. "Where to begin?" he said. "The man demanded that I be turned over to him because I killed his son, but Isabel refused."

"You did not kill his son."

Douglas put his hand on Jonathan's shoulder. "You know that and I know that," he muttered. "So does Davyss. But if you think I am going to let Lady Mira take the brunt of de Honiton's anger, then you do not know me at all. From this point forward, all you know is that we came upon Raymond assaulting the lady and I smashed his head in with a rock. Davyss? Do you hear me?"

Standing dejectedly with the empty wine pitcher in his hand, Davyss nodded. "Aye, Douglas."

Douglas returned his attention to Jonathan. "De Honiton thinks it is me and so does everyone else, so he demanded that Isabel surrender me to face his justice," he said. "When she refused, he threatened Axminster, Lioncross, and anyone else he could. He told her that she would never know a moment's peace for the rest of her life, that he would keep up the harassment in punishment for Raymond's death. When Lady Isabel tried to reason with him, he told her the only way he could be soothed was if Isabel was to give him one of her wards so that he could marry the girl and have another son to replace the one that was taken from him. He demanded Mira, given that she was the object of his son's lust, but Isabel refused."

By this time, Jonathan was scowling at him. "He said *that*?" he said. "He simply wants a woman handed over to him, just like that?"

"Evidently."

Jonathan shook his head. "Then the man is clearly losing his mind," he said. "Is that why he is telling the Axminster men that he will soon be their lord? Because he has gone mad?"

Douglas shook his head. "He is telling the men that because Lady Isabel, in order to save Axminster and Lioncross years of harassment from de Honiton, has made him the offer of marriage," he said. "She will not give over one of her wards, so she gave him the only woman she could—her. Once de Honiton marries her, he will be the Earl of Axminster. It is enough of an offer to still the man and make him forget about his vengeance."

Jonathan looked positively horrified. "Isabel?" he gasped. "And… *that* man? De Honiton?"

"Aye."

"But what does Eric say about this? He and Isabel are…"

He didn't finish even though it was the most poorly kept secret at Axminster. Douglas motioned Jonathan closer, indicating for him to sit, then sat down opposite the man as Davyss pulled up a stool. Their huddle was close and quiet.

"Eric is talking about challenging de Honiton to a fight," Douglas muttered. "He wants to fight the man for Isabel's honor. We all know how that will end."

Jonathan rolled his eyes. "Eric has not wielded a sword in years."

"Exactly," Douglas said. "I do not know de Honiton's skill level, but he arrived fully armed. That makes me suspect he is not afraid to wield a sword like Eric is. Therefore, the fight will be over before it begins."

"Eric will get himself killed."

"Agreed," Douglas said. "But the core of Eric's plan is a sound one. If we get rid of de Honiton, then we eliminate the problem. Isabel and Eric remain true to each other and there will be no harassment of Axminster or Lioncross or anyone else because de Honiton has no relatives. The line will be gone. Everything will return to the way it was before de Honiton and his unwelcome son pushed their way into Axminster for the night."

By this time, Jonathan was watching him carefully. "You have a plan."

It wasn't even a question, but a statement. Douglas fixed him in the eye. "Wolfie, I know you have worked with the Executioner Knights in the past," he said. "Not only are you Blackchurch-trained, but you are also an Executioner Knight veteran. I know you have worked with Myles because he told me. Something about a Flemish count who was providing money to the Welsh for an attack on Kirk Castle. You needn't deny it because I know it to be true."

Jonathan's expression never changed. "I will not deny it," he said. "But you are telling me this for a reason, I suspect."

"You would be correct."

"What do you want me to do?"

Douglas lifted an eyebrow. "Something unsavory."

Jonathan did grin then. "Isn't that usual for men like your brother and I?" he said. "You were never involved in anything like that, Douglas. Your father never recruited you like he did your brothers."

Douglas shook his head. "My father's path for me was different."

"How?"

"Papa kept Westley and I away from the Executioner Knights," he said. "I spent most of my youth in the royal household. I know nearly everything there is to know about every major house, every army, every foreign diplomat… anything that involves Henry and his politics. But I have been home on occasion, for long periods of time, especially as my father grew older. He always wanted Westley and I to be invested in the politics while my brothers—and men like you—were more invested in insuring England would always remain strong."

Jonathan understood. "Each man has a calling," he said. "Mine has always been to accomplish a task, whatever it takes, no matter how distasteful. My younger brother may be the Wolfe of the Border and my older brother may be an earl, but I am the one who ensures they have a country to defend."

Douglas smiled faintly. "And you do it well," he said, but

quickly sobered. "I realize that asking you to kill a man is unsettling at best, but it is a man who is harming good people. People who are our friends. And I would kill for my friends, Wolfie. Even you."

Jonathan put a hand on Douglas' shoulder. "I could not have said it better," he said. "Therefore, I am going to find Eric and ensure he survives. Did he have something in mind?"

Douglas nodded. "Luring de Honiton to the battlements and pushing him over the side."

Jonathan shrugged. "Simple and effective," he said. "But I would not trust Eric do accomplish this on his own. De Honiton will more than likely fight back, you know. It will not be an easy thing if Eric is not prepared for resistance."

Douglas lifted his eyebrows in resignation. "Although I admire Eric, the man is not a warrior," he said. "He admits that himself. I'm not sure if he had visions of grandeur when planning to save Isabel, but I am uncomfortable with letting him do this on his own. Save him from himself, Wolfie. But do not let him know it."

That seemed to settle it. Both Jonathan and Douglas knew what had to be done. As they stood up, preparing to move out, Davyss stopped them.

"I want to be part of this," he said. "What can I do?"

Douglas and Jonathan looked at the young knight with the flashy sword and a taste for blood. Jonathan put a brotherly hand on the young man's shoulder.

"If we fail, then de Honiton is yours," he said. "Do you think you are capable of what we are asking?"

"To kill him?"

"Aye."

Davyss grinned. "Slowly or quickly?"

In spite of the serious circumstances, it was the best laugh Douglas had in a long time. With a plan in place, the three knights moved out.

It was time to end this once and for all.

CHAPTER TWENTY-ONE

"WE'RE SORRY, MIRA. Can you ever forgive us?"

The soft plea came from Primrose, the most delicate of the younger wards of Lady Isabel. All of the wards, Mira included, were in the ladies' solar that was used for their lessons. Rather than hide in their chambers in fear because of the upheaval at Axminster, Davina and Helen had instead forced the younger girls back into their routines, so Mira found them all in the solar completing their poetry lessons. She'd only come to check with Helen and Davina before heading to the kitchens to see to the evening meal, but Helen and Davina had pulled her into the chamber and the younger girls—Ines, Marceline, Louisa, Primrose, and Theodora—needed little prompting to apologize.

They'd all heard the terrible truth about Astoria and her lies.

Truth be told, Mira wasn't in a particularly forgiving mood. She was very hurt by what the girls had done to her. But, on the other hand, Astoria had been a master manipulator, so she really didn't blame the girls too much. Astoria had managed to push everyone around with her demands and lies. Mira listened to Primrose, Ines, Louisa, and Theodora's apologies, and then Marceline's sobbing plea. Because she was crying, Primrose started to weep, and Mira gave up on her inclination not to forgive them immediately. They were genuinely remorseful, young as they were. She hugged both young women and assured them that they were, indeed, forgiven.

Standing by the open door as all of this went on, she caught a glimpse of Eric as he left the main solar and headed outside. She also saw Jonathan and Davyss enter, only to be quickly ushered into the main solar by Douglas. He didn't see her, but she took a moment to gaze at the man, feeling her heart swell with joy and pride. A man who would protect her and love her, something she'd never hoped for in her life. Not like this. She'd always planned to be married but never hoped for fondness in the union.

Love.

Though she'd never been in love, she suspected that's what she was feeling.

It was like a whole new world.

"Mira?"

Someone was calling her. Breaking from her thoughts of Douglas, she turned to Helen, who was standing a few feet away. The young woman smiled at her.

"Did you hear me?" Helen said.

Mira shook her head. "I confess, I did not," she said. "I saw Douglas and became deaf and blind to all else around me."

Helen grinned. "I am very happy that you have found such joy," she said. "We all are, truly. In fact, the girls were wondering if we would all be invited to the wedding."

Mira went to her and took her hand. "It would not be the same without you," she said. "Especially you, Helen. And

Davina, too. You were kind and supportive from the moment you found out, no matter what Astoria said or did. I shall never forget that. You are true friends."

Helen put her arms around Mira, giving her a hug. It was a sweet moment between them, and a friendship that had endured a great deal as of late. But Davina and Primrose interrupted because Primrose wanted Mira to hear the poem she had written, so the girls gathered around, embracing one another, smiling and listening attentively to Primrose's poem of a garden of flowers that talked to one another and magically danced with the fairies at midnight. It was meant to be sweet and humorous, and there was a good deal of laughing going on.

There was joy and friendship once again.

And that was how Isabel found them.

"Ah," she said as she entered the solar. "I see that we are all a happy family again."

The young women turned to Isabel in surprise. "My lady," Mira said, releasing Helen and going to her. "I was told you were sleeping. Were you disturbed?"

Isabel shook her head. "Nay," she said. "I found that I simply could not sleep, so I came to see to my young wards. What were you listening to?"

Mira pointed to Primrose. "Primmy has written a wonderful poem," she said. "Would you like to hear it?"

Isabel nodded. "Indeed, I would," she said. "You may continue, Primmy."

Primrose was always intimidated by Isabel, so her voice quivered a little as she recited her poem about the magic flowers. When she was finished, Isabel clapped politely, praising her imagination and critiquing it ever so slightly. As stern as Isabel could be, she was usually quite supportive when it came to the creative endeavors because she wanted to encourage them.

On the heels of Primrose's poem, Theodora was convinced she had one that was just as good, about a fox and a dog who became friends. Isabel took her usual chair in the chamber, but she took Mira by the hand as she sat down. She simply sat there, holding Mira's hand as Theodora spoke of the fox and the dog who were enemies and then friends. Mira glanced down at Isabel more than once, smiling at the woman, who smiled in return. Perhaps there were unspoken apologies in those gestures for the turn the night had taken, for the struggle Mira had gone through, and smiles of gratitude that she had emerged without serious damage.

Of course, Mira couldn't have known that Isabel was holding her hand for a deeper reason. She knew that the young woman had murdered a man in self-defense. She held her hand because of the terror Mira had felt, a silent gesture of solidarity and support. A gesture of relief because the night could have so easily have gone differently. It could have been Mira wrapped up in a shroud, stored in the very vault she had been killed in. So many things could have been different.

But they weren't.

And Isabel was grateful.

Primrose and Theodora's poems led to more recitations from Ines and Marceline, and finally Davina, who was very good at it. Poem writing and recitation was something all young women needed to learn and perfect, something Isabel considered a great virtue. It signified elegance and education. Looking around the chamber, she couldn't have been more grateful that life at Axminster had settled back down again. No matter if she'd had to sell her soul to do it, there was peace.

And would be for a very long time, if she had anything to say about it.

"Lady Isabel?"

A servant had slipped in unnoticed and now stood at Isabel's right elbow. She glanced up to see one of the kitchen servants who had been at Axminster since the time of Isabel's mother.

"What is it, Bets?" she asked.

The servant was older, with a rosy, shiny face and no eyebrows. She bent over to whisper to her mistress.

"Lord de Honiton has asked that we make special dishes tonight since he is to be our new lord," she said. "He wishes to have fish and fowl, and eels from Axmouth. He has instructed that someone go to the port to buy them. Shall we do this, my lady?"

Isabel looked at the woman as if she'd gone mad. "He said… *What* did he say?"

The kitchen servant was well acquainted with Lady Isabel's temper and it was a struggle not to cower. "He said that he is to be our new lord and—"

Isabel was out of her chair, her hand silencing the rest of the servant's explanation. "That is enough," she said. "Nay, we will not buy eels in Axmouth. What did the cook have planned for supper this evening?"

"The rest of the beef, my lady."

"Then what is what we shall have," Isabel said, storming off toward the solar door. "*Where* is Lord de Honiton now? Did he actually come to the kitchens?"

"Nay, my lady," the old woman said fearfully. "He sent a servant."

"Then he must be somewhere on the grounds," Isabel said.

"I will find him, and when I do, he will not go around telling anyone he is to be the Lord of Axminster again!"

She stomped out. Mira, who had still been standing next to the chair, watched the woman go with concern.

"I am not entirely sure she should go alone," she said to Helen, who had come to stand next to her. "When she is that angry… sometimes she says things she does not mean."

"Go with her," Helen said, also the slightest bit fearful of Lady Isabel's temper. "Find Eric. Mayhap he can keep her calm."

Mira nodded quickly. Leaving the chamber full of young women and their poetry, she dashed out after Isabel.

The woman wasn't difficult to track. She was cursing up a storm as she passed through the inner gatehouse, into the central bailey beyond. She was nearly halfway across the bailey when she caught sight of something on the walls and came to an abrupt halt. By that time, Mira had caught up to her.

"Lady Isabel," Mira said. "Would you permit me to summon Sir Eric? Mayhap he can help you straighten out any misunderstanding with Lord de Honiton."

Isabel pointed to the wall. "Lord de Honiton is up there with Eric," she said. "Douglas and Jonathan and the de Winter knight are with them. Why are they all up there? What in the world are they doing?"

She was stomping off again, making her way to a turret that had narrow spiral stairs that led to the wall walk. The walls of Axminster were particularly tall, taller still at this point because on the other side of the wall was a cliff. The twenty-five-foot wall was tripled in height between the top of the wall and the bottom of the cliff. It could be dangerous because, like many walls around England and Scotland, there was a minimal lip, which could give an enemy trying to scale the walls something to grab on to should they throw grappling hooks.

But if someone fell over the side, it would surely kill them.

Mira wasn't thinking about any of that as she followed Isabel to the turret. She could hear Isabel muttering the entire way up those narrow stairs. Once she hit the wall, she quieted, however, because the men were about twenty feet away from her. Mira came up behind Isabel, who, when she saw the young woman, tried to turn her away. But Mira wouldn't go. She thought Isabel might need her support. They were hissing at each other, arguing in mostly sign language, when Douglas caught sight of them.

"Lady Mira?" he said. "Lady Isabel? What are you doing here?"

Mira didn't know what to say. When Isabel turned to look at Douglas, Mira discreetly pointed at her and shook her head, hoping that would give Douglas a hint that something was amiss. He saw the miming and was smart enough to realize that Isabel wasn't pleased about something.

He braced himself.

"Lady Isabel, may we be of service?" he asked.

Isabel thrust her chin up, something she was very good at doing. "I've come to see Lord de Honiton," she said as she moved toward the men. "Am I interrupting some conclave? Something that, as Lady of Axminster, I should be part of?"

There was that imperious tone again, one that left no doubt as to who was in charge of Axminster. It *was* Isabel. There was no substitute. She was furious that the men were up on the wall, gathering, and she was not included, but she was more furious that Jerome might have called the meeting specifically to leave her out of it.

"Was this your idea?" she said to him. "This meeting, I mean. Was it *your* idea?"

Jerome was clueless about her question. "My lady?"

Isabel wasn't going to let him play stupid. "Clearly, you went back on your word to me that I could announce our betrothal, because the servants tell me that you are demanding fish and fowl and eel in celebration of the fact that you are about to become the Earl of Axminster," she said, growing louder as she went along. "I can only assume you are now trying to run Axminster without my input by gathering my knights. Well? What do you have to say for yourself?"

Jerome was taken aback. Eric had found him with his men in the central bailey, making arrangements to send Raymond home, when Eric had come upon him and very kindly offered to show him some of Axminster's points of interest.

It seemed like a nice enough gesture.

As Eric had explained, it was going to be Jerome's property soon enough, so he should get a look at what he was acquiring. Given that Jerome was thrilled with Isabel's offer, which had most definitely been spreading around, he'd readily agreed. He thought it quite sporting of Eric to take him around Axminster, which he had visited a few times in the past but had never been given a detailed tour of. He'd been so eager that he hadn't even considered Isabel's thoughts on the matter, and when Douglas, Jonathan, and young Davyss joined the tour, he felt important. Douglas and Jonathan had some good insight into Axminster's defensive features. Jerome had been so swept up in a glimpse of his future castle that Isabel's rather angry appearance had him completely off guard.

But he wasn't going to take her scolding. He didn't like bold women, and Lady Isabel was one of the boldest he'd ever seen.

If they were to be married, then she would have to understand her place in his world. She wasn't going to give him orders and she certainly wasn't going to embarrass him in front of his men.

A storm was brewing.

And it was about to get ugly.

ଓ

HE HAD TO get her off the wall.

Douglas never thought that Mira would be an unwelcome sight, but at this moment, her appearance, and that of Isabel, was not only unwelcome, it was also dangerous.

They had de Honiton where they wanted him.

Like a sheep to the slaughter, Jerome had been more than willing to follow Eric to the wall for a guided tour of the land around Axminster. When Douglas, Jonathan, and Davyss had emerged from the keep a short time later, they could see Eric and Jerome on the northern wall. Eric was waving his arms around, clearly describing the landscape to the future Lord Axminster, but more importantly, the place he'd chosen to explain the land was where the parapet of the wall was low for strategic reasons. It was also where the walls were built next to a drop-off that plunged down the side of a hill and into the River Ax.

The perfect spot if you wanted to push someone over the side.

But it was also a perfect spot for a not-so-skilled man, or cunning man, to make a mistake and fall over himself, so the three knights had headed up to join Eric as he gave Jerome the grand tour. They had tried to be as amiable as possible, within believability limits, in helping Eric explain the structure and defenses of Axminster. Eric was sharp when it came to the history of the castle and its abilities as a fortress, and that was where his education as a knight could shine. The truth was that he had been training royal troops for quite some time, so there was a good deal of merit in his knowledge. It was simply his applicable skills that were in question.

Douglas, as he listened to Eric, could only imagine how good the man must have been in his youth. It was clear that he knew a great deal, and Douglas found it a sad thing indeed that a knight like Eric, someone who had been part of Henry's army, should find himself in the position he did today. How far had the mighty fallen.

It just didn't seem fair.

All that aside, Jerome didn't seem to have a clue that his remaining life was being measured in minutes. Douglas and Jonathan had discussed it briefly as they approached the wall and decided that Douglas should distract Eric while Jonathan did what needed to be done. The problem was that, at this moment, Eric and Jerome were standing close together as Eric pointed out a rather large farm to the north. In fact, the two of them had been standing rather close together since the knights joined them, which was going to make it difficult for Jonathan to accomplish his task. Somehow, they were going to have to get them separated, but the addition of Mira and Isabel threw a rock into those plans.

Now they had women to deal with.

And one of them was particularly angry.

"Well, Jerome?" Isabel said again. "What *do* you have to say for yourself? I make you a generous offer and you are already taking advantage of me?"

Jerome struggled between defiance and surrender. "My lady, I do not think anyone could take advantage of you without suffering your wrath greatly," he said. "I will admit that our bargain has me quite pleased, so mayhap in my excitement, I said more than I should have. But it was not malicious, I assure you. I was not attempting to overstep."

That wasn't a good enough excuse for Isabel. She scowled at the man. "How could you *not* realize you were overstepping when you are telling my servants that you are to be their new lord?" she said angrily. "My offer to you was fair and just, but your lack of respect for me is clear. Mayhap I should rethink my offer if this is how you keep your word to me."

Jerome's slightly submissive stance changed quickly. He stiffened and his eyes narrowed. "We have struck a bargain," he said. "You cannot go back on it."

"And you made a promise as part of the bargain that you have already broken," she said. "Quite honestly, *you* have broken our bargain completely."

Jerome's frown grew. "I have done no such thing," he said. "What difference does it make if the servants know I am to be their new lord now, tomorrow, or next month? It *will* happen. I see no reason to keep it from them."

That was the wrong thing to say to Isabel. "You will keep it from them because I asked you to," she said. "I was to tell them."

"I still do not see what difference it makes."

Isabel was starting to turn red around the cheeks. "Is this how you treated Raymond's mother?" she said. "Lying to her to get your way and then breaking promises? Because if that is who you truly are, Lord de Honiton, I will be forced to revoke my offer."

Jerome advanced on her, and it took everything Douglas and Jonathan and Davyss had not to posture, to show that they were there to defend Isabel to the death. They didn't want him to be suspicious of them, so they had to stay still when they were positively aching to throttle the man. In fact, Eric started to move, but Jonathan held out a hand to him, stilling him. Enraged, but essentially helpless, Eric was forced to stand there as Jerome put himself in front of Isabel in a threatening manner.

"If you revoke your offer, then everything I told you prior to our bargain will stand," he said in a low voice. "I suggest you not threaten me in such a way. It will not go well for you."

Isabel wasn't frightened in the least. In fact, he only succeeded in stoking her smoldering fury into a roaring blaze. "Now I see why Raymond was the way he was," she hissed. "He came to us a child with little discipline and as the years passed, we found him to be a lying, vindictive, and shallow young man. No amount of punishment could change his character because, clearly, he has taken after his father, a dishonorable man."

Jerome smiled thinly. "I would rethink your words, Lady Isabel," he said. "The one thing I will not tolerate is a woman who does not know her place. And you shall know yours if I have to beat it into you every night for the rest of your life."

Isabel stiffened. "And you probably would," she said. "You came to Axminster yesterday under the pretense of being an ally. You pretended to be kind and amiable when the truth was much darker. Although I am sorry that your son was killed, it does not give you the right to behave as you have. The truth is that your son was killed in the course of attacking a weaker woman. He paid for it with his life. Instead of accepting that your son is responsible for his own death, you have blamed everyone else for it. You have threatened those you feel responsible to get what you wanted and, fool that I am, I let you. Now, the fact that you would break our bargain and fail to see the gravity of your actions tells me everything I need to know about you. You are not worthy of the earldom of Axminster, Lord de Honiton. I would rather give it to a pig than a worthless bastard like you."

Stinging words that should have been said much sooner in the situation, but Isabel had been trying to keep the peace. She had been trying to keep de Honiton from harassing Mira, Douglas, and anyone else he felt was involved in the death of Raymond. But that had been a mistake. Clearly, a very big mistake.

She was finished placating a fool.

But he was a combative fool.

After that, Douglas would swear that everything moved in slow motion when the truth was that events happened so quickly that he barely had time to react. For a man of action like Douglas was, his reflexes often saved his life, but in this case, things had moved too quickly for him.

Before he realized it, they were in a fight.

He and Jonathan and Davyss were standing several feet away from Jerome and Isabel, too far away to stop the man from slapping Isabel across the face. Her head snapped sideways and she stumbled back, stepping on Mira, who scrambled to get out of the way and ended up tripping. As Mira fell back and quickly crawled out of the battle zone, Isabel brought up a fist and clipped Jerome on the side of the head. As he reached out to grab her, she kneed him in the belly. Her hands were moving as quickly, and she slapped at him several times before he got a grip on her arms to stop her.

Meanwhile, Eric was rushing to save her.

But Isabel didn't need saving. She was using her hands and

knees to pummel Jerome, who had his head down so she wouldn't hit his face. He was trying to push her back, away from him, but she just kept coming. Her movements were almost frenzied, as if she were terrified what would happen if she didn't gain the upper hand, but that meant Jerome couldn't open his eyes. He didn't see that his right foot was nearly on the ledge.

But Douglas did.

He'd been so busy watching Isabel throw herself at Jerome that he noticed the position of the man's foot too late. He shouted, but Jerome thought he was shouting *at* him. Out of corner of a peeped-open eye, Jerome saw Douglas move and knew the man was coming to help Isabel. Jerome could survive an angry woman but knew he couldn't survive the knights who served her. In an effort to move away from Douglas, and Eric, he stepped sideways and his foot bumped into the low lip of the wall. It was enough to cause him to stumble.

Over the wall he went.

But it wasn't just him. Jerome was holding on to Isabel, and they went over together. Eric, who was closer to Isabel, screamed her name and grabbed for her, managing to get hold of her ankle, but Jerome's body weight had pulled her over the side. Eric refused to let go of Isabel, which meant he also went over the side as Douglas managed to reach out as a last-ditch effort and grab Eric's booted foot.

The boot came off in his hand.

Jonathan and Davyss grabbed Douglas before the momentum could take him over the side, too, and the three of them watched in horror as Jerome, Isabel, and Eric fell to the base of the wall, down the side of the cliff, and continued to the very bottom of the rise.

It was all over in a matter of seconds. As they remained frozen, staring at the bottom of the cliff, a scream brought them back to reality.

Mira had seen everything.

She had been witness to the fight, the fall, and Douglas nearly going over the wall after them. As terrifying as that was, the very real fact was that she'd just seen the death of Isabel, a woman she loved dearly, and she began to wail in horror. Douglas scrambled away from the ledge and went to her, half walking, half stumbling, and pulled her into his arms.

"Wolfie! Davyss!" he hissed, both arms around her and a hand over her head, holding it against his chest. "Get down to the base of the hill. Find them. Take men with you. *Go!*"

Jonathan and Davyss rushed past him, heading for the turret stairs, as Douglas picked Mira up and cradled her against his broad chest.

"I'm so sorry, love," he said, feeling as bad as he possibly could. "My God… I am so very sorry you had to witness that."

Mira was weeping loudly, her arms around his neck as he held her tightly. She couldn't even speak. Horrified and sickened by what he had just witnessed, Douglas took Mira down the stairs, carrying her toward the keep in a weeping, heaving mess even as the castle around him came alive with men rushing out to see what had become of Isabel, Eric, and Jerome. Douglas and Jonathan and Davyss hadn't been the only ones to see the fall—other sentries on the wall had seen it, too, and word had spread like wildfire. All of Axminster was in chaos as the main gatehouse opened, purging men and horses onto the road.

All the while, Douglas held Mira tightly and carried her to the keep.

There wasn't anything he could say. There wasn't anything he could do. He'd gone to the wall with his comrades in arms, preparing to rid Axminster of a viable threat for the sake of a woman who had become a good friend, but somehow, the fingers of fate had twisted up that plan and spit it out as a jumbled mass of pain and suffering.

He could hardly believe it.

Maybe this was their punishment for planning the death of Jerome, or mayhap this was simply a way to put Isabel and Eric at peace. If they could not be together, there was no point in living. They were together in death as they could not be in life. Douglas wasn't going to try to rationalize what he just saw. All he knew was that he was heartbroken by it. Absolutely heartbroken.

But it wasn't over yet.

Not in the least.

CHAPTER TWENTY-TWO

"SHOCKINGLY, THE FALL did not kill her," the physic said. "She did not land on the rocks like the others did. She landed on them and they cushioned her fall, but she will not survive this. The damage she suffered is too great. It is only a matter of time before she passes."

It was evening at Axminster as a hush settled over the land, and the castle, with torches on the wall and phantom shadows in every corner, remained still and solemn. Douglas and Jonathan were listening to the physic, the same physic who had tended Mira after her beating from Raymond. He was young but he was knowledgeable, and Douglas wiped a weary hand over his face after the physic delivered the news.

"Is she in any pain?" he asked hoarsely.

The physic shrugged. "The fall broke her back," he said. "She cannot feel much, but she is experiencing some discomfort. It is to be expected because her body is very broken up inside. Soon, her heart and lungs will begin to fail. She will simply go to sleep and it will all be over. It will be a relatively painless death."

That was the saddest thing Douglas had ever heard. They

were on the entry level of the keep, in a corridor outside a bedchamber usually used by the servants. When Isabel had been brought back to the castle, she was so badly injured that the physic didn't want to take a chance of jostling her up the stairs more than they already had, so it was decided to put her in a room on the entry level for her comfort.

As the night had settled, an eerie calm settled over Axminster. By this time, everyone knew about the tragedy. The rumor was that Jerome had lured Isabel up to the wall and then attacked her. When Eric rushed to save her, they all pitched over the side and crashed to their deaths. Quite honestly, Douglas didn't have the strength to correct anything. Castles were always rumor mills and this was no exception. The damage was done, so he was just going to let the gossip die away. People would believe what they wanted to believe, anyway.

But he knew the truth.

"Is there anything that can be done for her?" he asked after a moment. "Does she require anything?"

The physic nodded. "Douglas," he said. "She has been drifting in and out of unconsciousness and has asked for Douglas. Who is that?"

"Me."

"Ah," the physic said. Then he eyed Douglas for a moment. "We met when Lady Mira was injured, but we were not introduced. My name is Pinney."

Douglas acknowledged the introduction with a brief nod. "Thank you for your attention to Lady Isabel," he said. "If there is anything we can do to make her more comfortable, please do it. You do not even have to ask permission. Whatever she needs… Anything at all."

Pinney nodded. "I will, my lord," he said. "I need to prepare a pain potion to help her discomfort. May I use the solar for this?"

"Of course," Douglas said. "Do you require anything for this potion?"

"Wine."

"I shall have it sent to you."

Pinney nodded and headed toward the entry where the solars were, both of them. As he headed into the large solar, Douglas turned to Jonathan.

"You had better fetch Mira," he said. "I know she will want to speak with Isabel if she can. She is quite shattered."

"All of the young women are," Jonathan said quietly. "They are upstairs, in their chambers. The cook is seeing to the evening meal, simply to feed the men. I do not think the women want to be part of anything."

Douglas conceded the point. "That is understandable," he said. "The woman who has mentored them, trained them, educated them, is dying. I can only imagine the grief they must feel."

Jonathan watched him carefully. "And you?" he said quietly. "You are feeling grief, too."

Douglas nodded. "Indeed," he said. Then he snorted softly. "You know, when we first came to Axminster, I thought Isabel was a… was a not very nice woman."

"A boorish hag?"

Douglas grinned weakly. "Something like that," he said. "She did not want me here any more than I wanted to be here, but now I feel as if I am losing a sister. We tried to save her, Wolfie. We tried and failed. I am not accustomed to failure."

Jonathan shook his head. "We did *not* fail," he muttered.

"We had no part in what happened. We never touched Jerome. What happened with him and Isabel and Eric… It simply happened. But we had no hand in it."

Douglas sighed heavily. "I suppose you are correct," he said. "If we could have only separated Isabel and Jerome when they started fighting, mayhap none of this would have happened."

"Stop reliving it," Jonathan said. "You tried to save Eric. Had it not been for his cheap boot, you would have."

Douglas shook his head sadly. "The poor man," he said. "It seems to me that he just wanted to be happy. He wanted his dignity and the woman he loved. That is not too much to ask."

"It is not."

"Where did you put his remains?"

"In the vault with Raymond and Jerome," he said. "Though Eric has the dignity of being on elevated wooden boards, off the ground, while Jerome and Raymond are lying in the dirt where they belong. I have already spoken with the de Honiton escort, and they will be departing on the morrow, delivering their liege and his son home."

"Good," Douglas said firmly. "Let them go back where they came from. God, I wish they'd never come here."

"I am certain that is a sentiment they would both agree with if they could," Jonathan said. "But what about Isabel? What will we do with her?"

Douglas' gaze moved in the direction of Isabel's closed door. "You heard the physic," he said. "She does not have much longer to live. Once she passes, we will bury her with Eric. I think she would like that, and I know he would. In fact, send for a priest at St. Mary's in the village. It is possible that Isabel would like her last rites, and I want to be prepared if she does. The last thing she needs to worry about is her immortal soul."

Jonathan turned away. "I'll send for him right away."

"And don't forget to fetch Mira to me."

"I won't."

With Jonathan heading out to follow orders, Douglas went to the door to Isabel's bedchamber. He paused, hand on the latch, before taking a deep breath and opening the door. Inside, it was small and dimly lit by several tapers and an oil lamp. It smelled heavily of cloves, which physics believed had medicinal purposes. There was a servant inside, a woman who had been assisting the physic, but Douglas waved her out.

He wanted to be alone with Isabel.

The last time he saw her, she was unconscious, being carried between Jonathan and Davyss. Her dress had been torn, part of her hair pulled from her scalp, and both arms were broken. They were flopping at her side. It had been a ghastly vision, and Douglas had ordered a blanket thrown over her so others wouldn't see her in such a state before they got her into the castle.

He wanted to spare her dignity.

Now, she lay upon a small bed, arms at her side, the blood washed from her face, and a blanket pulled up to her chin. Her eyes were closed, her face softly illuminated by the light from the tapers. Quietly, he sat down on a small stool that had been pulled up to the bedside and sat for a moment, watching her face. He couldn't even tell if she was breathing. Sighing softly, he sat forward, his elbows on his knees, his chin resting on his clasped hands. Just watching her.

Waiting.

"Douglas?"

Isabel's usually strong voice was a mere whisper. He sat up, peering at her more closely.

"Aye, my lady?"

"It *is* you?"

"It is, my lady."

"Fancy a game of chess now?"

He smiled weakly. "I would only beat you," he said. "Mayhap you have had enough excitement for today."

Her eyes fluttered open, moving slowly until she found him sitting beside her. "You mean that I have had enough tragedy for today."

He nodded slowly, with resignation. "That is a harsh word," he murmured. "And I am sorry to agree with it."

"Douglas?"

"Aye, my lady?"

"Will you hold my hand?"

He didn't hesitate. He reached under the blanket to find her left hand, soft and warm, but he knew that her arms were broken and didn't want to jostle her, so he simply held it gently without moving it.

"I am holding it," he said. "Can you feel me?"

"Nay," she said. "I cannot feel anything."

"Trust me when I tell you that I am," he said. "Shall I prove it to you? Shall we arm-wrestle?"

He was rewarded with a weak grin. "I would beat you and then you would be ashamed because I would tell everyone," she said, but it was clear that she was having difficulty talking. She sounded weak and winded, as if she couldn't catch her breath. "But I will spare you that for today. I am not feeling up to it."

"Mayhap another time."

"There will not be another time," she said, the mirth fading from her eyes. "You needn't pretend, Douglas. I know that I am dying. I am at peace with it."

His expression went from one of warmth to one of sorrow very quickly. "If there is anything I can do for you, my lady," he said, "please ask. Anything at all."

"Do you swear this?"

"Of course I do," he said. "What is your wish?"

Isabel's gaze fixed on him, and for a moment he wondered if she had died right in front of him because she didn't move. Her eyes didn't move at all. But then she coughed weakly.

"I have been lying here, thinking," she said softly. "We must speak on a few things before I leave this world and I want to ensure that you carry out my wishes."

"As I said, I will do whatever you wish."

That seemed to give her the strength to continue. "You are a strong man, Douglas," she said. "I know you are the fifth son of the Earl of Hereford, but surely you are the strongest son. You are wise beyond your years, but more than that, you are a man of noble character. I admire that about you greatly."

"Thank you, my lady."

Isabel's eyes closed for a moment before reopening. When she spoke again, her voice was weaker. "Eric," she said. "He died trying to save me."

"I know."

"His family is in the north, but he is not close to any of them," she said. "Will you make sure he is buried near me?"

"I thought you would want him buried with you."

She nodded her head slightly. "He is not my husband, so that may be frowned upon," she said. "But if you can bury him within sight of me, I would be grateful. So would he. He was a good man, Douglas. I hope you came to realize that."

Douglas nodded. "I did, my lady," he said. "He has my respect."

Isabel smiled faintly. "He would have liked to have heard that," she said. "He was a great knight, once, but his wounding in battle… He was never the same. Men called him a coward for it, but he was not."

"I know."

Isabel took another breath, her smile fading. "I will be buried at St. Mary's in the village," she said. "That is where my brother and my mother and father are buried."

"It will be done, my lady."

Before Isabel could continue, there was a knock on the door. Douglas opened it to see Mira standing there, tears in her eyes that she quickly wiped away when he saw her. Reaching out, he took her hand and gently pulled her into the chamber, directing her sit on the stool that he'd been seated on.

Isabel smiled at her.

"Mira," she murmured. "The daughter I never had. How I will miss you."

Mira was trying desperately not to weep. Seeing Isabel fall off the wall had been bad enough, but to hear that she hadn't died right away and was suffering was worse than Mira could have possibly imagined. Isabel meant so much to her and she was trying very hard to be brave in this last meeting.

These last few precious moments.

"And I will miss you, my lady," she whispered tightly. "Are you in any pain? May I help you with anything?"

Isabel's gaze was soft on her, probably the softest it had ever been. "What have you been told about my condition, Mira?"

Mira swallowed hard. "That you were badly injured."

"I am dying, lass."

So much for being brave. Mira's face crumpled and she lowered her gaze, looking at her lap and sobbing softly. Douglas put his hand on her shoulder, rubbing gently, trying to give her some comfort.

Isabel was watching the both of them.

"I am glad you have come, Mira, because I have something to say to both of you," she said. "I must have your permission."

Mira's head came up. "Permission for what?" she asked, puzzled.

Isabel didn't answer for a moment. She was growing progressively weaker and was struggling to remain conscious.

"I have told Douglas that I was lying here, thinking," she finally said. "My greatest regret is not marrying and having children. I hoped to, someday, but with Eric… I was cruel to the man. I should have married him. Now that my time is limited, I would like to ask your permission to marry, Mira."

Mira wiped the tears on her cheeks, bewildered by the request. "Marry?" she said. "Why do you need my permission?"

"Because I want to marry Douglas."

Mira's eyes opened wide with shock and she looked at Douglas, who had the same startled expression.

"My lady?" he said, perplexed. "What do you mean?"

Isabel's gaze moved to him. "Listen to me, Douglas," she said. "I have no children. No one to carry on the Axminster title. No one to leave anything to. I want to marry you, and through me, you shall obtain the Axminster title. Once I am gone, you are free to marry Mira and she shall become the new Countess of Axminster. She will carry on my work here with the young wards. She will train them well. And you… you will be the greatest earl Axminster has yet to see. A de Lohr at the helm of our ancient title. I can die peacefully knowing Axminster shall survive… through the two of you. Will you grant me this honor, Douglas?"

Mira was nearly beside herself with shock, but that wasn't half of what Douglas was feeling. He looked at Isabel, his jaw hanging open.

"I… I cannot," he finally said.

"Why not?"

He looked at Mira, seeing her confusion, before looking to Isabel again. "Because men will think I am an opportunist," he said. "Marrying you for your title on your deathbed. They will believe I've stolen Axminster from you."

"Not if it is my wish," Isabel insisted. "Mira, find the physic. Bring him here right away. And grab any servant you can find. Send them to me. Hurry!"

Mira stumbled up from the stool and fled the chamber, leaving Douglas standing there, torn as he'd never been torn in his life.

"Do you truly think to do this to me?" he hissed. "I cannot do it!"

"Douglas," Isabel said in a voice that sounded more like herself. "Look at me—I am dying. I want to know that Axminster shall go on after my death. I want to know that the young ladies known as Axminster's Angels will continue through Mira. And I want to know that the next Earl of Axminster is a worthy man. You deserve this. You have been a good friend and advisor. I want to do this. Please."

"I will *not*."

"You promised me that you would do anything I asked. Will you now refuse to honor your word?"

He looked at her as if he wanted to wring her neck because they both knew, as an honorable knight, he was bound to follow through. Still, he protested.

"I promised you I would do anything you asked before you

asked me this… this terrible thing," he said. "You knew you were going to do this all along."

"I did."

"You knew I could not refuse you!"

"I knew."

Douglas was so angry that he had to turn away from her. He was ready to kick her bed and yell at her, but he couldn't bring himself do to that to a dying woman. Even if she *had* manipulated him. He struggled to calm himself before turning to her once more.

"I appreciate that you want to know Axminster will continue in good hands," he said. "I am honored that you would entrust it to me. But can you not see the burden you are placing on me by asking this?"

Isabel had started to open her mouth when Jonathan suddenly appeared. He looked between Isabel and Douglas.

"What is amiss?" he asked, moving toward Douglas. "Mira told me to come here right away."

Douglas sighed heavily and gestured toward Isabel, who turned her attention to Jonathan.

"I want to marry Douglas and pass the Axminster title to him, and he is refusing," she said. "What kind of man refuses someone on their deathbed? He promised he would do as I asked and now he is trying to go back on his word."

Jonathan's eyes bugged. "What's this?" he said, shocked. "You… you want to *marry* Douglas?"

"I have no heirs," Isabel said. "I want to die with the peace of knowing Axminster will continue with Douglas as the earl. The only way to do that is to marry him, but he seems to think that men will believe him an opportunist for this, so I will tell you, Jonathan, that I make this request with a clear mind. I make it selfishly, because I do not want Axminster reverting to the Crown. I want Axminster's legacy to continue, from de Kerrington to de Lohr, where I know life at Axminster shall go on as usual. You are my witness, Jonathan. Douglas has not asked for it. He does not want it. But *I* want him to have it. When I am gone, he may marry Mira and Axminster shall become theirs, remaining strong for years to come."

Jonathan understood a little more now. As he pondered the situation, Mira returned with the physic. Two servants wandered in after them, wide-eyed, going to stand in the corner. There were six people in the room as Isabel coughed again, struggling more to breathe as the moments ticked away.

As her life ticked away.

Time was of the essence.

"Jonathan," she said, weaker now. "Tell them what I told you."

Jonathan did. He explained Isabel's wish without mentioning Douglas' reluctance. When he was finished, no one seemed particularly moved or surprised except for Mira. Hearing it again, as explained to her by Jonathan, made her realize she'd heard it correctly the first time. But it also made her realize why Isabel had made the request—not on a whim, not foolishly, and not because she was in love with Douglas. She did it selfishly, as she had said. Much as she had negotiated a betrothal with Jerome to save Axminster, she was trying to force Douglas into a marriage for exactly the same reason.

She wanted to save her home.

As Douglas stood in the corner and fumed, Mira knelt down beside Isabel.

"Is this truly what you want, my lady?" she asked, putting a gentle hand on Isabel's forehead. "Of course we want to carry out your wishes, but this… this is something quite serious. Are you certain this is what you want?"

Isabel looked up at Mira. "Of course it is," she said softly. "You should have been my daughter, Mira. It is only right that you succeed me as the Countess of Axminster. How proud I am of you already. I know that you shall do great and wonderful things."

Tears formed in Mira's eyes. "Because of what you have taught me," she murmured. "You saved my life, my lady. You taught me everything I know, of course, but when my mother rejected me, you took me back to Axminster with open arms. You sheltered me and fed me and treated me as if… as if I was wanted. I can never thank you enough for that."

"Your mother does not deserve you," Isabel muttered. "Promise me that when I am gone and you are the countess, you will send your mother a missive announcing this so she will know the value I placed on her daughter. *Her* daughter, whom I love."

Mira blinked and tears splattered. "I love you also," she said. "Thank you… for everything."

Isabel smiled weakly. "You may show your thanks by convincing Douglas to marry me," she said. "The witnesses are here. All he need do is consent. Then you may have someone draw up a document stating that we wed by mutual consent and the witnesses may sign. That is all that is required by law."

Mira nodded, turning her gaze inevitably to Douglas, who was standing with his arms folded stubbornly across his chest. Kissing Isabel gently on the forehead, she left the woman's bedside and pulled Douglas out into the corridor where they could speak privately.

"Before you say anything, know that I do not feel right

about this," he whispered loudly.

Mira was patient with him. "Why not, if it is what she wants?"

He rolled his eyes. "Because it looks as if I stole the title from her upon her deathbed," he said. "Regardless of how it happened, I will appear morally corrupt, and I do not wish for that to follow me around for the rest of my life!"

Mira nodded calmly. "Then it is your reputation you are concerned with and not Isabel's last request," she said. "Douglas, she is going to die. She wants to die in peace. Axminster is her entire life and she wants to know that her legacy will continue."

He waved her off irritably. "I know that, but—"

"But you are more concerned about what others will think," Mira said, interrupting him. "Isabel is being selfish in her request, that is true, but I do not blame her. And you should understand, of all people. All that is left of us when we die is our legacy. She is begging for you to be hers. Why can you not see that?"

He eyed her a moment before sighing heavily. "When you put it that way, you make me sound selfish."

"You are if you are only concerned for yourself and not her dying wish."

His jaw twitched faintly and he leaned against the wall, pondering the situation, seeing both sides of it. Mira went to him, putting her soft hands on his arms.

"I do not care if you are the Earl of Axminster," she murmured. "I do not care if I am the Countess of Axminster. I was agreeable to marrying you without a title and I would be agreeable to marrying you when you have it. It does not matter to me. But you will make a great earl, Douglas, and you will make Isabel proud. And Eric. Let us fulfill something they no longer can. Let us create a legacy of love here at Axminster, honoring Isabel and her family as well as our own. The blending of two houses, carrying on the traditions and legacy of Axminster. That is all she wants."

He looked at her a moment before breaking down into a faint smile. "My father always calls me the wise one," he said. "I think you have me beaten in that arena."

Mira smiled back. "It is not of wisdom I speak, but of logic," she said. "And of love. Isabel is asking you to do this out of love."

Of course he couldn't refuse when she put it like that. Douglas was starting to come around now, starting to see it from Mira's perspective. But before he could reply, the door opened and Jonathan appeared.

"If you are going to make a decision, then do it quickly," he said. "She is growing weaker. The physic says she will not last much longer."

The tears returned to Mira's eyes. After standing on her toes to kiss Douglas on the cheek, she rushed back into the chamber, leaving Douglas and Jonathan alone in the corridor.

"What do you think about this madness?" Douglas asked. "Mira thinks I should do it."

"So do I," Jonathan said. "Not for the title, but because it is the right thing to do, Douglas. It is what Lady Isabel wants. The woman wants to die in peace. Let her."

"You do not think it looks as if I am taking advantage of the situation?"

"I think Lady Isabel is taking advantage of the situation," Jonathan said, grinning. "She knows what she wants and she's using her demise to get it."

"She is *using* me?"

"This is one chess game against you that she is going to win."

Douglas stared at him a moment before breaking down into laughter. "Very well," he said. "I suppose I will let her have this one."

"You'll do it?"

"I will."

"Good," Jonathan said, slapping him on the shoulder. "Come back into the chamber. You'll have to make this fast."

Douglas obeyed. He went into the chamber with Jonathan behind him, his gaze moving to Isabel. Mira was on her knees beside the woman again, hand on the undamaged part of her head. She was looking at Douglas rather anxiously, and he gave her a wink to let her know that everything was all right. Moving to the other side of the bed, he took a knee beside Isabel.

"As you wish, my lady," he said. "If you want a husband, I am happy to comply."

Isabel smiled as much as she was able. The spark of life had gone out of her eyes, and she was now living on sheer willpower alone.

"Thank you," she whispered. "We must say the words now. I suppose they were words I should have said with my dear Eric, but it was not meant to be. Not in this life. Douglas, are you ready?"

"What will you have me say?"

"It is simply a matter of my saying that I take you for my husband, and I do," Isabel said. "You must say that you take me as your wife."

Leaning over, Douglas kissed her on the forehead. "I take you as my wife," he said softly. "Thank you, my lady. For all you have done for me, and for Mira, and all you continue to do. You have been a true friend."

Isabel smiled faintly. "Make me proud, Douglas."

"I will, I swear it."

"Then I am content. Thank you, Douglas."

"Thank *you*, Lady Isabel."

Douglas kissed her on the forehead again, reaching over her to take Mira's hand. As Jonathan silently ushered everyone from the chamber, Douglas and Mira remained, holding hands that were resting on Isabel's torso as Mira gently stroked the woman's forehead. It was a waiting game now, but Isabel held out longer than she should have. When her eyes finally closed toward dawn and her breathing became erratic, Douglas leaned down and whispered in her ear.

"Go, my lady," he said. "Eric is waiting for you and you must go to him. Do not worry over the things you leave behind. I will take care of them for you. But you must go now. Be free. Be happy."

When Isabel breathed her last, it was to Douglas' gentle whispers.

The knight she had fought with, bargained with, and eventually grown to love as a dear friend was with her in her last moments as her husband, as fine and true a man as had ever walked the earth. Isabel knew that. Eric may have been her love, but Douglas turned out to be her legacy.

And that was the way she wanted it.

CHAPTER TWENTY-THREE

Three months later

THERE WAS A new Countess of Axminster.

The church bells of St. Mary's in the village of Axminster were pealing off their clear tones in celebration of the marriage of Douglas de Lohr, Earl of Axminster, to Lady Misery Isabelle Rosalie d'Avignon, now known as the Countess of Axminster.

The union, as rumor had it, was a love match.

Madly in love was more like it. As Douglas took his new wife, who was wearing the *my choice* pendant, from the church, he was positively radiant with joy. That was something his parents, who had both attended the wedding, noticed. Christopher and Dustin, the Earl and Countess of Hereford and Worcester, were thrilled to finally see Douglas' life come to fruition.

It was a glorious thing to behold.

Three months ago, they had been notified, by Douglas no less, that he had married the heiress to the earldom of Axminster under special circumstances. When Douglas told them of those precise circumstances, he made sure to have Jonathan with him so the man could confirm everything. He told the tale of how Isabel de Kerrington hated having de Lohr troops at Axminster after the Tatworth skirmish. Curtis, of course, had left them behind to strengthen Axminster's numbers, but Isabel had viewed it as an occupation. While grateful for the allies' help, she didn't want them taking over her castle.

Only Douglas could have softened that stance.

It was quite a tale Douglas gave his parents. Tales of chess, of broken necklaces, of unwanted visitors, of death, of threats from a former ally, and finally of the fall of Lady Isabel and her lover from the walls of Axminster. It had been a difficult and convoluted tale, one that left Christopher and Dustin quite shocked, but the most predominant thread in that tale was the fact that Douglas had fallen in love with a certain young woman. A ward of Lady Isabel who seemed to have been a tremendous influence on Douglas and his outlook on life. Upon finally meeting Mira, they could see why.

They loved her almost as quickly as Douglas had.

Now, three months after the death of Lady Isabel, Douglas had married Lady Mira. He'd wanted to marry her immediately after Isabel's death, but Mira wouldn't hear of it. She wanted to give Isabella a proper mourning period before she even considered taking the lady's place. Therefore, the new earl had to bide his time, which had been very difficult considering how badly he wanted Mira. Their three-month courtship had been very proper, however. Mira had seen to that. Considering she was now in charge of Lady Isabel's Axminster's Angels, she wanted to set a good example of propriety.

It just about killed Douglas.

But now they were married, and Douglas could still hardly believe it. Dressed in a fine silk gown that Douglas' mother had made, Mira had never looked more beautiful. In the great hall of Axminster, a wedding celebration was taking place, a celebration that included Grayson and Davyss de Winter, Antoninus de Shera, and most of Douglas' brothers and sisters. Jonathan was also there along with his brother, Robert, the Earl of Wolverhampton, who had come down from the northern Welsh marches to celebrate an alliance with Axminster, something he was quite thrilled to have.

The bonds of de Lohr and de Wolfe grew deeper.

During his wait for Mira, Douglas had kept himself occupied by making quite a few changes to Axminster. He had heavily recruited for its army until it swelled to almost two thousand men. Since Eric was no longer around to train the royal troops, Douglas gave that task over to his youngest brother, Westley, who took to it like a duck to water.

But there was more.

Jonathan, who had been sworn to Norfolk, was released from his oath at Christopher's request and swore his fealty to the House of de Lohr, and more specifically to Axminster. Douglas was thrilled to have a knight of such caliber as his army commander, and Jonathan also helped Westley train the royal troops. Since the king had been notified that Douglas was the new Earl of Axminster and was so confident in Douglas' abilities, he sent more royal troops for training than ever before. Within a few months, Axminster had grown to a significant power in Southern England.

And Christopher could not have been prouder.

Douglas, in addition to being the wise one of Christopher's sons, had also been the quiet one due to his slight speech impediment. The lisp was barely noticeable these days and Douglas had become a fine orator, so it was gratifying to see him rise to the opportunity that had been given to him. Christopher understood why the spinster heiress had asked to marry Douglas on her deathbed because he understood a little something about legacies. He had married his wife in his thirties and until then had not assumed he would ever even have a legacy. But he did, a great one, so he understood why the heiress had asked for Douglas' hand. He wished he could have thanked her because in her death, Douglas had found a new life.

Christopher was grateful.

Now, he was watching his son and his son's new wife as they toasted their new life together in the great hall of Axminster. Even though Christopher was quite elderly, nothing could have kept him away from this moment. Not even days of travel from the marches, jostling his old bones and exhausting him. Seeing Douglas happy was well worth it.

"How are you feeling, Papa?"

Jolted from his train of thought, Christopher looked up to see Douglas and Mira standing beside him. He smiled at his son and reached out to grasp his new daughter's hand, bringing it to his lips for a gentle kiss.

"I am feeling quite well," he said. "And how do you two feel? Like a married couple yet?"

Douglas grinned as Mira laughed. "We have felt like that for the past three months," she said, looking at her husband. "I cannot remember when Douglas has not been by my side."

Christopher smiled. "And he shall be there forevermore, God willing," he said. "This will be a time of true happiness for you, as you come to know one another as husband and wife. Personally, I can well remember the time before I married Dustin. It was a time of peace and rest for me, without a woman screeching in my ear, and… Ah, look. Here is my wife sitting next to me. I did not see you, my dear."

Dustin had been listening to the entire thing and rolled her eyes at her husband's sense of humor. "The truth is that he had no life before me," she said. "There has only, and always, been me. Though there were times when we first met that I would have gladly thrown him to the wolves. I still might."

Mira chuckled. "Like father, like son, mayhap?" she said. "I have had the same urge once or twice."

Dustin laughed and reached out to take Mira's hand from her husband. "This is why I love you, Mira," she said. "You understand these de Lohr men already. Now, come with me—we shall have them play a woman's dance and we can dance with my daughters."

"Wait, Mama," Douglas said. "It is growing late and Mira and I were hoping to retire. I need you and Papa to hold off anyone who tries to follow us to our chamber."

Dustin glanced at Christopher and they exchanged knowing expressions. It wasn't particularly late. Douglas was simply eager to be alone with his new wife, whom they knew had held him off for the entire courting period. That information had come courtesy of Myles and Westley, who had listened to Douglas speak of his frustration that Mira would not let him go beyond passionate kisses and some fondling. It had resulted in some very uncomfortable nights, and days, for Douglas, whose engorged manhood was never allowed to do what it was designed by nature to do.

Mira had made him wait until they were properly married.

Dustin had cheered her. Christopher had only laughed.

"Everyone seems to be having a good time," Dustin finally said, looking over the hall. "No one seems to be paying much attention to the two of you, so if you are to leave, do it now.

Your father and I will ensure that your guests are properly taken care of."

With a grin, Douglas grasped his wife's hand and pulled her away from the dais. He thought he heard someone calling his name, but he didn't stop. He didn't want to. He pulled Mira out of the hall through the servants' entrance so they were less likely to be seen, dashing with her across the central bailey and to the keep. He had taken over Lady Isabel's enormous chamber at the very top of the keep and, this morning, Mira's wards had swept and dusted and put fresh linens on the bed. By the time they reached it, the fire was inviting and the chamber was warm and intimate. Douglas let go of Mira long enough to open up the shutters facing the central bailey, looking out to see if anyone had followed them.

"Good," he said. "It seems quiet out there. I do not think we are missed."

Mira grinned as she sat down at a dressing table that had been prepared for her and carefully removed the repaired necklace that Douglas had given her. After laying it down on the table next to her, she began to carefully remove the pins from her elaborate hairstyle, courtesy of Helen.

"With the rest of Lady Isabel's fine Burgundy being passed around?" she said. "We'll be lucky if we see our guests three days from now. As long as that Burgundy holds out, they'll remain as drunk as pigs."

Douglas chuckled, turning away from the window to see how nicely the bed was made up. But something caught his eye and he peered closely at it.

"God's Bones," he finally muttered. "Someone has put weeds in our bed."

Pulling out the last of the pins, Mira came over to the bed to see what he was talking about. When she saw him point, she snorted.

"That is lavender, my dearest," she said. "It keeps the linens fresh. It is also supposed to aid in conception. Someone wants us to conceive a daughter this night."

He frowned and looked at her. "Daughter?" he said. "Why not a son?"

She turned back to her dressing table as she unwound the braid around her head. "If there is lavender on the bed, it will mean a daughter," she said. "Rosemary on the bed means a son."

He suddenly grabbed the linens and shook them violently. Lavender bits flew out all over the floor.

"Remove that rubbish from my bed immediately," he said. "I'll not have those weeds touching any part of me."

Mira started laughing as he finished shaking the lines and charged toward the chamber door. "Wait," she said. "Where are you going?"

He yanked the door open. "To find rosemary!"

Her laughter grew. "Stop," she said. "Douglas, shut the door and bolt it. Surely you know that lavender or rosemary will not determine the sex of the child. It is just a silly superstition people have. It means nothing."

He wasn't so sure, but he came away from the door and bolted it as she'd asked. Stomping vindictively on the little bits of lavender as he came back into the chamber, he began to remove his clothing.

"I hope it means nothing," he said. "If our first child is a girl, then I know you have lied to me."

Combing out her blonde hair, Mira laughed at him. "I have never lied to you and I never will," she said. "But I cannot control the sex of our child any more than you can. It is in God's hands."

Douglas didn't like the fact that he wasn't in control of something, but he knew she was right. He pulled off his tunic, his boots, and finally his breeches, climbing between the linens and making sure there were no remnants of the lavender. He lay back on the pillows, an enormous arm folded behind his head, and watched Mira as she finished brushing her glorious hair. When she stood up and saw him in bed, a seductive expression on his face, she fought off a grin.

"You are so eager that you did not realize I need help out of this dress," she said. "Get up and help me get this off or your wedding night will not go as planned."

He flew out of the bed, stark naked, and Mira caught a glimpse of his semi-erect manhood. She'd truthfully never seen a naked man before, and in the months they'd been courting, he'd never revealed his organ to her because she'd never asked to see it. He'd been very careful about not exposing her to something she was unsure about, or didn't ask about, but now she had no reason not to be curious about it. When she got over the surprise of seeing it, intrigue took hold.

"The ties in the back," she said, moving her hair aside so he could get at them. "Douglas, may I ask you something?"

He was so eager to loosen the ties that he accidentally broke one and didn't want to tell her. "Anything, my love," he said, wincing with guilt as he held up the broken tie. "What is it?"

"You know I have never… done this before," she said. "We've only talked about it in theory, of course, but you've never told me—have *you* done this before?"

He froze, eyes wide. "Why do you ask?"

"Because if neither one of us has done this, it may be a bit awkward," she said. "I've seen dogs mate, of course, and Lady Isabel was very factual in the way she told us about the joining of a man and a woman, but she had never done it before, either, to my knowledge."

He resumed loosening the last of the ties. "What makes you think that?"

"Because she was unmarried, of course."

With the ties completely loosened, he began to help her off with the dress. "Sweetheart, surely you know that a woman does not have to be married in order to copulate with a man," he said. "Isabel and Eric loved one another very much. I am certain Eric bedded her from time to time."

Mira turned around to face him so he could help her pull off the sleeves, her eyes wide with the thought of Isabel and Eric banging it out in bed. "Do you really think so?"

"I would bet money on it."

Her expression was full of contemplation as Douglas pulled off one sleeve and then the other. "They did love each other a great deal," she agreed. "Have you ever loved anyone enough to do what we're going to do?"

He stopped undressing her and looked her in the eye. "You know I will not lie to you," he said. "Surely you must know that you do not have to love someone in order to mate with them."

"I know," she said. "Well? *Have* you?"

He sighed heavily. "Aye, I have, but not with anyone I loved," he said. "That, my darling, has been reserved only for you. What we do tonight is out of love, not physical need or just because we want to. There is far more to it."

Mira had known that's what his answer would be, but it was difficult not to feel jealousy for the woman, or women, who touched Douglas before she did. She finished removing the sleeves that he had started.

"I do not like the idea of another woman touching you," she said, sounding unhappy. "I have saved myself for you, after all."

He fought off a grin. "And you wanted me to save myself for you?"

She knew that sounded silly. It simply wasn't the way things were done, a man saving his virginity, so she made a face and turned away to finish taking the gown off.

"That would have been the polite thing to do," she said. "Is it too much to ask?"

He chuckled as he came up behind her, wrapping her up in his big arms. "Probably," he said, squeezing her. "Young men are like rutting stallions. They have needs that women do not. If it makes you feel any better, I paid well to learn something of the art of love. How else am I to teach you? If I know nothing, and you know nothing, we'll make fools of ourselves."

She let him hug her a moment longer before pulling away and removing the dress completely. As it fell to the ground at her feet, she stepped out of it and Douglas picked it up.

"Then you had better be very good at this if I have had to sacrifice you to another woman so you could learn," she said, feigning seriousness. "If she has not taught you properly, then I will find her and demand your money returned."

He laughed as he put the dress carefully over a chair. "You probably would," he said. "You know, you act like Lady Isabel sometimes. I think her demanding ways have rubbed off on you."

Mira fought off a smile, pointing to the bed. "Show me what you have learned."

"You'll need to take your shift off first."

He was naked, so she forced herself not to feel embarrassed

as she rolled off her hose and pulled her shift over her head. He watched her intently, biting his lip with anticipation as she removed the pale garment, the last line of defense between her modesty and his eager eyes. He'd long dreamt of the moment. She was short, petite, and oh so curvy in the right places. More than a handful for his eager touch.

He was ready.

"God, you're beautiful," he breathed as he looked at her. "Get into that bed. Let me show you what I've learned."

Fighting down flaming cheeks, Mira crawled beneath the linens. Douglas followed. The moment he lay down next to her, he knew he couldn't wait. He pulled Mira to him and his mouth came down on hers, so firmly that he drove her teeth into her lip. He kissed her deeply, tasting the blood, tasting her sweetness. There was passion and lust and love in that kiss, feelings that made him gather her more tightly against him. Her arms went around his neck, and her breasts, soft and warm, were pressed against his chest. Their naked flesh touching for the first time spurred him to another level of desire.

Rolling onto his back, he pulled her on top of him.

Douglas loved the feel of her squirming on him, her wet heat against him, and it drove him mad. His mouth moved down her neck to the exposed cleavage, but it was difficult to go much further the way they were, so he quickly rolled her back over so that she was beneath him. He lifted her arms, snaring them above her head, as his free hand began to move. His mouth trailed away from her lips, down her neck, and to her breasts. Using his knees, he pushed her legs apart and wedged himself in between them. With one hand holding her arms above her head, the other hand moved to the delicate heat between her legs and he stroked her gently before inserting a big finger into her.

Mira shuddered.

He'd done that before, during times of passion when she had thrown propriety to the wind, but this time it was different. She wasn't going to stop him from going any further, as she always had in the past.

"Do you feel me inside of you?" he whispered, his mouth against her right breast. "This is where you will know pleasure. This is where our loves comes to fruition, wife. *My* wife."

He thrust two fingers into her, moving them in and out, mimicking what he would soon be doing with his engorged member. At the same time, his mouth found a nipple and he suckled firmly. Mira groaned with pleasure every time he thrust his fingers into her tight, wet heat, preparing her for his entry. It wasn't long before he could feel her body start to quiver, the beginnings of her first release, so he quickly removed his fingers and thrust his manhood firmly into her as she began to throb with pleasurable convulsions.

Douglas could feel her body pulsing around him as he carefully but firmly thrust into her. She was so hot and wet, so prepared for him, that she hardly felt the sting of losing her innocence. So many sensations were overwhelming her that all Mira could feel was Douglas' manhood inside of her, driving her to a new plane of awareness. Her gasps of pleasure filled the air until he slanted his mouth over hers, kissing her with the power of the love he felt for her. Douglas was so highly aroused that he released himself sooner than he had anticipated, spilling deep into her waiting body.

It was heaven.

The sounds of heavy breathing filled the air as Douglas slowed his thrusts, finally stopping completely as he struggled to catch his breath. Beneath him, Mira lay with her eyes closed, arms over her head where he'd let them go, her bare breasts reflecting the firelight. Douglas watched her, thinking he'd never seen anything more beautiful. She was finally his—his wife, his life, his all—and when she lowered one of her arms, her breasts quivered and the sight was enough to arouse him again. In little time, he was sensually thrusting in and out of her as his manhood began to pulse back to life. They were on their sides now as he held her against him. The pace was slower but no less passionate. Douglas buried his face in her hair, inhaling her scent, as his hips moved in the ancient, primal rhythm.

"Douglas," Mira gasped as he hit a particularly sensitive spot. "God… *Douglas…*"

She had one leg over his hips as her hands found his taut buttocks to pull him deep inside of her. Douglas responded by covering her mouth with his, his kisses hot but tender, sweet but powerful. He held her leg behind the knee, rubbing himself against her as he thrust, and when he felt her tremors began again, he thrust into her, hard, before releasing himself in another burst of glory.

The fire in the hearth snapped softly as heavy breathing filled the room. Douglas lay beside his wife, his body still joined to hers, thinking that this moment had been well worth the wait. He began to kiss her softly—her head, her face, her shoulders—while his hand came away from her knee and went to her breasts, tenderly fondling her. At some point, her soft snores rose up and he smiled, thinking that she was quite adorable when she snored. But he continued to kiss her, and fondle her, until he, too, drifted off to sleep for a time, only to awaken sometime later with another erection that demanded satisfaction.

Mira was more than happy to provide it.

It went on all night.

When morning finally came, they welcomed the sunrise with yet another lovemaking session. Douglas had counted five times in total, but still, he wanted more. Mira didn't seem to mind, though he had asked her repeatedly, so he was quite happy to make love to his wife yet again. When they were finally finished and contemplating rising for the day, Douglas ultimately wasn't sure he wanted to. He rather liked it in bed with her, and they probably would have gone again had Mira not reached down in the bed and pulled off a sprig of lavender that had been stuck to her foot.

It had been there the whole time.

As Douglas climbed out of bed and cursed whoever had put the lavender in the chamber to begin with, Mira laughed so hard she cried. Tears of laughter streamed down her temples as Douglas was now convinced their first child would be a girl.

Little did he know that he was right.

Almost a year later, the moment his mother put his new daughter in his arms after a swift and rather easy labor for Mira, Douglas looked at that little face and didn't care one bit that his firstborn was a girl. He was in love with her as only a father could be, grateful for a healthy birth and a healthy wife, already planning the great things his new daughter would accomplish.

Little Isabel de Lohr had quite a life ahead of her.

A great legacy for the woman she'd been named for, indeed.

EPILOGUE

Year of Our Lord 1268
Axminster Castle

DOUGLAS' ELDEST DAUGHTER was in a flood of tears.

"They are arriving and no one is ready to greet them," she sobbed. "Papa, they will think that Marcus is marrying into a family of animals."

Douglas was trying very hard not to smile at his dramatic daughter. Isabel was to be married on the morrow, to the heir to the d'Vant Cornwall empire and, much like her mother, she simply wanted everything to be perfect. Unfortunately, with nine siblings, things could be far from perfect.

A bit chaotic, actually.

"Your mother has everyone moving for the hall, sweetheart," he said steadily. "Your sisters will ensure the younger ones' good behavior. You needn't worry."

That didn't ease Isabel's tears. "What about Atlas?"

"What about him?"

Isabel began to weep anew. "Papa, he *throws* things," she said. "He throws food, his own waste—everything. I do not want him in the hall. He will embarrass me!"

Douglas couldn't help the laughter then. He chuckled, kissing her forehead as he tried to comfort her. "He is only three years of age," he said. "Sometimes children are a bit wild at that age. You are the eldest of ten children, Izzy. How can you not know this?"

Isabel did, and that was perhaps why she was so upset. Her sisters weren't so bad—all six of them—but the three boys were what her father termed as "lively."

Wild was more like it.

Nicholas, the eldest son at fourteen years of age, seemed to have outgrown his wild streak, because he'd been fostering for a few years and the master knights of Kenilworth wouldn't tolerate it. Dallas was the next son, at eight years of age, and he, too, fostered at Kenilworth, but he hadn't quite outgrown playing jokes on his sisters or stealing coin from his father. Atlas, the baby at three years of age, was the one Isabel was worried about. A feces-throwing, food-spitting abomination.

"Please, Papa," she said. "Not Atlas. Please don't allow him in the hall."

Douglas took pity on her. "He's too young for something like this, so do not worry," he said. "He'll stay in the nursery."

That seemed to ease her mind a great deal. They were standing in the foyer of Axminster, dressed in their finest, and as Douglas helped her wipe the last of her tears, the troops started to arrive.

De Lohr siblings, to be exact.

Aurelia, Matilda, and Beatrice were the first down the stairs. They were young women now, looking a good deal like their mother and their paternal grandmother with their blond hair and fine features. They were well bred, well mannered, and very excited about Isabel's wedding because a wedding meant young men in attendance. They were hoping to meet some. That particular hope was giving Douglas palpitations because all three girls—at nineteen years, eighteen years, and sixteen years of age—were considered marriage prospects. Carrying the de Lohr name made them more appealing than most.

He wasn't ready for that.

As the girls clustered around Isabel in the entry, smoothing her dress and making sure her hair was perfect, Douglas stood out of the way, turning his attention toward the stairs as two of his three sons descended. Nicholas, a tall and well-built young man, was the first one down, followed by Dallas, who looked very much like his grandfather. Nicholas was the one dark-haired sibling of the group, taking after his paternal great-grandmother, who sported nearly black hair. He had inherited that trait along with his grandmother's gray eyes, which gave him a strikingly handsome appearance.

Both boys flew past Douglas on their way to the entry door.

"We are going to the gatehouse, Father!" Nicholas said, opening the door for Dallas to rush through. "We will meet the incoming party!"

They were gone, the door banging back on its hinges. Douglas went to the door and called after them.

"They are being admitted by Lucius!" he said, referring to a knight who had joined him a few years ago after Jonathan returned to Wolverhampton. "Try not to knock anyone over in your haste! *Slow down!*"

His plea fell on deaf ears. The boys continued to bolt and Douglas shook his head at their enthusiasm. But he also caught sight of someone he recognized coming through the inner gatehouse and quickly shut the door.

"Iz," he said to his eldest. "Marcus is approaching."

Isabel lit up with excitement. "He's here?" she gasped. "Open the door, Papa!"

Douglas shrugged with uncertainty. "I did not know if you were ready to see him yet," he said. Then he waved a hand at her eager sisters. "Back away. Let this moment be between your sister and her intended. Go—back up the stairs."

He made a sweeping motion toward the staircase, prompting Aurelia and Matilda to grab Beatrice by the hand and pull her along. They rushed back up the stairs just as Douglas opened the door.

Marcus was standing in the doorway.

Big and blond, like all of the d'Vants, Marcus smiled when he saw Isabel, but his focus moved to Douglas standing by the open door.

"Good day to you, my lord," he greeted Douglas. "I hope my appearance is welcome. I simply could not wait to see Isabel. May I?"

Douglas smiled at the young man he'd grown fond of. "Of course you are welcome, Marcus," he said, indicating for him to enter. "Isabel has been waiting for you. Had you not come to us, I am sure she would have gone to you."

"Papa!" Isabel scolded. "Do not say such things!"

Douglas shrugged. "It is true," he said. "You want to see him as badly as he wants to see you."

"But you are not supposed to say it!"

She frowned at him until Marcus filled her field of vision. Then she could not see or hear anything else but him. With a smile at two young people very much in love, Douglas shut the door and quietly made his way to the stairs. He was just heading up when he caught sight of his wife and children at the top of the steps.

All of them.

He silently motioned for them to back up so they would not be seen by the couple in the entry.

"Back," he muttered at them as he reached the top of the steps. "Those two want to be alone, so let them be alone."

Mira, her blonde hair wound up attractively on the top of her head, had a three-year-old on her hip but strained to catch a glimpse of her eldest daughter and the woman's betrothed.

"I really must go down, Douglas," she said. "Marcus' parents have arrived and I should greet them."

Douglas shook his head. "Nick and Dallas are escorting them to the hall," he said. "It will take a few minutes, so we can wait. Let Izzy and Marcus greet one another after such a long separation."

Mira snorted. "Long separation," she scoffed. "It has only been a week."

"Back when you and I were courting, a week of separation was like a year."

Mira laughed softly in agreement, remembering well those days. On her hip, the Monster of Axminster stirred and rubbed his blue eyes sleepily.

"I want apple, Papa," Atlas said. "Apple!"

Mira lifted an eyebrow to support her child's request. "You cannot keep us trapped up here, Douglas," she said. "Iz and Marcus can go into the solar, but we must be able to use the entry."

The children behind her were in agreement. Douglas looked at his brood—the older girls Aurelia, Matilda, and Beatrice were followed by the younger girls, Alessia, Madeleine, and Rosamund. Rosamund had red hair, the color of molten metal, but the others were blonde. An entire family of blonds. Mostly, anyway. Even Atlas, when he would let them wash his hair, had a bright shade of blond.

Such a beautiful family.

And they were all his.

Reluctantly, Douglas stood aside, letting the younger girls down the stairs. Aurelia took Atlas from her mother and headed down the steps, followed by Matilda and Beatrice. That left Douglas and Mira standing at the top, watching Isabel become offended at the sight of her siblings invading her moment with Marcus. She dragged the young man into the solar, and when Madeleine and Rosamund tried to follow, she slammed the door in their faces. But that only lasted a moment because Marcus opened it again and kindly let them in.

That brought chuckles from Douglas and Mira.

"Marcus is like his father," Mira said. "He is kind to everyone, a gentle giant whom the world adores. Iz is a fortunate young woman."

Douglas nodded, putting an arm around his wife's shoulders and pulling her against him for a sweet kiss.

"She is," he said. "I was thinking the other day how much she reminds me of her namesake and how much Marcus reminds me of Eric sometimes. Quiet, tolerant of her spirited nature."

Mira nodded. "That is true," she said. "Sometimes—only sometimes, mind you—I swear I hear Lady Isabel in our Isabel's tone and manner. Don't you?"

"I do," Douglas said. "We've raised a strong young woman, Mira. She is kind and thoughtful, but she also knows her own mind. Marcus is fortunate to have her."

Mira was watching the entry down below as her children filtered out, heading for the kitchens and the hall. "This is a good match," she said. "When we named our daughter after Lady Isabel, I always hoped that our Isabel would know a happy marriage, something Lady Isabel never had. I'd like to think that somehow, someway, Izzy's match would fulfill Lady Isabel, wherever she is. For her to know that her namesake is happy with the man she loves."

Douglas looked at her. "I've been thinking of Lady Isabel lately because of Izzy's impending nuptials," he said. "It's because of Lady Isabel that everything for us is possible. I've always been grateful to her, but more so as of late, and I'm not sure why."

Mira laid her head against his bicep affectionately. "Because you see in our Izzy what Lady Isabel had hoped for," Mira said. "Life and love. There is nothing else that matters, Douglas. Our life and our love. Nothing is greater."

"True," he said, giving her another sweet kiss. "I would not have missed it for the world."

"Nor I."

Douglas gave her a big hug before leading her down to the entry, where Mira greeted Marcus with joy. The young man would make a fine addition to the family and Marcus knew he could not have picked a finer man for his daughter.

A daughter named after one of the finest women he'd ever known.

Isabel de Lohr and Marcus d'Vant were married the next morning and the wedding feast went all day and all night. Two of Douglas' brothers—Myles and Westley—joined the festivities and spoke of their parents, who had been so sorely missed over the years on occasions such as this. Even Jonathan had managed to make it down from Wolverhampton—still big and burly, but mellowed over the years. He and Douglas sat together, talking over old times, about Davyss, who had gone on to become a great knight, and about the Executioner Knights and how their lives and children had evolved. Axminster's great hall, on this night, was once again full of life and love, as Mira had put it, rising to meet the hope and happiness of a new generation.

Eventually, Douglas left Jonathan and returned to Mira, sitting at the dais with Marcus' parents, Dennis and Ryan. Their conversation drifted to the pride that they, as parents, had for their children and the wish that they should lead happy and productive lives. Douglas found himself wishing his father could have been there to see his granddaughter married, but he knew the man was there in spirit. Whenever anything major happened with the sons of Christopher de Lohr, he was always there in spirit. They could feel him.

And on this night, they could feel Lady Isabel, too.

Douglas and Mira knew how happy she would have been to see the legacy she'd left behind. Axminster was stronger than ever, Douglas and Mira had continued to make it a place of prestige and power, and it was everything Lady Isabel had hoped for. Perhaps she had left the world too soon, but she had left it a better place, something for Douglas and Mira to build on.

And build they had.

On a cold winter's night nine months later, Douglas and Mira were on hand for the birth of their first grandchild at St. Austell Castle in Cornwall. A fat, healthy boy with a crown of white hair, as sweet and docile as his father, but as loving and bright as his mother, entered the world. His mother, knowing for whom she had been named and the story behind it, had one final bit of honor for the lady who had made all things possible for her family.

She and Marcus named their son Eric.

When Douglas heard the news, he wept.

Make me proud, Douglas.

He had.

☙ THE END ❧

Douglas and Mera's children (Christopher lived to see the first two born):

Isabel

Aurelia

Matilda

Beatrice

Nicholas

Alessia

Madeleine

Dallas

Rosamund

Atlas

AUTHOR AFTERWORD

I hope you enjoyed Douglas and Mira's tale!

Of course, I didn't want to point this out in the foreword and ruin the surprise that Douglas would be the Earl of Axminster, but now you know. Isabel marries Marcus d'Vant, the firstborn son of Dennis and Ryan d'Vant from *Tender is the Knight*. Marcus' birth is shown in the epilogue of that book. The de Lohrs are related to a lot of my great families, and now we add d'Vant to that list.

I also realize that Astoria was simply banished from Axminster, sent home in disgrace, without making a big deal out of any punishment. It was implied that sending her home would be the worst punishment she could have. Maybe so, but I did that for a reason. I love to keep future villains in reserve, and she'd make a good one. Imagine her older and more embittered. Lots of possibilities!

I love that this book introduced you to Jonathan de Wolfe, the elusive middle de Wolfe brother. Who knows? Maybe he'll have a book of his own, soon, as an Executioner Knight. One can never tell in my universe!

Hugs,

Kathryn

Kathryn Le Veque Novels

Medieval Romance:

De Wolfe Pack Series:
Warwolfe
The Wolfe
Nighthawk
ShadowWolfe
DarkWolfe
A Joyous de Wolfe Christmas
BlackWolfe
Serpent
A Wolfe Among Dragons
Scorpion
StormWolfe
Dark Destroyer
The Lion of the North
Walls of Babylon
The Best Is Yet To Be
BattleWolfe
Castle of Bones

De Wolfe Pack Generations:
WolfeHeart
WolfeStrike
WolfeSword
WolfeBlade
WolfeLord
WolfeShield
Nevermore
WolfeAx
WolfeBorn

The Executioner Knights:
By the Unholy Hand
The Mountain Dark
Starless
A Time of End
Winter of Solace
Lord of the Sky
The Splendid Hour
The Whispering Night
Netherworld
Lord of the Shadows
Of Mortal Fury
'Twas the Executioner Knight
Before Christmas
Crimson Shield
The Black Dragon

The de Russe Legacy:
The Falls of Erith
Lord of War: Black Angel
The Iron Knight
Beast
The Dark One: Dark Knight
The White Lord of Wellesbourne
Dark Moon
Dark Steel
A de Russe Christmas Miracle
Dark Warrior

The de Lohr Dynasty:
While Angels Slept
Rise of the Defender
Steelheart
Shadowmoor
Silversword

Spectre of the Sword
Unending Love
Archangel
A Blessed de Lohr Christmas
Lion of Twilight
Lion of War
Lion of Hearts
Lion of Steel

The Brothers de Lohr:
The Earl in Winter

Lords of East Anglia:
While Angels Slept
Godspeed
Age of Gods and Mortals

Great Lords of le Bec:
Great Protector

House of de Royans:
Lord of Winter
To the Lady Born
The Centurion

Lords of Eire:
Echoes of Ancient Dreams
Lord of Black Castle
The Darkland

Ancient Kings of Anglecynn:
The Whispering Night
Netherworld

Battle Lords of de Velt:
The Dark Lord
Devil's Dominion
Bay of Fear
The Dark Lord's First Christmas
The Dark Spawn
The Dark Conqueror
The Dark Angel

Reign of the House of de Winter:
Lespada
Swords and Shields

De Reyne Domination:
Guardian of Darkness
The Black Storm
A Cold Wynter's Knight
With Dreams
Master of the Dawn
One Wylde Knight

House of d'Vant:
Tender is the Knight (House of d'Vant)
The Red Fury (House of d'Vant)

The Dragonblade Series:
Fragments of Grace
Dragonblade
Island of Glass
The Savage Curtain
The Fallen One
The Phantom Bride

Great Marcher Lords of de Lara
Lord of the Shadows
Dragonblade

House of St. Hever
Fragments of Grace
Island of Glass
Queen of Lost Stars

Lords of Pembury:
The Savage Curtain

Lords of Thunder: The de Shera Brotherhood Trilogy

The Thunder Lord
The Thunder Warrior
The Thunder Knight

The Great Knights of de Moray:
Shield of Kronos
The Gorgon

The House of De Nerra:
The Promise
The Falls of Erith
Vestiges of Valor
Realm of Angels

Highland Legion:
Highland Born

Highland Warriors of Munro:
The Red Lion
Deep Into Darkness

The House of de Garr:
Lord of Light
Realm of Angels

Saxon Lords of Hage:
The Crusader
Kingdom Come

High Warriors of Rohan:
High Warrior
High King

The House of Ashbourne:
Upon a Midnight Dream

The House of D'Aurilliac:
Valiant Chaos

The House of De Dere:
Of Love and Legend

St. John and de Gare Clans:
The Warrior Poet

The House of de Bretagne:
The Questing

The House of Summerlin:
The Legend

The Kingdom of Hendocia:
Kingdom by the Sea

The BlackChurch Guild: Shadow Knights:
The Leviathan
The Protector

Regency Historical Romance:
Sin Like Flynn: A Regency Historical Romance Duet
The Sin Commandments
Georgina and the Red Charger

Gothic Regency Romance:
Emma

Contemporary Romance:

Kathlyn Trent/Marcus Burton Series:
Valley of the Shadow
The Eden Factor
Canyon of the Sphinx

The Eagle Brotherhood (under the pen name Kat Le Veque):
The Sunset Hour
The Killing Hour
The Secret Hour
The Unholy Hour
The Burning Hour
The Ancient Hour

The Devil's Hour

Sons of Poseidon:
The Immortal Sea

Pirates of Britannia Series (with Eliza Knight):
Savage of the Sea by Eliza Knight
Leader of Titans by Kathryn Le Veque
The Sea Devil by Eliza Knight
Sea Wolfe by Kathryn Le Veque

Note: All Kathryn's novels are designed to be read as stand-alones, although many have cross-over characters or cross-over family groups. Novels that are grouped together have related characters or family groups. You will notice that some series have the same books; that is because they are cross-overs. A hero in one book may be the secondary character in another.

There is NO reading order except by chronology, but even in that case, you can still read the books as stand-alones. No novel is connected to another by a cliff hanger, and every book has an HEA.

Series are clearly marked. All series contain the same characters or family groups except the American Heroes Series, which is an anthology with unrelated characters.

For more information, find it in **A Reader's Guide to the Medieval World of Le Veque**.

About Kathryn Le Veque

Bringing the Medieval to Romance

KATHRYN LE VEQUE is a critically acclaimed, multiple USA TODAY Bestselling author, an Indie Reader bestseller, a charter Amazon All-Star author, and a #1 bestselling, award-winning, multi-published author in Medieval Historical Romance with over 100 published novels.

Kathryn is a multiple award nominee and winner, including the winner of Uncaged Book Reviews Magazine 2017 and 2018 "Raven Award" for Favorite Medieval Romance. Kathryn is also a multiple RONE nominee (InD'Tale Magazine), holding a record for the number of nominations. In 2018, her novel WARWOLFE was the winner in the Romance category of the Book Excellence Award and in 2019, her novel A WOLFE AMONG DRAGONS won the prestigious RONE award for best pre-16th century romance.

Kathryn is considered one of the top Indie authors in the world with over 2M copies in circulation, and her novels have been translated into several languages. Kathryn recently signed with Sourcebooks Casablanca for a Medieval Fight Club series, first published in 2020.

In addition to her own published works, Kathryn is also the President/CEO of Dragonblade Publishing, a boutique publishing house specializing in Historical Romance. Dragonblade's success has seen it rise in the ranks to become Amazon's #1 e-book publisher of Historical Romance (K-Lytics report July 2020).

Kathryn loves to hear from her readers. Please find Kathryn on Facebook at Kathryn Le Veque, Author, or join her on Twitter @kathrynleveque. Sign up for Kathryn's blog at www.kathrynleveque.com for the latest news and sales.

Milton Keynes UK
Ingram Content Group UK Ltd.
UKHW051447140724
445326UK00013BA/444